MEMOIRS

OF AN

EBONY COVER FAMILY

A NOVEL

BY:

V.A. PATRICK SLADE

MEMOIRS OF AN EBONY COVER FAMILY

Author's Notes

It takes a village to raise a child, and furthermore it takes just the same to form a writer. God, I'm grateful for the opportunities that I've been given and the blessings that I continue to receive. I was very privileged to have been given the opportunity at such a young age to hone my craft. I was allowed to tell stories, write stories and perform said stories in front audiences of family, community and friends. I was also given a protective atmosphere in which even my mistakes were guarded, and I was allowed to strive and become better at what I do.

I extend many thanks to my aunt Nell who gave me the gift of literature in my youth, though I was not thankful for it growing up. If it weren't for those books, and listening to books on tape as child, I don't think I would be where I am today and able to consciously tap into my imaginative self. It was she that got me hooked on the gift of words and the thirst for them.

Secondly, I want to thank my aunt Carol. It was she that recognized my gift in the arts at such a young age. Dance classes, acting and eventually reading my plays, screenplays and novels, I was able to grow as an artist with her protective eyes and discernment. I never make a literary move without her thoughts and input. I'm thankful for her successful streak. When she says something works, it works. And when it doesn't she's quite frank about it. And I love her for that.

I also want to thank my mom, Ms. J. She was front row at every play, recital and reading that I've ever had. She's supported me and believed in my dreams from such a young age. Her wisdom, input and mothering has been a blessing and she is what has shaped me into the person that I am today. She's always a shoulder I can lean on and without her I wouldn't be here, let alone be able to be the artist that I am today. She's an amazing woman, and many of my strong female characters are based on her and her zest for life. I thank her for never giving up on me and always there with a kind word.

I hate to drone on, but I just can't possibly forget Jessica-Cristal, Kristyl Tift, Christina Guillen, Leonia Wade, Beatrice Cook, Cheryl Manosa, Michael Pfirmann, Anthony Morgan, Jasmine Wells, Eugene Ochoa, my aunts Carol Cheatham and Nell Williams who took the time out of their lives to read my first novel in its raw form. It was their opinions on the piece and the corrections they gave me that helped shape this book into what it is today.

Lastly to the city of Atlanta and the beautiful topography that you have, I am appreciative to you for it. My home city is amazing and life there is like no other. It raised me well and gave me a good healthy understanding of life overall. It's a city that taught me manners, gave me great food and taught me how to enjoy all the simple things in life. It's in those simple things that lie life's greatest enjoyment and pleasure.

To you all that have supported me over the years, I want to say you mean so much to me and my life and my journey. If I've left out a name, please blame it on the glass of Cabernet that I'm drinking while I write this as the reasons behind it, and not that I don't love you equally as the people that I've mentioned. I love you all and I thank you with all of my heart. And I could not have done this without you.

Love,

V.A. Patrick Slade

6/30/12

Hilary,

Thank you for the support.
You're amazing and you are
the reason that I
can do what I do...

4.

"Accordingly, whatever you have said in the dark will be heard in the light, and what you have whispered in the inner rooms will be proclaimed upon the housetops."

-Luke 12:3-

V.A. PATRICK SLADE

PROLOGUE

He entered through an opened door at the opposite end of the warehouse. Echoes of the summer's balmy night reminded him subtly, as his clothing became tighter on his chiseled physique. This native of Atlanta knew of the famously hot nights, where the disappearance of the sun didn't necessarily mean the dissipation of the heat. But he still insisted on dressing as contemporarily as any Southern twenty-eight-year-old would: camel colored blazer, mocha button-down shirt, accented by Sean John faded jeans, and his coco-colored Timberlands.

Humidity wasn't the only cause for concern for Detective Kevin Dean, though. The dank warehouse added pouring perspiration to his forehead. Each wiping brought more to the surface. He was close, but any little mistake could blow his lead. He pulled his 9 millimeter from his side and cocked it, releasing a bullet into the chamber. He was prepared—for what, he didn't know. Pressed against the wall, he moved ever-so slowly, as though he was one with it. He was his father's son, just as dogged in his pursuits.

Zechariahs Dean, his father, was a foremost Southern contractor and architect, wealthy and its demure surrounded Kevin throughout his life. But he didn't want to make his father's wealth the only success in his life. Kevin Dean had become close to perfect as a detective. Graduating top of his Academy, awards lined his desk. Certificates mounted his wall at home, and Mayor Emory Westport had given the young detective the key to the city after a big bust a year prior. The youngest cop to make detective in years, he was given some of the most complicated cases the city had to offer.

He had been given this particular case six months prior, and it was beginning to feel like years for Detective Dean, with no end in sight. *PRAVELINE* was taking the city and country by storm. Finding its genesis in the Southeastern most portion of the United States, the drug took euphoria to another height and the disillusionments that it provided was better than any other drug combined. Relatively simple to make, ship and distribute, its white/pink crystals gave it the street name of *JEM*—from the eighties popular Saturday morning cartoon of the same name about a pink and white haired punk rock singer, who fought to be number one on the music charts against her nemesis THE MISFITS.

JEM was running rampant throughout the city of Atlanta, and Kevin felt obligated to protect the city he had grown up in and become its lover and protector. Many children of the city did not have the privileged upbringing he had, and he would do whatever he could to ensure that their humble upbringing would not be marred by drugs or other enemies. He wanted them to become productive citizens of the city and of the world, thus leading him to the warehouse.

The shining moon lit Kevin's path. The eeriness of the still silence added an extra sense of urgency and fear that Kevin had not felt in years.

The last time this "calm before the storm" feeling came was when he was five, and he had discovered his father's affair with their maid, and he was waiting on the minute, the hour, and day that his mother would find out and his family would be destroyed. Contrary to his thoughts, when his mother did find out, she did not disband the family unit as he had feared. Just as that moment did not become his greatest fear, he had soon hoped that this would not either. He clinched onto his gun, preparing for what would inevitably be around the corner.

Making his way to the belly of the warehouse, he heard voices, but he could not make out what was coursing through the wooden walls. He stopped...heart pounding, throat dry, struggling to listen to exactly at what was being said. As he got closer, he heard the word "Savannah." Then the next was "boat." The third was "shipment." He was in the right place. The drugs had been arriving in the city from their original drop off point in Savannah—the city that Civil War General Sherman declared as his Christmas present to then President Abraham Lincoln. Sherman's gift of the beautiful waterfront city with its luxurious mansions and cobblestone streets was now a breeding ground for a new recreational drug taking the Manhattan of the South by storm. Kevin was brought right to the source he had been looking for.

BAMMM!!! A force, resembling a black hole, sucked him into the room at which he had been listening to just moments prior. His gun was no longer in hand. His ear piece and weapon were on the floor in the corridor. The clandestine setup, he thought were remnant of something out of *Scar Face* or *The God Father* movies of which he was a fan.

He was forced onto a chair by a strong pair of hands that held him as if he were glued. He didn't struggle, but he was able to finally take in his surroundings. Wall to wall crates; he made out, surrounded the vast room. A similar crate was opened in front of him on a table. A bagged pink powdery substance looked as if were being readied for shipment and vending. This was the center of the drug cartel that was infectiously destroying generations of Atlanta's citizens and making other generations kill to bestow its power. As his ignorance of the situation waned, a new struggle began for the detective. An opaque blindfold was placed on his face, blocking out much of the world in front of him.

The lunar radiance that assisted him into the warehouse was the only illumination of the room. A blessing initially for Detective Dean, it was now a curse that impeded his vision and comprehension of his current situation. Shadows were easily seen through the netted blindfold, but no definite identifications for the figures that had his life in their hands. He looked, straining for an escape. He couldn't move. The humongous Michael Clarke Duncan figure was holding him in place as though he was a rag doll. He was very disappointed in himself seeing as though he was not a weak man by nature. He stood five foot eleven and his solid two-hundred pound frame was worked relentlessly at the *Run and Shoot,* a twenty-four hour gym in Atlanta's West Side, every evening after a long day on the streets following leads with a hard-hitting session of weights and a pick-up game or two on the courts with his after work basketball team. He shouldn't have been held down by this person, but he could tell this person was much stronger than he could ever have prepared for.

The other figures in the room moved around as though Detective Dean wasn't there. They weren't too upset by his intercourse, going about their normal activity getting the product ready for market. He began to recall how he had arrived at this exact point: remembering earlier of the raspy voice's quick insistences leading him to the warehouse. Perfectly he was able to stumble upon something that he had been trying for months to uncover. Right in front of him was the workshop of demented Santa's little helpers (elves) who were preparing gifts of disillusionments and life altering substances. This was too perfect. The scene was too eerie. It clicked with the Detective. He was brought here to be trapped. His lead: bogus.

The door crept opened. A figure entered the space and the helpers that were busied with activity moments before, stopped in reverence of the person. The giant that held Kevin turned to the central figure and said, "Boss, we did good, huh?"

"This mother-fucker has been messin' with my shit for too long!" The figure said. "Detective Dean," they continued. Kevin had heard this voice before, but couldn't place it. Kevin didn't say anything. He was still trying to take in what was before him: too much, too soon. The new addition to the room surveyed the worker's progress and was quite pleased: picking up a bulkier package sniffing, licking and placing it down. "This stuff just keeps gettin' better. We goin' keep bank! Believe it!" The clank of their hills came closer to Kevin, until the figure was dead center. "Take his blindfold off." The giant did as was ordered of him. Kevin could see the figure in front of him, but couldn't make out exactly who it was. The figure lit a cigar, and the lighting of the filter gave strong hint as to who this was that held him captive.

A surprised Kevin yelped, "You!"

A point blank shot to the head killed Detective Dean.

PART I:

CHAPTER 1:

Dontavious Dean's life was changing drastically, and everyday brought a new obstacle to his path. And the day he heard of his brother's death was no different.

He sat and surveyed the sunset-drenched room where each hue of pale pink, orange, and red ever-so gently hung on the furniture of the office. The mirror hanging over the fire place bounced a rainbow so subtly into his eyes. The rainbow wasn't annoying, though. He had been here more frequently this last year than he had ever before and that was the only thing that gave him solace every evening he was forced to be here.

Every crevice in this office he had discovered had some relevance to his life and what was going on in it at his present moment. The time he discovered the family portrait of his lawyer Lawrence Franklin, he would soon be brought up on charges. The day he learned of the undergrad institution that Mr. Franklin attended, he was trying very hard to understand why any one would do this to him. And last but not least, the court yard the office overlooked, with its menial topiary and marble fountain, was discovered when he was trying to escape the news that would inevitable shape his future as he knew it.

It was just a year before that he thought his life couldn't get any better. His thirty-sixth birthday was celebrated by the army naming him

Sergeant First Class—one of the youngest to do so. He had just completed his second tour in Iraq, and was brandished with many awards for having the lowest mortality rate of any unit during the unyielding "campaign." All of those physical mementos meant nothing to him. His freedom and dignity, he hoped, would stay in tact. This day was judgment day for a crime he felt he didn't commit.

He sat in the secure chair just able to relax. But thoughts of the days events floated ever-so closely to his temples and agitation begin to set in. The accusations flowed so easily in the Court Martial and there was nothing he could do. All of it was semi-truths. Were those nights really worth it, he thought. Bodies touching, each drop of sweat becoming liberations of sorts, undying ecstasy, followed by orgasmic sounds of pain and pleasure morphed into a world of passion and heat, this was a love, or so he thought: illegal in every way. After all, he was Sergeant First Class, and it was a Private he was lusting after. That moment of thought lead to pain all over again for him. What pain came from a night of pleasure, he thought.

He got up and walked over to the window overlooking the court yard. His unrecognizable visage stared back at him, and he noticed that his ebony veneer was not as sharp as it had been. His caramel complexion paled in comparison to what it once was. The vibrant sparkle that had captivated and inspired many most of his life was no longer there. His zest for life had dissipated along with his belief in the human race. He was and felt as if he was a shell of his former self.

Lawrence Franklin entered the office, casting a shadow into the constantly dimming room. Dontavious hadn't seen him in an hour. That hour was spent working out a plea agreement that he hoped would keep his client from losing everything. He turned towards Lawrence. Standing in front of him, clad in his navy-blue pinstripe suit, each hair mechanically placed in gel-covered rivets, Lawrence's shoulders were as stiff as they had been through the whole ordeal, and his flawless face, covered in sweat, now gave hints of what was to come.

"Dontavious, I have good news, and some bad." Lawrence stated ostentatiously, as did everyone who had just those two options.

"Give it to me straight, pardon the pun." Dontavious said jokingly.

"They said that you can get an honorable discharge."

"That's the least they can do for all of my hard work for them!" Dontavious snapped back at him.

"That's the good news."

"What's the bad?" Dontavious surprisingly inquired believing that was the bad news.

"You leave with nothing but a retirement package worth sixty-thousand."

"What?" Dontavious quipped.

"Your rank, gone."

"You're serious?"

"As a heart-attack, pardon the horrible cliché."

"My twenty years of service's gone, just like that—as though it didn't exist?!"

"It was that, or they would reveal what happened, and you would get a dishonorable discharge and have nothing. At least you have a package that you can start your civilian life with."

"All of my hard work, years of sacrifice, gone...gone because of an affair?"

"You knew the rules, Dontavious."

"I know. I knew." Remorsefully, Dontavious sighed. "I guess this is it. My life will never be the same."

"At least you have something."

"Yeah, but what about my career, my lively hood?"

"I have all confidence that you will find something. Why don't you call your family?"

"No!" Dontavious snapped back.

"Why not? They are family, right?

"I haven't seen them in almost twenty years. I don't want to see them either."

The stormy night was the perfect isolation to begin packing. Cardboard littered the small living room, waiting to be made into boxes.

He started to remove each picture from the wall relishing the moments that each captured: the first day as a Sergeant at training camp, military balls, and award ceremonies. When he looked at the photos he didn't have any sadness, but remorse that there wouldn't be any more of those moments to be captured in photos and be hung on this particular wall.

An hour passed. Dontavious sat in the middle of the floor surrounded by his memories. Packing each with care, as though, and he knew, were his only prized possessions in the world. Every medal, every ribbon of honor, and change of uniform had been his crown of glory that all men strive to find in life. His many mementos, he thought, would be the show of his life's work. They were now worthless to him, seeing that his rank was no longer valid for him. He was as normal as he was when entered the military almost twenty years ago at eighteen.

He thought about how he ended up where he had come in life—leaving home, leaving behind his father, mother, two brothers and a sister. He wanted to find himself. He, like many other children of prominent families, had to find a way to make a mark in the world without the influx of the power that his father's name and money carried to the rest of the world. Being in the military, climbing the ranks, earning respect, he felt was the way. He had been quite successful until the year before when he met the "Private."

Without letting the thoughts get to him, he thought of many ways to distract himself from his impending doom and degradation, he thought, that would be the calling card for the rest of his life. He dropped the last ribbon in the box and sealed it ever-so tightly with duck tape: one layer on top of the other. He took in a sigh of completion, for the work that he had done, but incompletion of the work that lay just before him. He would have to sell his house, and then determine what would be the rest of his life. Seeing that black men live an average of seventy-eight to eighty-nine years, he knew that the rest of his forty years or so would have to be somewhat enjoyable, barring getting hit by a bus, or such an occurrence that would end it earlier.

Distraction, I need a distraction, he thought. He also knew he needed to relax before the stress would overtake his body. He thought back to his childhood. His mother, the Southern debutant she was, always said, "A hot bath can wash all your troubles away, hon." He thought of this and knew that would be the perfect idea for a night such as this. After drawing a hot bubble bath, he cued Tweet's **It's Me Again** on his I-pod, an older album, but one he knew had always relaxed him when he was stressed.

Standing in front of the bathroom mirror, he noticed the t-shirt he was wearing was now covered in smut from the hours of packing he had just undertaken, even though the mirror was clouded with steam. Taking off his shirt, he noticed the hard work he had put in for years in the gym and on obstacle courses: a near perfect chest, sinews in place with the most precise spherical nipples on either side of the chest. He rubbed down to his stomach, where the scar from his childhood appendectomy was evident, but was not a distraction from the perfectly chiseled abdominals that Michael Angelo's *David* would have been envious of and men read *Men's Heath* and *GQ* to understand how they were created. He pulled down his jogging pants, gray, baggy, and they fell effortlessly to the ground. His boxers, his favorite and most lucky, green and blue stripes accented his body just right.

Slipping off his boxers, he slipped into the bathtub. **Turn Da Lights Off** welcomed him into the steaming bath. He knew that each beat of the opening chords would only relax him even more, just as each song on the I-POD with its mellow undertones, calmed his soul and body. He laid his head on the nape of the tub and fell asleep to the sounds of a familiar sounding **Cab Ride**—Tweet, the singer of the song, asking the cab driver to take her where she wanted go, escaping her world as she knew it. He so could relate, as he felt as though he wanted to be taken away from this place, his life—a complete escape...

BRINGGGGGG....The phone rang. *Who could've been calling this late?* He exited the tub quickly, wrapped a towel around him, and went to the other room where his cell phone was. (Why did he still wrap a towel around him even when he lived alone? He had always done it, habit.) But apparently he was not quick enough. The phone signaled that a call had been missed and looked to see exactly who it was. 770-555-3208—Home. He knew that a phone call from home was never a good sign.

His parents never called him, not even on the major holidays. They all had an understanding. He had his life. They had their life. And he knew this couldn't have been good with it being so late back East. So, he decided to recall and see what was going on with his family. But before he could, a voice message indicator popped up on the phone's screen—voice mail was left.

He retrieved it, fearing what was said. He knew his father had had a heart attack seven years prior, could his father be dead? Or he thought the worst: his family was bankrupt. He punched his pass code into the phone and listened to the message. He heard a Latina's soft spoken voice on the other end, "Hey, this is Sasha. I have some bad news. Mr. Kevin was shot and killed on duty last night. Get here, if you can."

His father was not dead. His family wasn't bankrupt. But he was informed by his parent's maid that his little brother, who had just turned twenty-eight, was killed in the line of duty. He was a detective for the Atlanta police department: decorated in his own right, the youngest cop to make detective so quickly. He had an affinity for his youngest brother. They were essentially alike: ambitious and not wanting to make a name off of their father.

He was on the next Delta flight to Atlanta. He hadn't been home since the first Bush was in office. Nothing was keeping him in Oregon any longer.

CHAPTER 2

Kevin's middle brother Malek was at home when he heard the news of his brother's tragic murder. He had his hands full when the news came to him, as were a few other things.

"Yes! Hit that right! Keep going...Yeeeeees, yeeeeeees! Coooooooooome on baby, cum for me..." Kameron's orgasmic panting echoed through the cavernous mahogany bedroom of her fiancée Malek, as she was riding him as though he was a buck and she a cowboy. Sweat poured down her supple breasts, as she and her fiancée were completing a competition in which they were not frequently a part. He, just as she, was drenched with the stench of love making, thanks impart to the humidity of Atlanta's balmy nights and their passionate sport. He liked how she had molded to him, and was the perfect lover he needed. She, on the hand, was earning her position in society on her back or from tonight's indication, on her lover's belly.

A final jerk spat his seed into her and the night's activity was over. Flopping down, each to their respective sides of the canopy-covered king sized bed. "That was the best...you've been in a while," Malek mustered from his exhilaration and exhaustion. Her eyes rolled, as they usually did, unseen by Malek of course, and she replied with a quick pat to his stomach. She rolled over, as not to incur any cuddling Malek usually wanted after he nauseatingly made "love" to her. Their roles were indeed reversed: she, the male, he the female. She was doing her part in order to crawl up the social ladder that had eluded her for most of her life.

It wasn't that Malek was hard on her eyes. He carried the same Dean qualities as his brothers Kevin and Dontavious. The only things lacking were a sculpted physique and the caring personality of each of his brothers. He was a good thirty-five pounds overweight and had been that way most of his life. Being sandwiched between an older brother who was likened to singer/actor Tyrese and a younger brother who was as ripped as daytime television star Marcus Patrick, he felt as though he was not worthy and couldn't compete on the same level as they. Insecurities set in as he got older, and he realized that his father's money and power could garner him all the respect and popularity that his brothers had naturally. His attitude reflected it as well, brash and disgusting to the outside world: he had no friends, and barely had a fiancée.

What he lacked in the physical, he more than made up for with his intelligence. Instead of the sports and dates that occupied his brother's social calendars, he was reading or watching television. He was inside so much so that he was forced to go outside as a punishment for various childhood offenses. His hermit behavior had its rewards, though. Becoming the valedictorian of his prestigious preparatory school Marist, he had been courted by Ivy Leagues and HBCUs alike. Settling on Howard, he learned the skills of a top-notched architect and civil engineer, completing a dual degree in five years, even with such complicated courses. He went on to a Masters program at Berkeley, which garnered him many job offers. But his loyalties lay with his family and the family business that his "perfect" brothers so easily abandoned.

He was finally in the good sight of his father. A position he had been striving to have since childhood. He was the middle child: a syndrome indeed reflected in the attitude he carried. He didn't know where he fit into the bigger scheme of things. But with such prestigious accomplishments under his belt so early in life, his attitude became more menacing and destructive to the outside world.

Kameron was one of his prizes, or so he thought, of his hard work in school. He met her during a random temp job she had done with the family business Dean Architect and Design, the company in which he had become the President and eventually the CEO. She was everything any man could want. Her five-foot four frame was wrapped in a butterscotch hue, with silky black hair, that touched her mid back, of course all weave. Kam, as her friends had called her since adolescence, worked every curve that she had. "A brick house" was an understatement when describing her. She had the perkiest, round, but not too big or too small breast; the waist that any man of any size could wrap around; and the most petite and attractive feet that didn't need to be touched by a manicurist in order to be perfect. Her porcelain visage was the adjunct complement to her near-perfect body. Each eye brow was arched just right, to fit her almond gray eyes, which were natural. Her nose, not too Anglo, or Negro, led to her

lips that were soft and sensual. No makeup was needed on her face, it
was a work of art, which God himself had signed and given to the world.

Kam knew of her qualities from childhood and was not afraid to use
what she had in order to get what she wanted out of life. This meant
doing things of which she was not necessarily proud. Her first foray was
as a teenage escort for the most elite of the exclusive neighborhood,
Buckhead's, married men. Though no sex was ever involved, she used her
beautiful presence to acquire couture clothes, expensive shoes, and
accessories. As college approached, she thought of going into the full on
prostitution, but rethought it once a girlfriend of hers got killed on the
corner of Pine and Spring Streets at the age of seventeen doing such
activity. So, she continued doing what she had been doing since the age
of fourteen, and it allowed her to live in a posh and luxurious high rise
loft in Midtown Atlanta and drive a sleek BMW to her day classes at
Atlanta Metro Tech. She never really worried too much about her
education, seeing that she could always use her looks to get any job she
wanted. But she didn't want to take any chances, as she remembered her
mother once telling her that her beauty would soon fade—which she
thought would never happen, but didn't want to be assed out if such an
occurrence should happen.

When she met Malek her first day as a temp, she could see straight
through his power suit and menacing personality to the insecurities and
heartbreak that she could easily take advantage of and would allow her to

access the core of society's elite: namely the Dean fortune and power.
She was not even in his department, but he so happened to come through
to yell at one of the random presidents about the newest figures of the
quarter. He locked eyes with her, and as they say, the rest was history.
The next day Malek's secretary of three years was dropped to the corral of
the secretarial pool and Kameron, who had no previous experience or
typing skills, was named Assistant to the Executive.

Though she had looks that could launch a modern Trojan war,
Malek soon realized that her candor and class left a few things to be
desired. She had no tact, and would say whatever came to mind. Being
able to transform her into his modern Eliza Doolittle, in essence making
over Kameron in a *Pygmalion* sort of way was a task he took on very
easily and was eager to do. He felt he had everything, the job, the mini-
mansion, the car, and now he could have the woman: some pretty young
thing on his arm at the company parties, dinners, and the Atlanta
Symphony Orchestra, where the company had box seats because
investment in the arts.

Etiquette was first on Malek's short list of things to teach Kameron.
She knew how to carry herself when she was in the presence of the
Buckhead elite, but she really didn't know how to conduct herself in an
office situation. Not just any office, one of the most influential
architectural firms in the United States: one that did well over one billion
a year easily through investments and the work that it did. Though she

protested the initial input by Malek and the way she should react to certain situations, she eventually caved seeing that it was the only way for her to have a secure foot in Atlanta's high society. So she took each prod and insistence from Malek with a smile laced grimace. Malek didn't make it easy for her by any means but both came to an understanding. It was almost a year before Malek realized that she was ready to meet the finest of society.

It was the annual Dean Architectural and Design Christmas party at the prestigious Mt. Paran Road Dean mansion where she was introduced to his family and friends as his girlfriend. Most importantly she met his mother Jordan Dean, the grand dame of Atlanta's Wealthy African-American set. As Jordan made the rounds of the party, she came upon Malek and Kameron. She looked Kam up and down, almost toying with her, as would a lioness before she devoured her prey. Jordan summed up what she thought of Kameron with one cruel and disapproving word, "No!" And she walked off. Kameron knew that Malek wasn't a mama's boy, so she didn't have to worry about him breaking up with her for that reason, but she knew that she couldn't climb any further in the company if one of the primary shareholders didn't like her. They didn't cross paths for another three years.

Malek had tried talking to his mother after Christmas dinner that year. He was trying to figure out why she had not taken to Kam as easily as everyone in the company and the family had. Malek got his answer, as his mother twiddled her thumbs and drank her fourth of Hennessey VSOP out of her cordial. She, as elegantly as she said everything in a deep Southern accent, ostentatiously stated: "I just don't like her. I have a sixth sense of about these things, hon. That gal ain't nothing but street trash. No matter how much Versace she wears on her back and how many Jimmy Cho's she glides on, she will still just be common street trash! If you choose to continue to see her, that'll be your mistake." And with that she dismissed her son to finish her drink in peace. That was the last thing that Jordan had ever said about the situation, and as anyone who knew Jordan Campbell Dean, that was the only thing she had to say about it.

The relationship continued to the chagrin of Jordan, but as Kameron soon figured out, she couldn't keep a virile young man like Malek at bay sexually any longer. Each day she gave him the excuse that she wasn't feeling well or was on her period. When those two things no longer worked, she decided to go for the gambit and tell him that she couldn't have sex with anyone unless she knew there was a real commitment to the relationship. With a feat that would have surprised everyone who knew Malek, he proposed to Kameron at her favorite Tiffany's store in Phipps Plaza, one of Atlanta's most luxurious and elite malls. He closed the store, in something that was reminiscent of a scene out of *Sweet Home Alabama*, or what Toni Braxton said her proposal was like, and told her that she could pick anything in the store. She of course went for the earrings, but he politely informed her that she should pick any ring she wanted. He proceeded to get on one knee and ask her to marry her. Though her libido wasn't there physically or emotional for Malek, a six carrot baby blue diamond from Tiffany's gave it a boost. That night was the first time she had given Malek his greatest desire. She wasn't thinking of her other wealthy and much better looking suitors to keep her motivated when she made love to him, but it was the thought of the huge rock on her left hand that made her pant and scream with ecstasy for hours on end.

Months passed and the ring's appeal waned, and she soon realized that even Malek looking at her could make her stomach hurt and her face cringe. Malek put the dots together soon enough and realized that she was no longer interested in him. He had to finally admit to himself what wasn't stated verbally. Each knew that they had a mutual reason for the relationship and each had to play the game in order to get what other wanted and was willing to give. She was using him, but in a sick way he liked it and knew that this was the only way to have someone like Kameron in his bed and on his arm. He knew what made her tick: money. She wasn't going to be satisfied until she had a lot of it.

He soon promoted her to President of Land Acquisitions, in which she became very successful. What skills she lacked in the secretarial pool, she more than made up for it in her cunning land negations and tactful strategy in which garnered the company profits in the millions. She more than exceeded what Malek thought she would do, but her success wasn't what Malek wanted initially. He wanted to keep her any way he could. He did this by enacting a clause in her contract that would tether him to her through her career at the company and kept her in the finer things of life. She signed the contact without any knowledge of it and didn't have any idea of its presence until she tried to leave him one day in April.

She had begun an affair with a mail room clerk after the promotion. Rory was everything that she wanted in a man. He was six foot three, two hundred pounds of solid muscle. The ex-con's tattoos gave reason to why he was trapped in the smoldering mail room at such a mature age. The affair was covert and Malek had no clue. No one knew about it. She was good at everything that she did. She had put it on him so much and so good that he could not and would not say anything about the affair to anyone, even his closest friends. She got cocky in her pursuits and thought that she could have the job and her stud. She figured that she could have the best sex of her life and the money from the job and support both of them: showering each of them with the most lavish things in the world.

It was a candlelit dinner in which she would try to make her move. As she was about to give Malek the dissolution of their relationship and go off with her stud (of course not giving her prized ring back) Malek presented her contract to her. She and he read the contract, he aloud, she to herself. She couldn't believe what she read in the fine lines and had indeed signed weeks earlier: *I, Kameron B. Hanes, do solemnly swear that by taking the position of President of Land Acquisitions, I will remain with Malek T. Dean in a civil union, either be it engaged or married, in his house, in his bed, or forgo the job title, its benefits and monies that the said party has become accustomed and they will be relinquished if said party dissolves said relationship in any form.* Shocked and applaud at the one-upmanship, she slapped him. She repeatedly hit him, releasing all of her stress and anguish of her recent discovery. Upon his last hit, he grabbed her arms and forcibly made her listen to him. "You will abide the contract, or you will be out on your ass!" He shouted at her.

"You would keep me in this relationship against my will?" She was at the weakest he had ever seen her. It turned him on even more. He had the power, now.

"You are not forced to be here. You can leave whenever you want."

"But without nothing?"

"Damn straight. Those are requirements."

"Fucking bastard..."

"Watch what you say baby. You chose this. We knew that we were both playing a game and knew what you had to do in order to stay in it."

"And you had a trump card."

"And you didn't?" He quipped at her.

"So, what do I do now?"

"It's up to you. Make your choice: me and the money, or you alone with nothing."

"I had lots of money and material things that I wanted and needed. I don't need you or your job to have it again."

"Your slight tricks, hand jobs, and seductive smile didn't give you all this. Trust me, that was small time compared to what this world with me could and will garner you baby!"

"You could be in a meaningless relationship, knowing I don't love you or want you in a sexual way?"

"It's all apart of life. Hopefully you will find love for and with me one of these days. But if not, I'll have a perfect specimen on my arm every where I go and in my bed. Deal or no deal?"

"You think I'm perfect?"

"Of course I do. Why do you think I'm trying so hard to hold on to you?" He let her go. In that moment she and he locked eyes. She no longer saw weakness and the insecurities in Malek as she had before. She did not think that he could not handle her any longer. She now saw the power and determination that could keep her interested in him on every level. And they made love for real. She rode him as though he was a buck and she a cowboy. She reached her climax finally. There was first time for everything, she thought, even if she he wasn't her first choice.

Malek had ended his passionate sex with Kameron when the phone rang. It was Malek's sister-in-law. His brother Kevin had been shot and killed. Though they weren't the closest of brothers, he still felt remorse for the loss of someone in his genus pool. He got out of bed to put on clothes to go to the family house. "You're going right now?" Kameron inquired.

"My family needs me. Someone has to be the sane one. My father won't be, my mother either." He relayed.

"Do you want me to come with you?"

"That would be nice of you."

They were dressed and headed to the Dean's Mt. Paron Road mansion.

CHAPTER 3

Paige Dean heard of her brother Kevin's death after her first performance as Nettie in *The Color Purple.*

She had been nervous all day before the performance. She had waited for the chance to grace the stage as Nettie, a role she had coveted since the performance she saw that originated in Atlanta in 2004. Being a chorus member in the revival of *Sweeny Todd*, the classic *Rent* as Mimi, and Nyla in Disney's *The Lion King,* the Julliard graduate had great luck when it came to the experiences that she had gotten so quick after graduation.

It wasn't just pure luck that she was as successful as she was. She was a top notch dancer and singer, having had her start in musical theatre camps as a child at the age of five. Playing the little Daffodil in *The Littlest Woods* and other syrupy-sapped musicals, where the children's dress personified their respective character attributes, her parents saw what she could possible be in life. It wasn't much of a secret either, when at the age of ten she stated that she would attend Julliard, taking up dance with a concentration in musical theatre, and would take Broadway by storm. Her parents and siblings supported her, by attending all of her, what they felt were God awful plays and dance performances, until she eventually became one of Atlanta's finest dancers and singers.

Relinquishing singing to the backburner, she soon realized that dancing would get her into any door on the New York stage that she wanted. The lean muscles that her body possessed easily allowed her to glide sensationally upon the stage. Each pirouette was accented perfectly by the gracious form that her body took. It was if her body was a ribbon, and the wind was blowing it. Winding and fluid as easily as the string, she was light on her feet and was the perfect partner for anyone of whom she was paired.

Her work was so immensely admired that the New York Times ran a piece in the Theatre reviews:

> *Paige Dean was as malleable as a lump of amorphous clay being molded into anything a playwright, character, or director could want. Her grace as a dancer is only paled by her intense facial expression and vocal wonders. She is the new toast of Broadway.*

This article was her validation of her long years of hard work and dedication even though she was only twenty when the article was published.

She, like her brothers, was very single-minded and destructive as she came to know that her position could be easily lost to more talented up-in-coming singers and dancers. She resorted to vile means in order to stay on top, which included sabotaging auditions, slightly poisoning her chorus girls and understudies if she felt they were getting to close to her

jobs and her position in any company she was apart. Though as cruel as
Jordan Dean, her mother, when it came to holding onto what she had
worked so hard for, this twenty-four year old was not above doing
anything, to retain her power including drugs.

No one would guess that a vindictive and destructive person
inhabited this particular petite woman, when first seeing her porcelain
coco-colored face. The portrait of perfection which she had become as
she matured into young adulthood was wrapped in the innocent veneer of
her roughly five-five frame. Her dimensions were what dancers strived to
have, and her feet were the perfect size as any dancers could be. Her gait
was that of dancer's and her strut allowed her rear end to reflect it as she
walked into a room. Her clothes fit as though she were a mannequin,
slightly smaller than runway material; but she could still command a room
with the radiance of her smile and personality. Her honey tinted eyes
showcased a possible charm that she was capable of exuding, but never
did, which was an ability that attracted her to the man that would become
her lover and dealer of the ultra sleek powder that could keep her at peak
performance.

She had gotten reacquainted with Marcus Tillsdale, her boyfriend,
at a post *TONY* bash, the theatre's equivalent to the *Academy Awards*. He
was one of the dancers in *Sweeny Todd* as she was in the chorus. He
caught her eye during their run of the show, but she never acted upon her
infatuation until the *TONY* party. He stood six-foot tall, athletically

built, and had the skin of moonless nights. When he spoke, he commanded, like Helen of Troy, the ships to move, and everyone to stand at attention at his prowess and lexis. He, like Paige, was groomed for his Broadway career from an early age. From chorus to headliner in *WICKED*, he was her male equivalent. Just as nasty, destructively talented, the two of them together on the stage only palled in comparison to their works in the bedroom. Their sinews tightly wrapped around the other, with agile limbs congealed into shapeless wonders, the two of them made passionate love for hours on end until one or the other had to be at a matinee or rehearsal.

They were not only congruent in their passions for their careers, but their unabashed and superfluous need to hold on to it by any means necessary. He introduced her to ***PRAVELINE*** aka ***JEM***, a high tech drug that would keep the body as lubricated as possible and allow for the complicated moves which were required every moment on the stage, without any recourse of pain or recovery time. Paige and Marcus were using these maneuvers to make them unstoppable and a tour de force on the Great White Way, which didn't easily bend to African-Americans too easily.

"One minute to curtain Ms. Dean." The stage manager filtered through the door. This was the moment she had waited for. Costume, wig, and microphone in place, she stood and gave herself a once over in the mirror.

"Paige, break a leg," she whispered to herself. She kissed the mirror, a tradition she started as a teen in drama camp. "I'll be right there," she called back to her stage manager. She looked at her family photos lining her dressing table and knew for certain that even though they were not physically, emotionally present, she had them there with her.

Marcus was at her first performance as Nettie. She saw him in the masses of the standing ovation she had at the end of the play. He greeted her backstage in her dressing room after a quickly getting rid of that show's perspiration. "You were magnificent Pagie," Marcus said in his baritone, as he brought her into a deep hug.

"I messed up in the second act. I wasn't supposed to..." She tried explaining, but Marcus cut her off with a quick kiss to her lips.

"Only you knew. The crowd went crazy for your performance."

"You think so?" She inquired.

"I know so. So, what's on tap for tonight, Sardy's, The So-Ho Club, home to work off the adulation..."

"I'm starving. I was too nervous to eat all day."

"Then Sardy's it is."

Her cell phone chimed from her ragged duffle bag she had had since her early days in Julliard. "I'm Changing" from Broadway's *Dreamgirls* allowed her to know her phone had a caller. "Who could be calling this late?"

"Probably someone who wants to congratulate you."

"You're right." She rifled through her bag to find the phone, but it was too late. She had missed the phone call. She looked at the missed call list. The last number was from her parent's home. She knew this was never a good sign. The Deans didn't disturb each other unless a dire emergency was in affect. She listened to the voicemail. She got the same one that her brother Dontavious had gotten from the family's maid. Her brother Kevin was dead and she was urged to return to Atlanta as soon as she could. She fell into Marcus' arm distraught, for it was her favorite brother that was killed.

Paige Dean was on the next flight Atlanta to be with her family to mourn the death of her brother Kevin.

CHAPTER 4

Jordan Campbell Dean, Kevin's mother, was finishing her planning of The Annual Peachtree Harvest Ball when she heard of his tragic death.

She had planned the ball since its infancy some thirteen years prior. Originally a way to show off the Mt. Paron Road mansion her husband had designed and built for her, the ball had morphed into a profitable fundraiser for The Alzheimer's foundation, a disease in which her mother had passed away from, or at least that's what she had told people.

She was meticulous with every immaculate detail from napkins, gobies (spotlights that reflected a particular stencil on the walls), to the color of carpet that each guest would mingle upon. This day in particular she was trying to work out the venue details at the FERNBANK MUSEUM, which this year's ball would be held.

The FERNBANK MUSEUM was a wonder of architecture that held vaulted glass ceilings, fossils, and a Star Gallery that would amaze every guest. In Atlanta's Eastside, it was, as Jordan thought, the perfect venue for Atlanta's upper-crust to socialize after dark. Tongues would be wagging, as well as the positive social critiques in the *Journal-Constitution* the day after of how beautiful the event looked, felt and tasted.

The museum's aesthete blended well with the wonderment of scientific discovery—spiral stair cases leading from the gallery into the main hall where the center attraction, the skeleton of a Brontosaurus, left many stupefied. Its bones only shadowed by colossal bay windows that overlooked a lake reflecting the light of a night's magical moon. Jordan knew the perfect mixture of the fall colors of oranges, reds, and yellows coupled with the low lights that illuminated from the vaulted ceilings would set the stage for a ball that would top all balls she had ever thrown.

"Brianna Davidson, are you paying attention to me!" Jordan snarled as she poured Hennessey into her now empty snifter.

"All apologies Mrs. Campbell-Dean," Brianna tried to get herself out of hot water with much failure. "But you are going quite quickly..."

Brianna was a cute brown skinned young lady of thirty-three years. She was a thick woman, who wasn't afraid to show her curves in every outfit she wore, and dared anyone to say anything about it. She had become known as the planner to have, and Jordan recognized her talent at a benefit Brianna threw at the Egyptian Ball Room, located at the prestigious FOX THEATRE off of Peachtree Street in Downtown Atlanta. She was smart, and her eye to detail matched Jordan's well. They had the same taste, and a degree from Carnegie-Melon didn't hurt Miss Davidson's position in the Dean family inner-circle. But what most attracted Brianna to Jordon was her ability to withstand the hurricane force gale winds Jordan had in her arsenal for anyone she felt was out of her league, which usually was everyone that wasn't in Atlanta's upper-crust, and even then some of them.

"Oh, am I now? You can't keep up?" Jordan retorted.

"But being accommodating doesn't equal speed Mrs. Campbell-Dean. Just like a good rump in the sack, it needs to be slow, methodical and decisive. You just can't have everything you want and expect to come with ease. You have to work at it, and that takes patience."

Jordan like the analogy and like the two year's prior, Brianna had softened the tone that was now laced with more than a half a bottle of Hennessey. Brianna knew of Jordon's famous drinking and rude behavior, and knew exactly what would appeal to her womanly side, more than anything, that would keep her over the top persona at a somewhat human level.

Jordan wasn't a tyrant to those who really knew her. But it was rare that anyone really got close to Jordon in order for her to reveal her admiral traits. She was the most insufferable human being to grace the earth since Grindal's Mother, for those who didn't know her. She tried really hard to filter things she said through a "pleasant sieve," but she tended to treat people like the gum that someone had scraped off their shoe, put in the trash and sent to the junkyard, only to be rescued by mice that made a nest out of it, and raised their children. Her behavior wasn't her fault, though. Her father treated her as a princess, and knowing how lucky he was, her husband, Zechariahs, made her his queen. Zechariahs knew he had a good thing when he found Jordan and latched onto her. The mother of four was graced with a body that bounced back fairly quickly after each child. And the one unnatural mark on her body was from a c-section done to remove her last child, Paige, from her twenty-two years prior.

At fifty-eight, she stood five-foot-eight, and had a twenty-two inch waist. Menopause only enhanced her breast, which were already a supple double-b, now they bordered on a low c. Her short hair, always cut in the latest style, was pepper gray in color, and each curl set so perfectly on her head, it was if God himself had laid the foundations of them himself. Her lips were perfect for her, though in childhood she couldn't stand them because of their supple nature and the fact that they were quite full: bee stung, for those who were trying to describe them.

And here she was planning the ball, and finishing off a bottle, and was still lucid and as brash as she was when she was sober, which was hardly ever. And Brianna was now immune and pretty much laughed off the behavior. "I've got the FERNBANK meeting tomorrow, with the specifications you've set up, Mrs. Campbell-Dean," Brianna continued once she saw she had pleased Jordan. "And I will get back with you later on in the day to work out the rest of them. Is that okay?"

"Perfect darling. It's indeed getting late. Have a good one and I'll see you tomorrow."

"You too Mrs. Campbell-Dean." With a quick placement of her Louis-Vuitton notepad in her attaché case of the same brand, she sauntered off to her home where she was prepared to do more hours of planning for this year's big event.

Jordan sat on the chaise and regaled in thoughts of the upcoming ball and what would be Atlanta's premier event of the fall. But she remembered that it was early June. Months of planning still lay ahead. Her excitement waned, as well as the fifth of Hennessy that she had poured into her snifter.

She drifted off to sleep with her snifter in her hand, something she had done many nights before. A slight tap on her shoulder jostled her awake.

"What is it?"

"Mrs. Dean wake up." Sascha said softly, as not to incur Jordan's wrath. Five hours had passed, it was almost three in the morning. It wasn't her husband that woke her up this eve.

"Can't you see that I'm sleeping?" She snipped. She sat up groggy, struggling to stabilize what she saw in front her, as not to expel the contents of her stomach at the same time.

"Mrs. Dean, I have some really bad news..."

CHAPTER 5

Zechariahs Dean's secretary buzzed into office to let him know he had a call the morning that would be the untimely death of his youngest son Kevin.

Paper work and phone conferences abound, and he politely let her know to take a message. If he had known that would be the last time he would speak with his youngest son, he would've told his secretary to pipe the call through. But he didn't and Kevin was killed tragically that evening and he hadn't gotten to talk with his son one last time.

It wasn't that Mr. Z—as many in the business world called him—was too busy to talk; he had a lot on his plate at present, more than this fifty-seven year old man had ever bargained for. It had been one month since he officially threw his hat into the Atlanta mayoral race. Turning over the day to day activities of Dean Architecture and Construction, a company he had vested blood, sweat and tears into to his middle son Malek, was his current concern. He didn't want his legacy to go to waste and his company led astray by new hands.

He knew Malek would lead the company into a new era seamlessly, but he wasn't certain that this particular moment was the right time to make such a drastic decision. He poured over paper work that would entitle his middle son the money, power and respect that made him THE leading contract builder and architect in the world. His son knew the business, and he knew the ins and outs of what it took to be just as cut throat, if not more menacing than his father. But regret and second thoughts drifted closely in the back of his mind. He regretted that his other children didn't want anything to do with the company, even though they had benefited greatly from the wealth and grandeur it procured throughout the beginning of their lives.

Somehow he felt responsible for turning them away from a passion he had had growing up in Statesboro, Georgia some forty odd years earlier. After being given a book on Roman architecture from his parents when he was ten, he was in forever entranced by the man-made creations and their beauty. He dreamed of one day creating masterpieces of his own that likened to the Greco and Roman templates and would someday be the pillar of architectural wonder that future generations referred to as the stencil and which they would copy.

He had long days as a child investing in the future that would make him one of the richest African-American men in the world. Mornings were spent in the fields helping his sharecropping family tend to the year's crops. Late mornings and early afternoons he drifted off into his own world of structure and architectural innovations, while he was to be paying attention in his primary school classes of reading, writing and arithmetic. He got plenty of detentions for the doodles, as his teacher called them, and his mother incorporated many beatings, to break him of the creative habit he was developing.

When he told his mother what he wanted to pursue as his life's goal, she became angry, and told him to concentrate on the fields and bringing up a good crop. She was mad at his ludicrous dreams, as she thought they were, and wanted to bring him back to the reality of his present situation: sharecropping and living very inadequately. It was the only world that she had ever known. She also knew her son would have a hard enough time in the world being a black male, let alone in the Jim Crow South, where her mother was bought and sold only a few decades prior to his birth.

It's amazing what time does, he thought, as he read over papers he had asked his lawyer to draft just a few days prior. He dropped the papers and walked over to the window on the other side of his desk. He overlooked the city of Atlanta out of the picturesque window that covered more than half the length of the wall of his forty-second floor office in the middle of downtown Atlanta. He had come very far since he left Savannah for Morehouse and had climbed to the top of the business world one design at a time.

He regretted not being able to instill in his children, beside Malek, the great happiness and satisfaction he received from drawing blue prints, or making a sketch for a future project. He couldn't understand why they hadn't jump at the chance to be apart of an empire that rivaled Donald Trumps' and one of the biggest African-American businesses in the world. But like sugar to a child who craves it, the world of Dean Architect and

Construction excited them for a minute, but in the end its appeal waned and left them groggy and regretting their involvement in the first place. Because this craving would come with consequences, it was like a curse within itself and the time and energy required was not worth its appeal, at least not to Dontavious, Kevin, or Paige, as it was to Malek.

It was ten in the morning, and he had done what many had done in an eight hour work day. He was ready to reveal his plans to the board of Dean Architecture and Construction and tell his wife over dinner that night, if she wasn't too drunk to comprehend, that he would be entering into the political arena.

Though very few moans of concern were uttered, the new leader of Dean Architecture and Construction was installed. And by eight, Mr. Z. was on his way home to have dinner with his wife. When he arrived home he found her in the parlor passed out, as he believed that she would be. He didn't bother waking her, and was relieved, yet unsettled that she would discover his announcement on the front cover of the *Journal-Constitution* in the morning.

Zechariahs retired to the bedroom and took a long hot shower. He looked in the steamed laden mirror and wiped the rising humidity to view his once athletic body. It was still in tact, except for a small pooch brought on by years of eating well and lack of exercising as strenuous as he did in the fields of his childhood. He realized that his face hadn't changed, and his subtle graying hair gave hints to the decades of growth he had actually incurred. He was still sexy, and Atlanta Magazine agreed with his thoughts by naming him "Sexiest Businessman of the Year" three years in a row, a title he flaunted quite mercifully on the golf course with his business buddies, who of course, teased him about the dubious honor as well.

He put lotion on his various body parts, slipped into silk pajamas, and got into the bed. He didn't care if Jordan came to bed or not, he was tired, and he was going to get some rest before the next day would begin his political career and shape the rest of his life as he knew it. But what he didn't know was that the next day would change his whole family's life for what would seem like was the worst.

It was almost three in the morning when the cavernous halls echoed Jordan's horrific screams. He jolted from the bed and followed them, only to find her in the parlor where she was held by Sascha exuding her grief, tears rolling from every part of her body, shaking and nodding her head in disbelief. This couldn't be good, Zechariahs thought, and once he learned of what happened, his heart sank to the ground and a single tear rolled down his cheek. His youngest son was dead. He went to comfort his wife. They both melted in each other's arms as their common grief welded them together for the next two hours.

Kevin Dean's death brought the family together. But the mystery that surrounded his death and the events that followed affected the Dean family for generations.

CHAPTER 6

Dontavious' flight arrived in Atlanta bright and early Sunday morning. He hadn't been to Hartsfield-Jackson since the grand renovations, and was quite surprised at the small city the airport had become. Making his way down the concourse; he was dragging behind him his only piece of luggage. Each step brought him closer to a reality that he just didn't want to face, but the gait of those behind him insisted that he plow along faster than he had wanted. What would he say to his parents, his siblings; and what did the world hold for him in the city he so quickly abandoned years prior to joining the army?

He stopped at a shop on the concourse to buy gum, and to his surprise he saw his father on the cover of the *Atlanta-Journal Constitution* that was in the newspaper rack next to the counter. "Dean to Run for Office" he was not taken aback at his father's latest venture. His father had always had a passion for politics, and had critical analyses for what changes could be done to make the city, county, state and country a better place. While waiting in line to pay for the pack of gum, he picked up the newspaper and sifted through the cover article. A feeling of nostalgia rushed over him. He hadn't thought about this place, his family, or their bond since he left. His father's smile and mother's dulcet look took him back to his childhood, where he was protected and felt he could do anything.

"Sir…" the clerk's voice snapped him out of his venture down memory lane. "You ready?"

"So sorry. Just the gum." He handed her the gum, paid for it and continued to exit the huge airport. He walked outside and to his surprise he hadn't remembered the Southern humidity he had grown up with. The instant dampness of his forehead was wiped with his sleeve, and he unbuttoned the top of his collared shirt to help him cool down. He motioned for a taxi, and was surprised that it came quite quickly.

"Where to sir?" The Arab cab driver asked him in a distinctive accent.

"456 Mt. Paron Road, Atlanta," Dontavious answered back after looking at his text message of the new address he had yet been to.

"Pretty nice area," the cab driver said baiting trying to coax Dontavious into a conversation about his destination.

"Yeah, so they say…" Dontavious said in a manner as not to incur any more questions, and he sat back in the seat as he was driven down I-85 towards Mt. Paron Road, and his family's house. He noticed familiar surroundings, as he continued down the topiary-lined interstate. He noticed the exit for Stewart Avenue was now Metropolitan Avenue, and Lakewood Freeway was now Langford, Jr. Parkway as he passed both, and was quite surprised at the changes. Though they were just names, the freeway felt unfamiliar, and reminded him of the subtle changes that had occurred in his life as well—not just his brother's death, and family's estrangement, but a constant growing understanding of who he was as a person. The city for the most part was still the same, and its beautiful skyline with the gold-topped capital building, Peachtree Plaza Hotel, and Georgia Power building adorning part of the city's skyline, was still just as beautiful that bright Sunday morning as it was every night as he remembered.

He passed by Georgia Tech University on his left which he remembered from his childhood, and noticed the Varsity Restaurant to his right. He remembered the greasy fast food he had consumed there as a child, and the nights of hanging with his friends at the establishment in his teenage years. But quickly that fond remembrance was jolted by the new visual addition to the city to his left: *Atlantic Station*. As he would soon learn this was Atlanta's newest premier shopping, eating and living venue. A few more exits later, he arrived at his destination. He paid the taxi driver and exited to face his family's multi-million dollar home that was just a few yards down the driveway from the street he exited upon.

He walked up the driveway surrounded by high pine trees and emerald grass. Bushes shaped into various animals greeted him as he walked closer to the mote-like fountain in front of the Dean home. Asphalted and resembling a highway to heaven, The Dean's driveway with its vast greenery and shaded paths opened up to vastness of the abode. He hadn't seen the home in twenty years after its construction and was quite impressed by the vastness of it. The two story mansion boasted some forty rooms.

The house itself was menacing from the outside with it gothic arches and high-paned windows. If anyone was lucky enough to get this close to the home, they couldn't see anything due to the high shrubs that guarded the home better than any security fortress. He looked over his shoulders and noticed cars parked in the driveway. He knew there would probably be a house full helping his family deal with their grief. But was he really ready to deal with the crowd that would await him?

His heart pounded and palms became sweaty, and it wasn't due to the humidity either. He reached up to the door and knocked. It was quite soft as he told himself that if they didn't answer, he could turn around and not face his family. No answer. But he knocked again, this time louder.

The door crept open. He recognized the face on the other side of the door. Sascha Galardo, the family's maid, greeted him with a warm hug. She had changed; her now padded physique was not of years prior. But she was still as sweet and welcoming as she had always been, just a little touch of grey and slight wrinkles among her eyes and mouth gave clue to the years that had passed. "Mr. Dontavious, I'm so glad you've come, mijo."

"Sascha, so glad to see you. You haven't changed one bit."

"But you have Mr. Dontavious. Look at you, Músculos y una cara muy Hermosa." And from the Spanish he remembered, he responded bashfully to the fact that recognized his hard muscled body and handsome face. She hugged him once again, and brought him into the house.

The vastness of the outside of the house couldn't have prepared Dontavious for what awaited him on the inside of the home. A cascading staircase incased in marble, led to a grand foyer made of the same material. The vaulted ceilings were nearly fifty feet high, and its windows, seen on the outside, allowed the sun's beams to bounce so beautifully off of the maple-paned walls that traveled from the floor the ceiling. Dontavious knew his family had money, but this was, in his opinion, a very decadent show of wealth and demure.

Sascha closed the door behind and led him to the vast family room off of the main foyer. It was as grand as every room was in the immense mansion. The fireplace was surrounded by antique furniture and his parents littered the Queen Anne-chairs closer to the entrance of the room where Jordan sat on the couch being held by Zechariahs. Jordan almost didn't notice him because of the cloud of grief surrounding her. But peering up she saw the face of her first born and glided to him, as to welcome him back to the fold.

"My baby's returned...Dontavious, I missed you so." She wrapped her arms around him, trying to not let him go: making up for the years he had been away. He had missed her touch and smell: A mixture of cigarettes, Hennessey and Chanel number nine that he had grown to love as a child. He remembered the nights of her tucking him and his siblings in the bed and the smell being the last thing and the first thing that would hit him the morning. This was before the money, the maid and the big house.

He held her. She was still a lot smaller than he, and she disappeared into his muscled frame. He was somehow protecting her from the world that had recently dealt her an awful blow by taking her youngest son away. He felt guilty in that moment because he wasn't there when the news came down, and couldn't have shielded her from this current hurt.

"I came as soon as I heard mom."

"My first born has come home." She wiped her cheeks, smiled and hugged him once again.

"I just wish it wasn't under these circumstances."

"We all do son," his father piped in as he approached. The two embraced in the middle of the family room. Awkward at first—balancing between a hug and handshake—his father and he agreed up a happy medium between the two. Dontavious was looking into a mirror, as he had grown to look like the father he had tried to be nothing like. He was younger and more physically fit than his father, but the similarities outweighed those topical differences. "How have you been son?"

"Good. Life's great..."

"I've been keeping up with you Sergeant First Class Dean." Dontavious was taken aback at his father's knowledge and even caring of what had been going in his world. "I'm proud of you son."

"Thanks pop." Dontavious embraced his father more tightly. His grief compounded by the mere affection and caring of parents made him weep openly the tears he had been concealing since his first cry a day ago.

"Can I get you something to drink Mr. Dontavious?" Sascha asked.

"Water would be nice. Thanks Sascha," he replied.

"Look, who's back!" Dontavious turned around to see the smiling face of his little sister Paige.

"Paigey is that you?" He asked with uncertainty. When he had last seen his sister she was only five and was going into first grade. He had never imagined that she would transform into a woman he would not recognize in a line up if given the chance. But he did recognize her from photos online he found on Broadway.com, that he visited very rarely, but where he kept up with his sister's flourishing stage career. She was even more stunning in person, he thought. They embraced.

"It's been years D." Paige whispered, as she held back tears that welled inside her eyes.

"Too long Paigey...too long." He held her as he did his mother moments prior and felt an instance guardianship over her, as to make up for lost time when he should have been protecting her from the world as the role of big brother commanded him do so. She was now an adult, a thriving citizen of society with the same woes as anyone of her age, but he still saw the little girl who he was begrudgingly asked to watch swim laps in the family pool when his mother was too drunk to do so. The same girl, he remembered, he helped with her ABC's, when she thought L, M, N, O, P was one letter. He couldn't believe that time had passed so quickly, but indeed it had.

He was only back for a few minutes before pangs of guilt racked his body. He had been gone for so long: missing all of the triumphs and milestones of his family's life. Though he had rationalized why he had to be absent, he hadn't really rationalized why he hadn't been back to this place. He had missed them. He understood them, and they he, without any explanation or heirs.

"For my brother was dead, and he is alive again, was lost and now found…" The snide voice of his brother Malek sounded behind him. Dontavious turned to face him. "Dontavious, it's been a long time my brother. Welcome back." Malek made no effort to embrace his brother. He stared at him waiting for him to make the first move. Kameron watched curiously as the act before her unfolded. This new person she had heard about, but the actuality of his presence she could never really imagine, until this moment.

"Malek…it's been…" Dontavious started.

"Years, almost twenty and you haven't called, visited, or sent a damn post-card."

"This is not the time Malek!" Zechariahs sternly said, his voice building a barricade between the two.

"Just to let you know..." Malek continued, "I've taken care of the press release with Brianna's help. Everything's in order father and mother just like you asked for me to do so." Malek retreated into the kitchen followed by Kameron.

"Who was that with Malek?" Dontavious inquired.

"Some trash that your brother found, dressed up, and called a treasure..." Jordan snarled, as she tried to mask the venom that lay underneath with little success. The conversation continued as each of them reconnected with old family business as well as life since they were absent from each other.

While Dontavious reconnected with his parents and Paige, Malek poured himself a glass of orange juice from an awaiting carafe on the table. Kameron poured herself a glass of Hennessey from Jordan's open bottle on the counter. "This early?" He said in response to her drinking.

"Your mother does it," she didn't miss a beat. "So that's the absent brother?" She continued.

"My oldest brother, Dontavious."

"You don't look too happy..."

"This nigga hasn't been back here in twenty years, and..."

"And what Malek?"

"Nothing...I'm just giving my mother and father time to reconnect with their oldest." He lied trying hard to cover what was brewing underneath, trying not to show weakness. He hated that his eldest brother was back and that his father and mother were doting over him. He had worked almost twenty years to gain an iota of respect and admiration from them, and he felt that it was now being stolen by his brother's emergence out of no where. He was no longer the confident man he had grown into being, and had taken years to become, but he now retreated back to the insecure adolescence and teenager he was when he was cast into the shadow of Dontavious and his great accomplishments.

The green eyed monster was easily seen by Kameron, and she knew this would be the perfect exploitation to get what she wanted and to easily break down the strong hold that Malek now had over her. She knew the presence of Dontavious could be used best to her advantage and would do whatever she could to make sure her future was secure even in the short time Dontavious would probably be in town. She was thinking about herself as she always did and what it would mean for her future in the long run, even in this moment of grief.

Malek sat on the chair, despondent and Kameron came over and hugged him. "He'll be gone after the funeral, hopefully, and everything will go back to normal," she lied as to appease her fiancé. But she secretly hoped he would stay around for quite a bit longer, at least until she could work her magic and make Malek crumble to his knees.

In the family room everyone was getting settled from the initial welcoming that had taken place when Dontavious arrived, and the subsequent storm that had brewed in when Malek had entered. Jordan and

Zechariahs draped Dontavious as Paige sat on the fainting chair taking in the surroundings. Each was more interested in Dontavious with each passing moment trying to figure out what had been happening with him and why he hadn't returned home. Dontavious tried downplaying the absent years as just time getting away from him and nothing peculiar. But he was constantly trying to mask the pain and the real reason he left. He didn't want to share with his parents that he needed to get from the shadow of the Dean wealth and power and requirements of both. He didn't want to sound ungrateful and make their years of hard work seem in vein.

"Does anyone know what happened to Kevin? How he was murdered?" Dontavious inquired. His mother began to weep. And Dontavious felt badly for the question he had just posed. "I'm sorry. I wasn't thinking..." But secretly he knew that this question, of all questions, would take the focus off of him and the reason for his absence.

"It's okay Dontavious." Zechariahs said putting a comforting arm around his weeping wife. "Wrong place, wrong time." A deafening silence infiltrated the room at that moment. It was a collective gasp that they had all waited so long to release. The truth wasn't out, but definitely some understanding or at least some appeasement of the brutal act was now in the open. They all realized the senseless act that had taken their brother's life could have been prevented if he hadn't been where he was at that exact moment. It made them question their belief in fate and what exactly was the beginning of the end for something more in all of their lives.

The doorbell rang and moments later Mya entered. Dontavious hadn't seen this face in years, and it had not changed. Her sweet countenance looked as though she had slept for years in a honeysuckle and buttermilk cocoon. Her petite frame, topped by long flowing black hair, touched the small of her back with effortless abandon. The half black-half Korean beauty was the perfect compliment to her late husband Kevin.

She hugged her mother-in-law, and then moved on to Zechariahs, who held her tightly. And as quickly as he started to hug her, he quit. No surprise to Mya, she smiled and softly said, "It's okay dad, you won't hurt this little one." She touched her belly every-so gently in contrast to the words she had just uttered. Her flawless frame only gave hints of an early pregnancy with a soft-ball sized bump that stopped her body from flowing so perfectly in her dress, as it once did before she and Kevin discovered their latest blessing.

"Girl, you're even more beautiful pregnant." Paige said, coming behind her and hugging her.

"Thanks Paige. And you're looking good. I might need some dance instruction after this little one comes to get my shape back."

"I wouldn't even know you were pregnant if it wasn't for that blip in your dress."

"I feel like a small country...Is that you Dontavious?" She said noticing the Dean she had not seen in almost two decades.

"How are you Mya?"

"I'm well, considering." She hugged him. "How have you been Mr. Dean? You still look the same..." She said coyly as she let her mind go back to the first time she had laid eyes on Dontavious in high school. He was a senior on the football squad, and she a freshman junior varsity cheerleader. Double occupancy of the football field allowed the athletes and the athletic supporters to commingle during practice and this is where she saw him. She noticed him first out of the corner of her eye, and made no qualms about finding him quite attractive.

"You haven't changed a bit either." Dontavious said breaking her free from the memory that she allowed herself to partake.

"Life is so fleeting..." She whispered, almost to herself.

"Brunch will be done shortly, please come into the dining room. You all need your strength." Sascha said as she retreated back into her domestic domicile.

"I can't eat anything. I'm going to my study." Jordan said as she stood up from the couch.

"Do you want me to join you?"

"No, Zech. I'll be okay. Get something to eat. I just need to be alone." She disappeared out of the room.

The family sans Jordan had brunch in the palatial dining room. Each sat around the twelve person table, seats in between the other. Eggs, fried chicken, biscuits and grits were scooped up from plates, and only the clang of forks against china was heard. Not a word was uttered and no one dared to invent small talk to purvey the grief filled room. Each was trying to find their way of dealing with the loss of their love one. The Southern comfort food did help ease the pain, but this escape was fleeting as the clang of the grandfather clock brought them back to the reality of the situation.

"I have to be going. They want me to view the body today and choose the suit." Mya said placing her linen napkin over her plate and backing away from the table. "Are you sure you and Mrs. Dean don't want to come with me?"

"You'll call if you need anything, right?" Zechariahs said.

"Everything'll be fine. I'll call you later, dad." She said as she gave him a kiss on the cheek. "And it was so great seeing you again Dontavious." She hugged him once again and exited the room.

Brunch continued. The clang of china continued until each left for their respective places to ready themselves to bury Kevin Dean.

CHAPTER 7

By nightfall, Dontavious found himself trying to adjust to his bedroom in a house he had only seen in blue print years before he left. He tossed and turned, trying to put a sieve through the things that placated his active mind. Familiar obligations; keeping secret his life away from them, and the funeral kept his mind active in the still Georgia night. The chirping crickets were his only company, as he failed to obtain sleep. Maybe it was the change in time or the surroundings, but he knew that this was not going to be an easy night.

He abandoned his chances of sleep, and took a walk down the hallowed halls of the structure that his parents called home. He looked at the sepia toned walls and beige carpeted floors and soon realized that his father had a prowess for decorating, as he did designing, even though he knew his mother probably had more influence on the interior, than not. He found himself going down the grand hallway to the foyer and down the spiral staircase. He decided that a night cap that would relax him and the bar in the family room where he was earlier would be the perfect place to get it.

He poured himself a shot of gin, and took it with little effort. He hadn't taken a drink in years, but he felt the current situation prompted it. He poured himself another, and was almost to take it when his sister entered the room. "What are you doing up so late?" Paige questioned.

"I could ask you the same question baby sister."

"I couldn't sleep."

"Same here. Want a drink? Are you old enough?" He said jokingly.

"I am. Very funny...I didn't think military men drank..."

"They're the worse. You have to have something to take your mind off of your current situation—especially in wartimes."

"And from the look of you and Malek earlier, is this the beginning of World War Three?"

"Malek and I have always been distant if you remember."

"I was five when you left. I don't remember much."

"God, how time flies. You had pigtails when I left. "

"Yep..."

Dontavious looked up and noticed a painting he hadn't seen before when he was in the room. "I can't believe it."

"What?"

"They kept it all these years: The *EBONY* Cover."

"Oh, that. Mama had it commissioned about ten years ago. She said she wanted it on top of the mantle. I was just born when this picture was taken."

He took a closer look at the commissioned painting that was made to look like the cover of the *Ebony Magazine* the family had pose for over twenty-two years prior. The family was picked as a premier black family who *EBONY* felt represented the values, achievements and reflected the

positives aspects of the African-American family and experience in the
United States: Jordan seated on the couch holding a baby Paige, was
flawless in her two piece Armani suit, and standing behind her,
Zechariahs in a tailored three piece suit, and his three boys in polo shirts
and khakis—Dontavious-fourteen, Malek-twelve, and Kevin-seven—were
holding up the pillars of the family on either side. The ***EBONY*** red-boxed-
white-lettered trademark emblem atop of the painting made it an
authentically recreation from the actual photo that had the cover title:
"The Dean Family: Constructing the African-American family one brick at
a time." Though the title of the article was not transferred to its oil based
recreation, the family portrait of sorts took Dontavious back to when he
was once apart of the family unit.

"I hated it...the day we took this photo."

"Why?"

"You wouldn't shut up for one. No matter how we tried, you kept
on screaming and mama didn't know what to do with you."

"I was born, what, three weeks prior. I was a newborn. I wasn't
ready for lights yet. I barely got eyebrows or lashes..."

"And Malek and I kept on bickering about something that day. I
don't know what it was, but dad had to threaten us quite a few times with
a severe ass whopping if we didn't straighten up."

"That's not hard to believe."

"And Kevin was standing there, saying nothing. Not wanting to rile feathers, just trying to do what was right, and do his part to make the bigger picture look better..." Jordan swept into the room unnoticed until she brokered the silence with her observance of Dontavious' foray into the remembrances of the painting.

"Mama..." Paige went to her mother and hugged her. "We didn't see you for the rest of the day." And once Jordan's mouth opened, Paige knew as to where she had been for those twelve plus hours.

"I just needed to escape. And if I leave town they will think I'm heartless. And if I drive around town they will surely lock me up for driving under the influence. My only refuge is my study."

"Mama, can I get you water or something?"

"Honey if I drink anything else I will float away." She said trying to keep her balance, as she held onto the back of a Queen-Anne chair. She smiled, and Dontavious' memories of his drunken mother took hold of him and jolted inside of him one of the reasons why he had to abandon his family and their never changing issues and drama.

"Mama, let's get you to bed."

"I'm not sleepy."

"We all need to sleep, mama, come on. Dontavious is right. Let's get you upstairs." Paige said trying to rationalize with her unstable mother.

"I don't want to go to fucking sleep! Shit, I can't go to sleep. I see him. I see his face!" Jordan blurted with a tear stained grimace, as she protested the nightmare induced weeping she knew she would face once she allowed herself to drift off to sleep.

"I understand mama." Dontavious tried empathizing with his mother, but he soon realized that nothing short of drinking three bottles of Hennessy and smoking three packs of cigarettes would get him to truly understand how his mother was feeling at that moment.

"Just leave me! Please. I need to be alone. Please!" She sat on the Queen-Anne chair that was holding her up moments earlier and she sat staring at the painting above the fireplace. She hadn't grieved in nearly twenty years since her father's death from cancer. And it had been twenty years before that since she had grieved for her brother Josiah, who died in Vietnam.

Dontavious and Paige did as they were instructed and left the room, leaving their mother to grieve in her own way. The door closed to the family room and the two heard their mother cursing God for what he had done, and she finally let out a wail that released what pain the Hennessey filled cordials had not. "Do you think that she'll be okay?" Dontavious asked his sister as the two refrained themselves from entering the closed room.

"She has to do this her way..." Paige didn't understand the grieving process, nor did she know what it felt like to lose a child. She just knew that her mother needed this time to take her voyage down the road of acceptance and understanding of the situation, at least in private this pain could be let out in its natural context. Because anyone who knew the Deans knew that they kept a front to the outside world at all times and the motions her mother was going through in that closed off family room dared not emerged on the spotlight of the funeral of her brother.

Dontavious returned to his room and closed the door where he sat with his thoughts in the dark. Moonlit shadows crept up his bed spread, but sleep did not. He tried repeatedly to invite it into the room, but it refused to enter.

But sleep did come for Paige when she went to her room. She closed the door and removed her bottle of *PRAVELINE* from her bag. She knew this drug was the only thing that could relax her, and make her forget about the things that were now plaguing her mind. Once taken intravenously, she was out like a light. It wasn't until the next afternoon that she woke.

CHAPTER 8

As Dontavious wrestled with sleep, and Paige drifted off into a drug induced stupor, Malek sat at home reading over reports sitting in his bed. It was as though the news of his brother's death was a slight speed bump before he continued with his day of corporate maneuvers and business as usual. He looked over a new deal that was presented by Kameron a few weeks prior and given the green light: one of his father's last actions as the acting head of the company. Though he doubted Kameron's prowess and utility in her position as Vice President of Acquisitions, that he had given her to ease her into his bed, combing over the numbers and the proposed profit margin for the newest potential acquisition was proven to be a profitable decision for the company. He smiled to himself and soon realized that his bed partner was not just a great arm piece or someone to keep him occupied in bed, but she was quite intelligent and could be a tremendous asset to the company and his life as a whole.

"I brought you some chamomile." Kameron smoothly said as she glided into the room with piping hot tea on a tray service reminiscent of the turndown service at The W.

"Didn't think you knew how to boil water, Kam?" He said condescendingly.

"I don't. But I figured it out." She facetiously sprayed back.

"That was nice of you. It's not poisonous is it?"

"I'm not completely heartless; unlike you reading over work the day after your brother was murdered."

"Work doesn't stop because of a death, even my brother's."

"So you say." She continued as she watched him place his work on his lap, and then sip on his tea, blowing on it trying to cool it off. "How did I do?"

"It's tea, not crème brulee."

"I'm trying to be the dutiful fiancée."

"Thanks." He said unwillingly.

"Why are you such an ass to me Malek?"

"Why do you care, Kameron?"

"I wish I could answer that..." She heard the familiar buzz of her blackberry calling to her from her briefcase that she kept by her side of the bed. "But work calls Mr. Malek, and we will get into it later." She laid on her side of the bed and reached down to her briefcase and produced the blackberry. She looked and saw that she had a new text message. She retrieved the newest message and read its contents: "Shawty hit a nigga back when u git dis shit. Need u like 4 reals." She recognized the text's sender without even looking at the number that she didn't dare store fearing the prying of eyes of Malek. She politely replied back, "Not tonight!" And she pushed send, deleting its contents immediately.

"Who's sending you a text this time of night?" Malek had grown steadily suspicious of Kameron since the time she tried to leave him and he had to produce the contract to stall her advances. He knew she wasn't dumb enough to risk it all again, especially since she had knowledge and was no longer ignorant of the legalese of their relationship.

"A message from earlier from Wanda, my secretary. I have a meeting bright and early in the morning to discuss the new Swedish Acquisition. See." She showed him the blackberry and Malek saw that the message, in fact left earlier by Wanda, was what Kameron was reading, or so he was lead to believe. Not being a fool, she had quickly deleted the anonymous text that she had actually received at that moment and covered with the one she luckily had read earlier that day. "Are you jealous?" questioned him.

"No, just protecting my investment." He snidely said as he turned over and placed his stack of papers on the night stand, turning his back to Kameron.

She was so angry at the pigeon hold that Malek had over her and his smugness that he exhibited towards her now. He held all the cards, and unless she did something, she thought, she would be under his tutelage forever, and she will never be happy. Sure the money was great for her, and the power, but the control she missed and would do whatever she could in order to gain it back. That was the purpose of the new deal that she slid to Zechariahs on his last week and he instantly approved based on facts and figures that she knew no businessman in his right mind could ever turn down.

Malek's thoughts were no longer on Kameron as sleep came over him. Kevin's memory clouded his mind. The outside tough exterior was just that, and Malek let out a single tear that flowed down his cheek with the thoughts of his brother. He was privately grieving for his little brother, the one he had grown closest with over the past few years working together on various fundraisers under the insistence of his father and mother. He realized that the two of them were a lot a like, though Malek's hatred and sibling rivalry would have him suggest otherwise to himself in thought.

His brother was dead, and the grieving time was at that moment, though it was private and unheard by anyone, even Kameron his bed partner. This was the last time Malek would even show his emotions. As a good Dean, those were tucked away.

CHAPTER 9

It was one week before all the plans were solidified for Kevin's funeral. Every detail, overseen by Mya, was put together meticulously, as to befit her husband's legacy and impact he not only had on her life, but those who came in contact with him daily. She asked Reverend Reginald Newman to allow her to use their home church *Fountain of Faith Missionary Baptist Church* to house the funeral and he agreed.

The mourners processed into the church. It appeared smaller with the sheer mass of the people: local celebrities, rappers and politicians abounded for the state funeral of Kevin Dean. Dressed in his Atlanta Police Department issued Blues, Kevin laid peacefully in his mahogany casket that was draped in an American flag. Flowers, cards and other mementoes from mourners as far away as Savannah and those youth he had touched at the *Boys and Girls* club who couldn't make it to the massive turn out, surrounded the casket, and conveyed the love, admiration and brevity of this young man life, that was tragically cut short.

After a long hour wait in the line, his wife, mother, father, two brothers and a sister and her boyfriend Marcus Tillsdale came in and took their respective seats. They, all covered in black, held their grief in with silent stoic faces that were warned to stay in place by Jordan in the family car on the way to the funeral. She relayed to them the need keep up appearances from the awaiting news hounds that now plagued the family as though they were Britney Spears or Kim Kardashian. It was American's obsession with wealth and power that Jordan feared would take away from the day they needed to bury her son.

As expected local news sources were there, and many who were present seemed to be checking out the local celebrities and delegates as though it were a club instead of a church. The mourners shook the hands of the family and made their well wishes known before they took their seats. From the pulpit family and close friends gave fond remembrances of Kevin's life and how he had been such a positive influence on Atlanta and her people. So much he was loved and admired, that Kevin could have easily run for politics, got elected and served his city well.

It was almost thirty people who spoke of his greatness before the eulogy was given by Reverend Newman. He regaled the crowd in endocrine words of wisdom, love and made people feel at ease during the mourning process as many, like Mya, tried to figure out how and why his life was cut so tragically short. He finished with the inspired words, "Be of good courage, and press forward. Kevin would have wanted you to." With that he came to the family, shook their hands and walked to the door, where he would await the exiting procession.

The service lasted almost two hours. His flag was draped over the casket's entirety and taken out by his fellow APD detectives and officers. The family followed and the rest of the mourners filed out.

The funeral procession arrived at North Lawn Cemetery minutes later where they lowered his body into the ground. Zechariahs followed by Jordan, scooped dirt and dropped it on his lowered casket. His siblings and other mourners, who were permitted to the private burial followed suit, as "dust to dust and ash to ash" adjourned them from their solemn task of that day.

Kevin Dean was buried.

CHAPTER 10

Cocktails and food abound to help the mourners with their grief at the repast at the Dean Mansion. Zechariahs, Malek, Paige and Mya were flanked by those who wish them well and regaled them of the memories that they had of Kevin. Mya was constantly surrounded by people. And she reassured them that she was fine and was going to be. "He's in a better place." She explained, becoming more exhausted with each passing person, as she tried to feign gratefulness for the people's well wishes. Though she cared about what they were saying about her husband and the memories they all shared, her only true wish was that of having her husband standing right next to her and him not dead.

Dontavious, sensing that she was becoming overwhelmed, swooped in and rescued her from the onslaught of well wishers. "So, how's everything?" He asked as he handed her a glass of orange juice. The other mourners dispersed, leaving the two to their conversation.

"I'm okay...I just wish I had a moment to myself."

"If you need to, I can distract them while..."

"I'm so sorry I couldn't have protected Kevin! Forgive me please Mya." Cole said as he appeared in front of Mya and Dontavious, interrupting their conversation.

Kevin's partner and friend Coleman Denavar, who stayed relatively out of sight since the murder, stood in front of Mya. Cole, as he was known to Kevin, had become his best friend and confidant since the academy, and promised that he would watch out for him like a brother.

"You two work a very high risk job." She hugged him, and Cole's tension and grief seem to ooze at that moment, releasing his guilt that racked inside of him.

"Are you okay Mya?"

"I'm fine. The question is are you?

"I didn't think you could forgive me for allowing this to happen. That's why I have been out of sight."

"You couldn't have stopped what happened to him Cole. No one could have. Don't beat yourself up."

"I'm so selfish." He said as a single tear rolled down his face. He wiped it as discretely as he could with little success.

"No, you're okay." She hugged him and Dontavious could finally see the person who was in front of him very clearly and was taken temporarily out of his moment of grief. He looked into Cole's eyes and realized that his grey eyes were allowing him to see inside his soul: all truthfulness, as though he was tethered to a lie detector. What he further realized is how handsome Cole was. He was extraordinarily beautiful for a man who chose to live his life as an officer of the law. He should have been a model or a movie star, Dontavious thought, as he stared at the man that was once his brother's partner. How could anyone not stare at Coleman Denavar, a product of mix heritage, and a mind to match his beautiful exterior? The thirty four year old stood six foot even, and his Egyptian father and black mother gave his skin an olive hue that balanced his gray eyes perfectly. His glistening bald head lead to perfectly placed eye brows and curled eye lashes that led to perfectly molded lips. Dontavious was so entrenched in the new arrival that he didn't hear Mya introduce to the two. It wasn't until Cole held out his hand that he knew something had been said.

"I'm Cole. I was your brother's partner."

He didn't know what his name was. Distracted, but not for long, it came to him as he spat out: "I'm Dontavious. Kevin's older brother."

"I figured as much, since Mya just said that." He laughed. "Nice to meet you, man. Your brother was something else."

"He was..."

Mya faded back, as she allowed the two to talk. She walked around the party taking in the sights as she made her way to the food that was plated on silver trays and walked around by cater waiters. She took a mini quiche, ate and immediately remembered she had not eaten all day. She rubbed the little one inside her, and was quite surprised that she hadn't been reminded to do so earlier than that moment. She took another one as the small one moved a little, almost awaking from the slumber that it kept to allow its mother to mourn for its father.

Meanwhile upstairs, Paige was coming to grips with her mourning with Marcus in the bedroom, shooting up trying to numb that pain of sadness that racked inside her. Marcus, like he had the first time he turned her onto the product, administered it with care into her delicate arm. Her face took on a hue of euphoria that was a consequence of the drugs that lay inside her body. She didn't need to speak. They both understood.

Her relationship with Marcus was one of dependence, not just the drug factor, but that of the emotional tie that held them together beyond anything else that was in her life. Though she had accomplished great things in a short amount of time, Paige still had insecurity and a need to be accepted by someone, and Marcus gave her that assurance that she was loved unconditionally, though he was secretly using her for his greater gain. Another product of the cold Dean upbringing, Paige was wrapped easily around Marcus' finger as he pilfered money from her account to fund a lavish lifestyle that a struggling artist in New York could hardly afford.

And now sitting in the bedroom of the monstrous mansion, Marcus grasps the reality that he had hit the lottery. He realized that if he kept her doped up and kept her motivated long enough that a tiny piece of this rock could easily be his one day. What he didn't reveal to Paige that day as she sat mourning her brother, is that he was actually mourning himself for the newest loss of the wealth that his family had as a result of bad investments and stupid mistakes that drained the nouveau riche Tillsdales that had made their money during the technology boom of the early nineties. They both were using each other: one for emotional gain and the other for financial.

Brianna Davidson was the most stressed of everyone at the repast that evening. Trying to keep tabs on everyone as does any good PR person/ Personal Assistant for a family that was synonymous with privacy and decorum was increasingly more difficult with the more people who arrived. She knew if anyone were to get any dirt on the wealthy Dean family, they could spin it and create havoc for Zechariahs in the upcoming mayoral elections in the fall. She didn't allow any press into the affair, because she knew they would only exploit the family's pain and anguish of losing their member. She stayed back, not being seen, but always ready to jump in if the situation warranted.

Mya escaped to the back veranda with ease, where she saw Zechariahs sipping on a smoothie and smoking a cigar. She closed the door behind her and stepped closer to the railing that overlooked the spacious twenty acres of trees and grass behind the Dean mansion. "I thought I was going to be alone back here."

"Me too. I guess we both had the same idea."

"How are you?"

"If I get that question one more time..." She harshly said as she sat down, taking a load off.

"I didn't mean to..."

"Sorry, but all of these people walking around like automatons saying what they think you want to hear, and not giving a damn if you are okay or not."

"No one in that crowd knows how it feels to lose a child so young. And to lose him so tragically. And they sit there gulping Champaign, eating free hord'oeurves and trying their best to see inside the elusive mansion they had only read about in *Home and Garden*. It's pathetic."

"Have you seen Jordan since we've gotten back from the graveyard?"

"Held up in that study of hers...She's not taking it well. She was on a bottle and a half of Hennessy this morning. I can only imagine how many she's been through since we've returned."

"I miss him dad."

"He was lucky to have you. You were the best thing for him."

"More like the best thing for me. How am I going to survive dad?"

"Kevin would want you to. If not for him, for my grandchild you're carrying." He placed an arm around her shoulder. She turned into him and let out an emotional outpouring that she had not released all day. He stayed by her as both allowed the other to be naked emotional with each other as they watched the sun began its journey to dusk.

Malek and Kameron held their place by the grand staircase where mourners entered and exited as the day drew on. About six in the afternoon, Malek leaned over to Kameron: "I think I'm going to go and check on mama. She's been out of sight since we've been back."

"You go do that. I don't think I'll be particularly wanted there."

"Why would you say that?"

"Maybe the fact that your mother grimaces every time she sees me?"

"It's just your imagination."

"I must be really good at seeing things that aren't there then. Maybe I should be in another career, maybe a genie...magician..."

"So, will you be right here when I return?"

"I think I'm going to head to the office. We do have a meeting tomorrow and I must be prepared."

"I admire your tenacity."

"I'm trying to prove myself."

"Don't want people thinking you got your position on your back now, do we?" He said biting, trying to stir some kind of retaliation in her.

She said nothing at first, just smiled, trying to see where this goading was going to lead. Seconds later she kissed him on the cheek and slyly responded. "I'll prove you wrong as well. You'll see." With that she grabbed her clutch, placed it under her arm, and walk towards the door to leave.

"I'll see you at home later?"

"Like I have a choice." With that she was out of the house. Once on the other side of the door she got her blackberry out and typed in "*Meet you in ten minutes."* She knew what her real motivations were for leaving the repast early, but coincidentally so did Malek, but he was too afraid to admit it even to himself.

He walked up the staircase to Jordan's study that lay right at the top of the steps. He slightly knocked on the door before he entered the study that many dare not enter, especially on a day like today. "Mama, you okay?" He said as he closed the door behind him. Billy Holiday streamed in the background, as the fire place crackled in front of him. There he found his mother sprawled out of the chaise sipping yet more Hennessey from cordial of choice. "Are you okay Mama?"

"Baby, I'm fine. Come here." He walked over to his mother. Sweat began to seep from his forehead, and he began to wipe it off. It was humid outside, but with the fireplace lit in the middle of the summer, it was ten times as hot in this room, and he couldn't figure out how his mother was still in the room sitting and drinking. "You came to check on your mama?"

"I did. I haven't seen you all evening."

"Just needed time baby. You okay?"

"I'm well mama."

"Where's that gutter snipe?"

Not missing a beat he responded, "her name is Kameron."

"I couldn't care less what it is. Where is she?"

"She had to go and handle some business. Mama, I really do wish that you would be nicer to her. I am marrying her."

"I thought I saw a ring on that girl's finger. We all make mistakes don't we?"

"Mama..."

"I'm not arguing with you today Malek. This is the day we mourn your brother. Your fiancée and your lives can come another day."

"I understand mama."

She pressed her lips against her cordial and took another sip, finishing the fifth that she had begun that afternoon. "Could you leave me please Malek?" She put her cordial on the table and laid her head down on the fainting chair.

"Sure mama. Get some rest." He kissed her forehead and backed out of the room.

He walked into the air conditioned hallway, and it felt like an Artic wind, a much needed relief from the sauna he had just exited. Wiping his forehead, he proceeded down the stairs to the guests that were mingling below. Some had left, but many people still remained at the repast for the youngest Dean son.

"I'm so sorry to hear about your brother Malek." Alex said as he tapped Malek on the shoulder.

"Alexander Gallardo, how are you this evening?"

"I'm well. Your brother will truly be missed."

"Our brother, don't you mean?"

"We were raised like brothers weren't we?"

"They called us the Dean five if I recall in high school."

"'Who is this Mexican boy,'" Alex said laughing. "That's what that rude girl said who your brother Dontavious was dating, remember?"

"Yep. Dontavious said, 'that's my brother, got a problem?'"

Alex continued to laugh at the old memories that flooded back to him. He hadn't remembered those things in years, and really had no reason to. He was so busy with his life after graduating high school that he didn't look back to those days with nostalgia, but as motivation to get a better life for himself and his mother, who was the Dean's maid Sascha.

He had come to the United States at the age of five, skipping over the border with his mother, and moving in with his aunt in Texaco, Texas. Not knowing any English, he and his mother went to Georgia to find his father, who unbeknownst to them, had died in a horrible cannery accident a year prior.

Mourning hit them quickly, but the need to support her son, drove Sascha to look for work to feed and shelter the young Alex. The Dean's old maid had quit, and a week later Sacha showed up on their doorstep.

Jordan had a soft spot for the shivering Alex on that February afternoon and they soon were taken in as help for the Dean family. Alex and his mom stayed in the back house where he took his lessons of English he learned at school and in the Dean house back to his mother and the two grew into American citizens day by day. By high school, Alex was a spry five foot-nine, taller than his Mexican mother and father, and had an athletic body that all the girls wanted. He was a top track star, and many would joke, "If all Mexicans had his speed, they would have no problems jumping the border." This joke, he initially let slide, but eventually he was suspended from school for fighting a fellow classmate after that particular classmate called him "Speedy Gonzalez" and taunted him with, "ARRIBA, ARRIBA!"

He was not only a star athlete at Marist, but he graduated valedictorian of his class. His mother was so proud, she was even more proud of him the next year when he enrolled at UGA with intentions to study law. Law School at Yale came three years later, and he passed three state bars, and became a fantastic lawyer, starting off as a public defender in Connecticut, and eventually moving up the ranks of Assistant D.A. in Boston, followed by a move back home to Georgia where he worked his way up the ladder once more to General counsel for the State board. A person of his age had never accomplished this feat, let alone a Mexican. He held that post for three years and insisted that his mother quit her job as the maid for the Deans and promised her that she could have her own maid if she so desired.

"I will not leave this family. They've been so good to me, us, mi jo." His mother said when he made the suggestion. She did however revel in the fact that she now owned her home and could commute to the Dean mansion each day in her own candy apple red Mercedes. It was their background and his remarkable rags to riches story that laid the groundwork for the grassroots campaign in which he ran for the new District Attorney for the city of Atlanta. The previous November he was victorious and had become the first Latino D.A. in the state of Georgia.

"That was so many years ago." Malek continued taking Alex out of the trance his memories had left him.

"A lifetime ago brother."

"Yes and look at us now. You are the D.A. of Atlanta and I am the CEO of the biggest Fortune five hundred companies in the United States."

"I bet you love saying that one every day."

"You know it man."

"Where is that beautiful fiancée of yours? Kameron is it?"

"She had some work to take care of, and I let her go and do it."

"Keep a leash on that one. If I remember anything from meeting her at the Christmas party, she looked damn good."

"Remember you do have a wife."

"We're separated, or have you forgot?" Alex clued Malek.

"I forgot."

"So, how is the family?" Alex said, changing subjects, as not to rouse any unneeded insecurities out of Malek. (Alex knew he was handsome, and the constant dates he had been on, internet pages created in his honor, and multiple letters from female constituents reminded him that he looked good. His manicured hair, sculpted eyebrows, and Crest white smile, accompanied his well built body that his suits hung on perfectly each day in the D.A.'s office. He knew that he could get Kam, but didn't want Malek to fear his intercourse with the course the conversation was taking.)

"Mom's not doing well. She's held up in that study, trying to get her life together."

"It'll take time man. These things usually do. I remember my mom was in mourning for almost a year after my father died."

"I'm trying to be the rock for my family right now."

"And you're doing a great job brother." Dontavious said as he approached the two with Cole.

"Dontavious?"

"Alex?"

"Yeah. It's been what? Almost twenty years?"

"Man. Tell me about it. But you..."

"Look the same." They both said completing each other's sentences. They hugged, as long lost brother would, unlike he and Malek when he returned to the fold.

"I'm going to get something to drink. Want anything Alex?" Disgustedly Malek said as he looked at his brother who had interrupted his reunion with his Mexican brother.

"A glass of Merlot would be great, Malek. Thanks."

"No problem."

"Could you refresh my juice Malek?" Dontavious inquired.

"I didn't ask you!" Malek walked off towards the kitchen to retrieve the glass of wine, leaving his brother in his dust.

"Wow, what was that about?" Alex inquired. Cole looked on just as confused at the situation as his counterpart.

"So you two know each other?" Cole tried changing the subject.

"Yes, he is like a brother to me." Dontavious said explaining the connection.

"That's interesting. How small this world really is. Kevin really never explained how he knew you."

"We tended to keep business, business. You know."

"I understand."

"So Dontavious, how do you know Mr. Coleman Denavar?"

"We just met today. Mya introduced him as my Kevin's partner." Dontavious stated. "We've been talking for an hour now.

"Where is Kevin's widow?"

"I don't know. Last I saw her she was heading toward the back patio." Cole said.

"What have you been up to Dontavious? No one knew what had happen to you. Not even your mother."

"Well..." Dontavious started to expound upon the reasons why he hadn't been in contact all those years and why he stayed away. Of course he left out all of the juicy details that could be fodder for tabloids and racy autobiographical books that set atop bookshelves at *Borders* or *Barnes and Noble* and would go for millions of dollars to be retold. He sugarcoated everything and the three of them sat talking for a while.

Mya walked back into the kitchen after being outside on the back patio with Zechariahs where she left him smoking his second cigar. She saw Malek pouring the glass of merlot, and himself another cordial of Hennessey. "Malek, I haven't seen you all day."

"Mya, I've been busy. Entertaining is not an easy job, especially when you're the rock of the family."

She smiled, but what came out was not happiness induced, "When have you been anyone's rock?"

"Mya, today's the burial of your husband, my brother, let's not do this."

"You're right. My husband would want me to behave."

"Yes, by all means, pretend as though you have some couth."

"Relay that on to that girl you're engaged to." With that she dismissed herself and walked out of the kitchen. Not even the day of her husband's death could keep her malice for Malek at bay.

"Bitch!" Malek muttered to himself. He didn't care if she was carrying his future nephew or niece; he knew that their hatred and animosity for each other would not go away. By the time Malek made his way back over to the spot where Alex, Dontavious and Cole were talking, Alex had disappeared, as well and Cole and Dontavious.

On the back patio Zechariahs finished up his second cigar and stamped out the left over butt on the bottom of his shoe.

"I wish you wouldn't smoke, Mr. Dean." He turned around to see Sascha standing there with another smoothie in hand. "It's a terrible, terrible habit." Sascha continued, as she handed the smoothie to him.

"I get a reprieve today right, Sascha?"

"Of course mijo. Drink up. You haven't eaten all day. You need your energy."

"You're so good to me."

"I have no other choice, no?"

"Right." He said putting a kind hand on her shoulder. He was now staring her in her eyes. The blue eyes sparkled against her aged face, but her beauty had not waned. She looked just as beautiful as she had some thirty years prior when they met on that cold February day when she came looking for a job.

"Your **wife** is doing a little better. I just checked on her. She's sleep."

"She'll be okay. It's you that I'm worried about." He said as he neared her face.

"Not today Mr. Dean."

"Then when?" He said as he tried to get closer for a kiss. As he neared, the door crept open and he backed away. It was Alex, who had come in search for his mother.

"Mama, I've been looking all over for you."

"Hola mijo, when did you get here?" She said as she embraced her only child.

"About thirty minutes ago. I'm sorry I couldn't make it to the funeral Mr. Dean."

"I understand son. A District Attorney's job is never done."

"And when you become mayor, you'll understand." Alex stated with confidence.

"Well, I'll leave you two." Zechariahs continued. "Thanks for the smoothie again. Thanks again for coming Alex."

"He was my brother Mr. Dean. And I promise to catch the bastards that did this to him without cease!"

Zechariahs hugged him and he exited into the interior of the house, closing the door behind him. Alex looked to make sure the door was closed and the coast was cleared before he continued with the conversation with his mother.

"You doing okay, mijo?" She asked stroking the good-looking face of her son.

"What if someone had walked in on that little scene I saw?"

"Everything's okay. I was just comforting him in his time of pain, mijo."

"You're the maid, not his wife. His wife is in an alcoholic stupor upstairs, or don't you remember. He will never leave her, no matter how bad she gets."

"I know that Alex." She said trying to quiet her son. She didn't want to hear anything else he had to say on the subject. "Just let it go, mijo."

"¿Cuanto tiempo usted será actriz para esta familia?" He said trying to make it blatantly clear he was serious about his non-approval of what his mother was doing.

"I'm not an actress for this family, mijo." She said translating what he had said to her, throwing back in his face that she was now just as educated as he was, not by Yale or the D.A.'s office, but by life. "They've been so good to us. They took us in when no one else would. They gave you a superior education and gave us anything we could desire. It's my duty to be here for them in their time of need and give them whatever they so desire."

"Including keeping his bed warm at night mama while his wife is passed out on the other side of the room?" Alex retorted in Spanish, trying to strike a nerve. She in turn slapped his jaw for the disrespect he had just shown.

"Soy su madre. Merezco respecto y usted me lo demostrará."

"Lo, siento, Mama. Lo, siento." He said. She placed her hand on where she had just struck him and kissed him. She, as Zechariahs had done a few minutes before, retreated into the house. Alex was left on the porch alone. He rubbed his jaw. He hadn't been hit by his mother like that in years, since he was in junior high school. He hadn't meant to disrespect his mother, but he had to say something about an affair which he had unexpectedly walked in on some seven years prior when he had returned to Atlanta.

At the base of the stairs of the winding staircase, Zechariahs clanged his empty smoothie glass minutes later. The awaiting crowd turned to face him. They were quieted. No one dared move in the presence of this powerful man.

"Thank you all for coming today. It's not an easy day for my family," He started, his voice bellowing through the walls of the house as though he was talking into a microphone. "With you all here, it makes it that much easier to deal with the pain of losing our son, brother and husband. To know that you all cared so much about him brings such a relief to me and my family. Because without you'll this would be so difficult to go through. Thank you. Give yourself the applause you so rightly deserve." The resounding applause awakened the solemn house as it was once again was filled with at least the hope of love and inspiration; it had before Kevin was killed. "I also want to raise our glass for a toast to my son. Would you care to do it Mya?"

"Thanks dad. But I can't. Not right now anyway."

"Mr. Dean, may I?" Cole asked stepping to Zecharias, feeling guilty for not being there for his partner that fateful night.

"Coleman, by all means, please do give the toast."

He raised his glass of orange juice to the crowd of mourners. "To Kevin, a great son, husband, friend, and detective, you will be forever missed. Rest in Peace Kev. There will be no one like you!"

A resounding "cheers" was heard through the cavernous halls of the Dean great room.

In that moment Jordan appeared at the top of the stairs. She was barely holding herself up on the banister. She looked as though she was hit by a truck, in her case, a case of Hennessey that was now taking its toll on her physically. "I want...to...say...something...about...my son..." She slurred as she tried walking down the spiral staircase to the base that lead to the great room. She didn't make it though, as she splayed onto the stair case, falling backward.

Cameras flashed from an unknown guest, but the flurry in which Brianna came to Jordan's aide, masked the flashing light bulbs, or at least she thought.

It was the next day that the proof of that night hit the papers. The cover page of the Atlanta Journal-Constitution's *Life & Style* section read, "Is this our Future First Lady Atlanta?"

CHAPTER 11

It was 4:15 a.m. when Mya sat straight up in the bed. The last few weeks she was living, she assumed, had all been a nightmare. Her arm caressing Kevin's side of the bed gave evidence that he was not only absent, but that he would never return to warm her on cold nights or to calm her when she was feeling stressed. She held her stomach, her baby, their baby, growing inside her, and tears ran down her cheek. The baby's father was gone; her man was gone, her best friend gone, never to return again.

What she regretted the most was that she had thought about the moment when she would receive a call saying her husband was dead in the line of duty. She had run the scenario in her mind countless of times, only to have her subconscious knock the unfathomable event right out of her head, and now the subconscious was made conscious and the realities of the situation would not dissipate as they had earlier when it was thought to have been unfathomable.

Her sabbatical from work was another five days. The pain racking inside of her mind and thinking of what she could have done to prevent his death would plague her the rest of her time away from her work. She would think that maybe she could have asked him to stay home that day. Maybe she could have told him that she loved him one more time. Maybe she could have just told him to come home early that night like she wanted him to.

She was alone now. Her baby, tears and memories were the only thing that kept her company when the clock struck 5:30 a.m. the day after Kevin's burial.

CHAPTER 12

Zechariahs sat at the dining room table later on that morning. Sascha poured him more coffee and she exited into the kitchen to prepare his breakfast. He sat reading the morning paper, dissecting it just as he had for years: Financial, Sports, Cover Pages and then lastly the Life & Style page. When he begin reading the *Life & Style* page, to his chagrin he saw his wife laid out on the stairs, drunker than he had ever seen her, at his son's repast no less. He was there at the actual moment of the picture, but the actually reality of the moment pressed into his soul even greatly, as he became more angry at his wife for her choice to get **that** drunk. He was disgusted by the title of the article, but became more nauseated by the caption underneath the photo. "Jordan Campbell-Dean, mayoral candidate Zechariahs Dean's wife, passes out at son's repast, her version of mourning." He drank his orange juice, letting the chill of the fresh juice calm the heat that was boiling within him.

"Good morning pops. How are you doing?" Dontavious said as he entered the dining room. He was quite surprised to see a breakfast fit for a king already laid out on the table. Fruit, bread, and various other pastries lined the mahogany table that was last used for the brunch on the day of then family coming together after Kevin's death.

"You're up early. How did you sleep last eve?" Zechariahs broke him from his food induced trance.

"Better than the night before, but still not the best. But you get used to that getting up at dawn for twenty years."

"This house takes a second to get used to. Stick around longer, and you will have many a good night's sleep. I promise."

"Pop, I don't know how long I will be here. I have a life in Oregon I have to get back to." He lied, trying to mask the uncertainty of his future.

"Just give it some thought. We need you around here, especially now that Kevin's gone."

"What's on the agenda for today anyway pops?" He said ignoring his father's insistence.

"I have a board meeting, my last one as CEO, and then I was thinking some golf, and then maybe lunch. When you're retired you can make decisions like that." He laughed. This was the first time he had done so since his son died.

"I never thought that you would retire." Dontavious said as he bit into a dry piece of rye bread that he had picked up from the table before he sat.

"I didn't either. But it was time. Malek was poised to take over. I had gotten the company to the place where he could take it to another level. I have complete trust in him that he will do our family name proud."

"I think he will do a great job. He's been waiting for this all his life."

"And if his brothers would have been there, they could be where he is now." His father said accusatorily, but no so much as to instigate a fight between the two. A little barb to begin the verbal sparring was his only intention.

"I was wondering when that would come up."

"I don't see why you and Kevin chose to leave the family business. That's all I'm saying."

"Kevin and I weren't built for it. Malek, on the other hand, was."

"If Kevin would have only taken the business path, he would be, could be, alive right now." Zechariahs choked back tears, trying not to let them well up in his eyes, and eventually wetting his face.

"Pop, let's not play would have, could have. It's too early." He was speaking of the time of day, as well as eluding the fact that it had only been a day since they had buried Kevin.

"You're right Dontavious." He cleared his throat. "I'm just so angry he's no longer here."

"We all are Zech." Jordan said as she sauntered into the room, holding her head. She was indeed hung over and hadn't remembered what happened the night before."

"Look who decided to join the land of the living!" Zechariahs quipped.

"Ma, you okay?" Dontavious said as he went to the aide of his mother. He helped into her seat at the table.

"I'm fine, baby." She kissed his hand, as he returned to his seat. "Sascha," she billowed. "I need a mimosa right now! My head is killing me. Hurry!"

"Starting already Jordan?" Zechariahs asked.

"Oh, please don't start with me this morning Zech. I don't feel too well."

"I wonder why? How many bottles of Hennessy did you go through last evening? Or do you even remember?"

"I'm in mourning Zech. My baby is dead! Our son was murdered, or don't you remember!"

"We all have to mourn, but damn, Jordan. It's one thing to drink to numb the pain. It's another entirely to drink until you pass out." And with that he threw the *Life & Style* page at her. To her dismay she saw herself, in all of her glory, splayed on the stairs, in the most embarrassing pose she had taken in years. Dontavious looked on the scene that was before him with shock, as he hadn't seen his parents at this disparaging or rude to each other ever in his life, not even as a child.

"Who took this, this, this monstrosity? We should sue!"

"The question should be why you didn't stay upstairs when you knew you were too drunk to talk, let alone walk?!"

"Go to hell Zech! I'm mourning my son my own way!" She spat back at him.

"Next time pass out near the bedroom. I'm getting too old to carry you up the stairs!"

"Sascha, I will take my mimosa by the pool. I need some air!" She yelled, penetrating the walls of the dining room, shaking everyone present to their core. She got up from the table and made her way back out of the door she entered only moments before.

"Pops, what in the hell is that about?" Dontavious said finally coming away from his shock at how his father was treating his mother.

"She's been getting worse son. She always drank. And you know that's why I don't even touch that stuff. But ever since Kevin died she's just been drinking herself into place where she can deal with it."

"Can't you empathize with her? She just lost her son?" Dontavious remembered his mother's infamous binges when he was younger, but he didn't realize how badly she had gotten. But behind the drunken rage and alcohol laced conversation, he still saw his mother: the one who had given birth to him and nurtured every wound he had as a child, emotional and physical.

"I'm at the point now that I can't even sympathize, let alone empathize. She's spiraling out of control, Dontavious. And I can't do anything to help her."

"Rehab, something?"

"It doesn't work. She's been to God knows how many programs, even when you all were children, if remember."

"Just like you like them, with a hint of milk Mr. Dean." Sascha said as she placed the plate of eggs in front of him on the table.

"Thank you Sascha." Zechariahs had calmed down a little. "And please take care of Mrs. Dean today. She's going by the pool to get some sun and air. Give her whatever she wants. She's in mourning."

"Don't I always Mr. Dean?" Sascha said kindly, as she exited the dining room.

"I'll finish my eggs. Then we are going to D.A.C. for the meeting and then we can head to the golf course." Zechariahs said smoothly as to not incur any more questions of the day's events thus far. Dontavious didn't say anything as he sat trying to take in what had happen and how his father so easily masked it and continued on eating without going to check on his wife. It was what the Deans were always known for, and Dontavious' memory of these things came back to him with a vengeance. He knew how his family's money not only helped them ignore the problems they were having, but the fact that their problems could easily be masked by pretending they didn't exist.

CHAPTER 13

Malek sat at his dining room eating a piece of dry rye toast and drinking a class of grapefruit juice. Just as sour as he, he had gotten used to the white grapefruit juice and required it every morning to start his day. He was dissecting his newspaper just as his father was doing on the other side of town. His shock and dismay was shown on his face when he saw the picture of his mother on the front page of the *Life & Style* page. He threw it to the other end of the table to get it out of his visual path. He went to grab the phone to call his father, but was stopped when Kameron came into the dining room smelling of freesias and humming Deborah Cox's "We can't be Friends."

"Good morning, Malek."

"Morning to you too, Kam." He said queerly as he tried to figure out her mood. She was too happy.

"I bet you wonder why I'm so upbeat, huh?"

"Took the words right out of my mouth."

"The Swedish deal is going through today."

"With any luck."

"I need no luck. This deal is fool proof."

"Yet instill you made it." He fired back at her.

"Not even your trite put downs will get me upset this morning." She sat at the opposite end of the table. She picked up the *Life & Style* section, which he had thrown to that end of the table, and she began to read. "You really must tell your mother this isn't her best angle."

"You will not talk badly about my mother! You will show her respect!" Malek said in a subdued tone, even though he wanted to send a verbal thrashing that would beat any other thrashing he had given her before.

"Why should I do so? When was the last time she showed me any respect?"

"I put up with a lot of shit from you Kam, but that's one thing I will not."

"Fine. It's a moot point anyway. I don't like a fight that I can win so easily."

"Baby, when I tell you my mama can mop the floor with you in that condition, or sober, you better believe it and heed my warning."

She poured hot water into her tea cup and soaked her passion tea bag, in silence. She knew Malek was serious and he would hear nothing else on the subject. And with his reign over her with the contract she ignorantly signed without reading, he had control over her future as she knew it. So she had to play her cards right in order to stay in the game.

"What time did you get home last eve?" He questioned her after about fifteen minutes in silence.

"It was two thirty or so. You can check the security tapes at the office if you really need to make sure."

"I trust you. I just wondered. Because when I came home, you weren't here. I called and no answer, both the office and your cell."

"You trust me. Sure you do." She squeezed out with enough sarcasm to kill an elephant. "Well for the phone calls missed, I was engrossed in work. And as far as me coming home late, I was engrossed in work, Malek. You'll see during this presentation today, I am ready to lock and secure this land deal that will make this company a few more billions in the years to come."

"You can only hope Kameron." He spat sarcasm right back at her.

"Ye of little faith."

"Was it Ludacris that said, 'you can't turn a ho into a Land Acquisition Specialist?'" He laughed at his joke. She was not amused.

"But YOU did!" She threw it back in his face. A few seconds later she started in, "Malek you are not a good person. And soon and very, very soon what you have been putting out will come back on you."

"Is that a threat?"

"No, just stating karmic facts. I'm leaving. I'll see you at the meeting later on today. Don't be surprised if you can't brake this morning while driving. Have a great morning Malek." She sipped the last of her tea and she was out of the door. Malek wasn't fazed as he continued to read his paper as he had done before she entered the room.

Moments later after she had left the house and he heard the door slam, he dialed a number on the cell phone and put the phone to his ear: "I don't care what you have to do! Just find out what the hell is going on!" He slammed the cell phone down on the table—the echoes hit every wall of the cavernous dining room.

Outside Kameron entered her midnight gray Mercedes SL-C, and put on her seatbelt. Her blackberry buzzed. She had a message. She pulled it out and looked at it as it was flashing in front of her:

Yo, thanks for last eve ma. You mean a lot to me.

She knew who it was from without even looking at the number. She started the engine and pulled out of the driveway into the busy Roswell Road, in which Malek's house resided. She dare not return this phone call on her "master's" property. She dialed send, and she spoke very sexy, as would a phone sexy operator. "Hey, pa, what you doing up this early?"

A slight baritone greeted her ear and soothed it on the other side of the phone. "Was just up and thinking about you shawty. This dick too."

She let out a slight giggle at the urban dialect that was reverberating through the phone. She knew what she had put on him the night before. She hadn't seen the mailroom clerk in a few months time, not since she discovered the clause in the contract and how she tried to get out of it. But last eve, the night of Kevin's funeral, seemed the perfect time in which to catch up on the habit she had so greatly missed. Every muscled it seemed she rode the night before. Every position and every orifice was used in the passion that lasted from seven that evening until twelve when she had to get home before Malek would begin to worry. And even then, they continued for two more hours, hence that's the reason why she had come home at two-thirty in the morning.

"So, do you have time to come by before you go to work?"

"No baby. I have a big meeting today. This is just the beginning for us. You know. I'm doing my part. Now it's up to you to do yours?"

"You talking about what you asked me last night, ma?" The mailroom clerk asked.

"Yeah. It's not that much to ask, right?"

"For you, anything Kam."

"That's what I like to hear baby." She said as sweetly as she could muster. "But got to get going daddy. I'll see you later on. Okay?"

"You got it shawty." The mailroom clerk was left to his own devices that morning to get rid of the rigor mortis that had settled into his pants.

She click off the blackberry and threw it on the passenger seat. The wheels were in motion for her plan to finally have the life that she had always wanted. As she drove down Power's Ferry Road, she began to think of how great life would be once Malek was out of her life for good. She thought about not having to depend upon him for nothing and the things that her and her mailroom clerk could do with her money, her power, and his body that was made on the jailhouse grounds, made her smile.

She gripped the steering wheel tighter. She thought of the night before when passion came over and over and over and over again. She thought of the moans, the laughter and the tears of passion that came so effortlessly to the lover that was unique to her. She also regaled in the fact that her prediction to Malek about his downfall was not only a reality, but it would be at her hands in which it would happen.

CHAPTER 14

Jordan sat by the pool until she was almost beet red. Mimosas flowed like manna from heaven and they washed away all of her pain from the day before.

"Sascha is she going to be okay?" Paige asked as she watched from the back porch overlooking the pool.

"Mija, don't worry. Your mother will be fine."

"Thank you tia Sascha. You're so good to us." She hugged Sascha and melted into her supple frame. "I'm going to check on her. See if she needs anything. I'll take this round." She grabbed the mimosa from Sascha and headed to the pool. She sat on the chair adjacent to her mother. "Hey Miss J., how are you doing darling?"

"Fine baby." Jordan took her sunglasses off her face and was looking her daughter in the eyes. "How are you today?"

"Rested."

"Wonderful baby. The sun's shining. The wind's blowing. And I'm getting a perfect tan."

"You really need to put on some suntan lotion before you burn."

"Honey, Sascha took care of that long time ago. You need to get some lotion. You're just as faire as me, if not lighter."

"You're right. Being in the New York apartment all day, and the theatre all night has made me as pale as a ghost. Why are all these white girls looking darker than me nowadays?"

"I blame it on the Negrorization of America." Jordan sounded lucid for once in a very long time. Paige had remembered her mother talking about how the races in the country were trying to be each other without the other knowing it—how the white people would go to their tanning salons or sit on the beach for as long as they could to get darker. She continued with examples of collagen being pumped into their lips and their roots dyed darker to look more African-American and breast implants and ass implants. She spoke of the blacks in America dying their skin, or wearing a lighter foundation, straightening and dying their hair and investing in body shapers to conceal the obviously Negro features each one had. Paige laughed at the comment.

"I haven't heard that in years ma."

"See your mama's not losing it."

"I know. We all just have to deal with our things our own way." Paige said sounding like a full fledge adult, which sort of surprised Jordan.

"When did you get so mature?"

"Eight shows a week will do that to you. Growing up fast in the big concrete jungle does that to you."

"Baby, give me some time. Let your brothers and your father know, I just need time. And Paigey, give me my mimosa and I need some time right now. I'll be okay. I won't drown myself I promise. One embarrassing situation a year is enough." She kissed her daughter on the cheek, took the mimosa and drank.

Paige left her to bake in the summer's sun. Something inside her told her that her mother would be fine.

Paige got back to the porch and was greeted by Marcus who was wearing a suit, much like one that he wore at the funeral the day before. "Why are you so dressed up, Marcus?" She inquired.

"I have a quick meeting with some music producers, a possible solo album for myself. Why not strike while I'm in the Motown of the South?"

"When were you going to tell me?"

"I'm telling you now, aren't I?!" His look of scorn matched his indignant tone.

"How long will you be gone? I wanted to spend some time with you Marcus."

"Shouldn't be more than three hours max." He saw the disappointment in her eyes. He went to comfort her. "We should go get dinner at the Sundail when I get back. I heard it's great. Does that sound okay?"

"Sure Marcus." She said coyly as she tried to mask her disappointment. He kissed her and he was off to his unknown destination, because he sure as hell wasn't on his way to meet with producers about a solo album.

CHAPTER 15

It was almost an hour before the presentation was done and the contracts were signed. Kameron wasn't sure if it was her skin tight two piece Donna Karen suit or the presentation that kept the board glued to her, but all she knew was that she had their undivided attention. The board, including Zechariahs, voted to push forward with the plans to buy Weber Inc. in Sweden to procure more lands for the D.A.C. Empire. Her insightfulness to business as well as her knowledge of the European market, not only impressed Zechariahs during her initial setup and meeting, but this presentation as well. He was also impressed by her eloquence and determination.

The meeting was over and the board adjourned. Kameron had closed the deal with Malek sitting on the sidelines. She had done what he thought she couldn't and made a reasonable enough deal for everyone involved. The Swedish land deal as it had come to be known was solidified and Kameron B. Hanes was the liaison for it and her rank in the company, contract or not, was solidified.

Zechariahs approached her with Dontavious who had sat in on the presentation and signing as well.

"I was very impressed Miss. Hanes." Zechariahs said holding his hand out for a handshake. She was delighted to complete the exchange.

"Thank you Mr. Dean. It means a lot that you would think so sir."

"Malek, thank you for bringing such a strategic and intelligent woman on board, son." Zechariahs turned his attention to Malek, who stood up in reverence of his father.

"I always knew Kameron would do us proud pops." Malek lied, as he hugged his father.

Dontavious interrupted, "Kameron, your ideas were quite concrete and lucid. My brother is lucky to have you in his corner."

"Thanks, Dontavious." Kameron said. She was now blushing. She had the Dean men in her corner. She knew it was just a matter of time before she would have everything else she wanted.

"Well, we must be going. Dontavious and I have a golf game to get to. My job is officially done as CEO." Zechariahs said ending the elation.

"All right pop. You all have a great one." Malek continued. "I have much to do today or other wise I would be right there with you." He knew he wanted to be there, because any more time with his father and he knew that Dontavious' previous status would ease back into play.

Zechariahs and Dontavious exited the board room.

Kameron and Malek were left alone. Kameron proceeded to pick up the presentation binders around the board table.

"I was quite impressed Miss Hanes." Malek regretfully uttered.

"I'm not some run of the mill ho off the streets Malek. If that's what you thought, you are sadly mistaken," Kameron said, baiting him. She was ready for battle.

"I never had any doubt that you could pull this off, Kameron. But you remember who got you all of this. And if you want to keep it, remember our contract, stick to it, and we will be all good." He whispered heavily into her right ear as she turned away from him picking up binders off the table.

She glided her ass back into his crotch. He pulled back, he knew she knew what she was doing. He controlled her financially, but his member is what she controlled, and controlled it she did at every turn. She picked up the last binder and exited.

Check mate.

CHAPTER 16

Jordan's afternoon by the pool only made her darker, and her mimosas made her drunker. She had tried numbing the pain, but the echoes her grief still panged. Her mind's images of her youngest, montages of his birth, life and death only haunted her as she tried to nap on the lawn chair. It was the third nightmare of the day in which she was awakened from by Sascha, who had another mimosa in hand.

"Mrs. Dean, you have a visitor."

"I don't want company. Tell whomever it is…I'm not accepting callers." She spat out.

"Mrs. Dean…"

"Don't worry Sascha, she'll be okay." The booming Southern voice made Jordan sit up and pay attention. She was staring at Emory Westport, just as tall and dashingly handsome as he had been when she first laid eyes on him some forty years prior. Though his gray hair and spectacles where now center stage and showed how he had aged, he was still as handsome as she remembered him being—butterscotch with not a flaw in sight.

"Mayor Emory Westport, what brings you slumming in my backyard?" Jordan said taking off of her shades and taking in a better look at him.

"I hardly call this mausoleum your husband has built for you the slums. But I came to give you my condolences personally for Kevin. He was a wonderful person and an even better detective. He's a great loss to the city of Atlanta."

"That was kind of you. But If Zech knew you were here..."

"We are political rivals. That doesn't mean that we can't be civil towards each other. Plus I just saw him at the golf course with your eldest an hour ago. I knew he would be gone for a while." Emory said reassuring her as he sat down next to her on the chair. He handed her the mimosa.

"I'm not just talking politics."

"He won you fair and square. What's the big deal? We are still friends, aren't we Jordan?"

"You know the only reason why he's running for mayor is because of this rivalry you two have that goes back to Savannah and that summer." Jordan said as she sipped the mimosa.

"He will always be a sharecropper's son as far as I am concerned."

"Why can't you just be happy for him, for us?"

"Because he doesn't deserve anything he's gotten."

She got a hint of why he had really come: "Emory, I'm in mourning right now. My son is dead, and you want to exhume some shit that happened over forty years ago. Not today, not right now! Please leave." She placed the mimosa down on the table next to her chair. She got up, and pointed towards the door to guide him on his way. She stood up too fast and swayed backwards, Emory caught her.

"Sweetie, you really must be careful." Emory said staring her in her hazel-green eyes.

"Thank you." She regretfully said.

"I remember holding you like this on Tybee Island that summer. Feeling your porcelain skin, never wanting to let you go."

"You're married Mayor Westport, if you don't remember! This is the third, much, much younger Mrs. Westport, if I do recall."

"That didn't stop us before, did it?"

"If you came here to wish me condolences, you've said them. Now leave! You're bordering on aggravation Emory."

"That was only part of my visit. I know your husband's campaign started a few weeks ago."

"And your point being?" She slurred out as best she could trying to keep her dignity and composure.

"Don't you think he should quit because of your son's untimely death?"

"Zech doesn't like to think about things. He likes to stay busy. It's his way of dealing."

"And yours is drinking yourself to numbness, I take it."

"Emory, you can go!"

"Before I leave I want to give you a warning for your husband. I think that you should try to convince him it would not be in his best interest not to run for mayor this term. For the family and for his sanity."

"I'm not having this conversation with you today. Get the hell out!"

"It was always great seeing Jordan." He leaned in for a kiss. She slapped him, leaving her whole hand print on his face. "Have a good one!"

He left. She fell back to sleep. Sascha watched the whole ordeal from the back porch. She knew what a past they had and what had transpired even more recently some twenty years prior. She was not surprised at the intense battle that the two had. She remembered walking in on them hot and heavy in Jordan's study a night that Zechariahs was running late, and that was the night that Sascha solidified her place, not only in the family's inner circle, but in Zechariahs' bed as well.

CHAPTER 17

Golf lasted almost four hours but the time flew by for father and son. By the three o'clock lunch that Zechariahs and Dontavious sat down to at the Sotto Sotto Restaurant on the Northern end of Highland Avenue, both were famished and ready to partake in the Italian Cuisine. Two peach juices started off the late lunch, followed by an order of Ravioli Nudi for Zechariahs and a broiled fish dish, Pesce Arrosto, for Dontavious, who was trying to eat healthy on his undetermined furlough.

They ate as they hadn't eaten in years, and conversation purveyed the afternoon delicacy was easier than both had thought it would. They had a lot of years to catch up on and the father and son wasn't going to take for granted that they had more time in which to do so, as the testament of Kevin's short life proved.

"You know, I really missed you son." Zechariahs said genuinely as he ate the last bit of his Ravioli and wiped his mouth with the linen napkin from his lap.

"I did too. I just needed time to explore myself. You know."

"I hope you've found yourself and are ready to come home after almost twenty years." Zechariahs insisted.

"I told you pops, I don't know how long I will be here."

"Your family is here. We need you. You can get stationed here in Atlanta. Hell, you can even come and do civilian work at D.A.C. I know your brother can find some place for you."

"I plan to be here for another week. If anything we'll cross that bridge when I get there. Deal?"

"You drive a hard bargain son. Just like your father. Deal." They shook on it as if they were decided an acquisition of sorts.

"Is everything okay, ya'll," Joshua said with his light Southern drawl. Their waiter was just as flamboyant as any woman and just as soft spoken. He was average height and thin as a rail. He couldn't have been more than one hundred and fifty pounds, wet. He grabbed Zechariahs' empty plate. "Was it good?"

"It was great Joshua. I'll take the check whenever it's convenient."

"Will do, sir." Joshua made his way to the kitchen with the dirty plate.

"I swear this city gets populated with *them* more and more each year." Zechariah's said plainly, drinking the last bit of peach juice.

"Who pops?"

"*Those* boys." He said making a supposed joke about Joshua's obvious homosexuality. "Those boys that sing in the glee club; you know what I mean."

"I'm not following." Dontavious said, though he secretly knew where this conversation was leading. In that moment before his father could answer, out of his peripheral, he could see a familiar face, and it wasn't until the two of them walked passed that he knew who it was. He thanked God for the pseudo interruption.

"Alexander Gallardo." Dontavious quietly said as to get Alex's attention. Alex stopped in his tracks and walked up to the table of the father and son. "Funny running into you here."

"Hello Mr. Dean, Dontavious. Just had a late lunch meeting with the Senator here. We're going over some documents for the new session of the city council beginning next month."

"Always busy Mr. D.A., aren't you." Zechariahs said greeting Alex with a hand shake.

"And what brings you all here besides the obviously great Italian cuisine?" Alex pondered.

"A golf game that went too long." Dontavious laughed. "But it was fun. Had time to hang out with my pops and get to catch up on old times."

"Zechariahs I'm so sorry to hear about your son and what a tragedy it indeed was." Thoreheart Kincade said trying to ease his way into a conversation he was not invited into. The Senator and Zechariahs had no love loss between the two. The rivalry that started in business moved into the political arena once Thorneheart became City Council Chairman years ago.

"I thank you for your condolences Thornehart. But as you see we are having lunch, my son and I. So if you could excuse us. Alex, as always, it was a pleasure to see you."

Thorneheart tucked his tail in between his legs and made his way to the door to exit the restaurant as not to incur a scene. But he made a mental note of the tally that he and Zech kept of the one-upmanship the other had inflicted on the other during the years. Alex excused himself, not wanting to get in between the two clashing titans. He knew of their history and how ugly the battle could get.

"Before I go, Dontavious, I would really like to catch up with you." Alex said turning around before he continued out the door.

"Anytime, I'm here for second."

"Meet me tonight at *HALO*, it's off of 14th Street. It's a small bar I like to go and have drinks after a long day. Here's the card. Call me if you get lost." He said as he handed the bright orange card to Dontavious. "I should be there around nine or so. They close at three."

"Sounds like a plan."

"Have a good one you all." Alex said as he continued outside to meet back with the Senator.

"Glad you're reconnecting with old friends. Hopefully he can convince you to come back home. You see Alex returned."

"What was that about pops? You and the Senator?"

"That goes back to the Olympic Committee days. Thorneheart Kincade has been a pain in my ass ever since."

"That long ago pops?"

"Yep. Bill, who was the old mayor of Atlanta, wanted someone he could trust to do the job right. Construction companies from all around presented their presentation about the Atlanta Renewal project, but he didn't entertain them too long as Bill reassured me that I would soon be a very rich man and my company would blossom with this new contract with the city."

"And what was in it for him for giving you the contract?"

"He didn't want Thorneheart to get it. He knew what would happen if that were to go down. I got it. Thorneheart couldn't stand that a poor black tenant farmer's son was getting the contract for a deal that was worth almost a billion dollars. And his old white money couldn't even buy him a parcel of land in the deal. He voted me hands down. The rest of the board voted for me, and the Dean Architect and Construction's newest phase was born and we became what we are today."

"It's been almost twenty years pop."

"Yes, and not a lot has changed. Once a snake, always a snake, son. Remember that!" He took the last sip of his juice. He was done with the subject.

"And here's your check." Joshua said as he placed the bill of about fifty dollars down on the table. Zechariahs took a look at the bill, and placed a hundred dollar bill in the check presenter and closed it and gave it to him. "I'll be back with your change." Joshua continued.

"No need Joshua. Have a good one."

"Thank you very much Mr. Dean. And I definitely will be voting for you in November." Joshua said as he smiled. He winked at Dontavious, unseen by Zechariahs, and continued on with the rest of his tables at the busy restaurant.

Dontavious was quite nervous. Could Joshua have picked up on some vibe or something, he thought. He ignored it and finished the juice. He and his father continued with the rest of their day.

CHAPTER 18

Paige sat at the Sundial Restaurant for almost an hour waiting for Marcus to show up. What was originally thought of as a three hour meeting became, "babe, meet me at the restaurant." Paige was already on her second glass of Pinot Noir, when the charcoal knight arrived the table. He kissed her on her hand, and she took it away from him, she was mad. "Where have you been?"

"The meeting ran longer than expected." He defended himself.

"Thee hours morphed into five and now six hours Marcus. Thank God the waitress recognized my picture from the blog *Young Black and Fabulous* or it would have been a complete embarrassment me to be sitting here all alone."

"I'm here now babe. Let's order and enjoy ourselves." Marcus said as quietly as he could as not to attract a crowd of onlookers.

The waiter was called over. She took Marcus' drink order as well as their order for food. Rack of lamb, new potatoes, and string beans in a spicy cabernet reduction intrigued the two, and tasted even better. They were silent while they ate. Some would say it was because the food was so delicious that it didn't require an accompaniment of conversation, but Paige's searing anger towards Marcus' tardiness made her silent. It was Marcus who broke the silence, as he hummed a few bars from "Can You feel the love Tonight" from the *Lion King,* a show she had just starred in as Nyla. She smiled. The tension was broken.

"I could never stay mad at you for long, could I?"

"I would like to see you try." Marcus said as he bit into the tender string bean.

"Marcus, this has been one of the worst times in my life. My brother's death has taken so much out of me. Thank you for being here for me."

"No problem, babe. You know I will cross the ocean for you, swimming, if you asked me to."

"I know baby. On top of all of this...and I haven't even properly grieved...and today I get a call from Sy, telling me that *The Color Purple* is closing at summer's end."

"Why?"

"He said revenue isn't what they thought it would be, and they're going to cut their losses."

"You have to get back up to New York babe. The show may be closing, but there are plenty of them on the Great White way that will give you a job. You will be in much demand—even though you took that secondary role as Nettie, even with your star power."

"I adored that role, it was the one that spoke to me, secondary or not." She explained to Marcus.

"Regardless, you have to go back to New York. We have to go back home. Atlanta is not our home." Marcus chided her.

"Maybe this is a blessing in disguise. I'm not ready to go back there, to the hustle and bustle. I need time with my parents, and for me to get over my brother's death."

"That door you've pried open will not stay open long. Some new girl will swoop right in and take your position."

"Producers will understand grief and bereavement. I've made a name for myself. I'm Paige Dean. I sell tickets. I bring the media and the people." Paige said as she sipped her wine.

"And the show will go on with or without you."

"Why are you fighting me on this? My career will be there Marcus. And if it's my banking account you're worried about, my trust fund is more than enough for me and you to survive for eons."

He sipped quickly on his merlot, trying to whet his dry throat that had instantly become Sahara-like. He knew if she would ever find out that he had siphoned millions from her trust and used it for bad investments, than he would not only lose her, but he would be on his way to jail. "It's not the money babe. I'm thinking about your career." He lied.

"I say, give me a month at the most. Everything will be okay."

A few minutes went by before the two spoke another word. The dessert tray came around, both passed on the suggestions, and the check was brought.

"Is this on me Marcus?" She asked.

"Babe, if you want me to get it..."

"I was just playing." She kissed his hand that he had extended to get the check holder. That moment Marcus' phone rang. "Go on, dinner's over."

Marcus picked up his cell and the quick conversation that ensued left him with a perplexing look on his face. He returned to the present world when he hanged up the phone. "That was my agent. They need me back in NYC immediately. My understudy just got into a terrible accident."

"I'm so sorry to hear that about Jamey. I hope all is okay."

"Just a broken femur and the second understudy doesn't have the show down pact."

"So I take it you're leaving tonight?"

"Yeah, the red eye."

"I won't say I'm disappointed Marcus." Paige whispered trying hard not to cry. "But you do have to work."

"Thanks for understanding babe."

"Oh, look, it's raining." She looked out on the Atlanta skyline that was now under the black clouds that had invaded seemingly out of no where. The rain washed against the window.

"Wow, where did that storm come from?"

"Summer storms in Georgia do that. It's peaceful and serene one moment and then all of sudden thunder and lightning and huge drops of rain."

What Paige didn't realize was that her statement would become an analogy for the events that would soon take place in her life.

CHAPTER 19

The clouds moved in quickly. The starry night was soon devoid of light as the massive clouds took over. Rumblings of thunder, followed by flashing lightning woke Jordan in panic. She was still sitting by the pool. But it wasn't the storm that was brewing that woke her with such a jolt.

She had seen Kevin in a dream. He told her to come and rescue him. He told her he was not dead. She took it literally and woke to go to save her son from his eternal resting place. Still not recovered from her day of drinking, she fell on the ground, but continued to press her way towards the interior of the house to leave to go to the graveyard where her son was just laid to rest.

CHAPTER 20

Dontavious barely beat the rain as he entered *HALO*, the bar in which he was told to meet Alex for drinks. As he entered he saw that the warehouse, turned bar, was quite modern, surprised that even something like this was housed in the modern Terminus. The color gray concrete walls reflected the changing lights that emoted from the bar's light fixtures, and the diverse crowd was a welcome sight for Dontavious, who hadn't seen a younger Atlanta crowd since his return.

He saw a lesbian couple kissing, and then two guys huddled in the corner, and he had wondered if Alex had secretly brought him to a gay bar. He sifted through the crowd until he came upon Alex, who was up the stairs, and was already engaged in a conversation with Cole, who he had met at his brother's repast the day before.

"So, it's being handled." Alex asked Cole.

"I told you it would be." Cole responded, as Dontavious made his presence known.

"Hey, Alex." Dontavious cautiously interrupted.

"Wassup, my brother. I'm glad you made it." Alex said as he greeted Dontavious with a handshake.

"I needed the escape. Thanks for the invite."

"I'm being rude. Dontavious, you remember Coleman Denavar, right?"

"Yeah, I remember you. We met at Kevin's repast." Dontavious said as he extended his hand to Cole."

"How are things going Dontavious?" Cole asked.

"Well as could be expected. I'm coping. One day at a time, they say."

"We're all still dealing with his death day by day."

"So what do you think about my hang out Dontavious?" Alex asked, trying his hardest to change the subject.

"It's different." Dontavious said taking a seat, and looking around.

Alex laughed and took a sip of his Corona. "Good different or bad different?"

"I mean, it's not my typical hang out spot. It's cool. Well, I saw these two women kissing and these two men..."

"You've been gone from the Empire City of the South way too long brother. We all mesh around here, straight, gay, bi...etc. It's a good drink spot, and plus many high class people come here. If they just so happen to be gay, so be it. I like people. After all I'm an elected official. I must commune with the people." Alex explained and took another sip of his Corona.

"I guess." Dontavious, kind of understood. "What's good to drink here?"

"I like the mijitos personally." Cole interjected. "I'm actually on my second."

"Sounds decent enough."

"I'll go get you a mijito Dontavious. I'll leave you two to talk." Alex said as he got up. He finished the last of his Corona. "I'll get me a refresh myself."

The two sat. Music played and the population around them became denser as the minutes went by. "It was so strange walking into the station today and not seeing your brother at his desk." Cole said sipping on his drink.

"He was a stranger to me. I left home when he was seven. I knew he would do great things, but I never knew he could become this great person. I don't know what I'm mourning for more: his life or the time I didn't spend with him."

"He was a good man. If I could have done anything to stop this senseless act, I would have."

"And I will stop at nothing to bring your brother's killer or killers to justice." Alex said as he handed Dontavious' drink to him.

"Thanks man." Dontavious said as he took the drink and took a sip. "This is good."

"Told you." Cole said as he finished his. "Well, I'm going to get round three. I'll be right back."

"Why didn't you tell me to get you one while I was there?"

"Cause I didn't think I was staying, until now." Cole said as he left.

"Cole's a cool person. I met him a few years ago when I moved back to Atlanta. Determined, arrogant and ambitious, but he's a decent person."

"He seems like he is."

"So tell me about the military my friend? How does the son of well off parents go from being waited on hand and foot, to being a soldier?"

"Just like any other. But the early mornings were a pain in the ass. I'm used to them now." Dontavious said. "Tell me about being a lawyer sir. When did that come about?" Dontavious continued.

"Took a poli-sci class following some girl, trying to impress her."

"It's always about a girl isn't it?"

"Yep. Funny thing is that I lost interest in the girl, and gained interest in the law. Hence that's why I am D.A. of Atlanta today. Among a few other factors, but that's the gist of it. "

"You've come a long way, Alex."

"I said my mother wouldn't have to be a maid for the rest of her life. And that's why I chose the field that I did. Don't get me wrong, your family was great to us, but I felt that my mother should have the best. You know."

"I know what you mean. "

"The bartender really outdid himself on this one." Cole said as he took his seat, sitting next to Dontavious. Surprisingly, he was not uncomfortable at all.

"Be careful Mr. Detective. No drinking and driving. I can't knowingly allow you to break the law."

"You know my taxi's on speed dial man." Cole pulled out his phone and showed evidence of his latest statement, which appeased Alex, who himself took the last swig of his Corona.

"Well, it's getting late, or I'm getting old, either way, I need to head home. I have a rally tomorrow. You two be good." Alex said as he put his coat on.

"Alex, you going to be okay?" Dontavious inquired.

"Yeah, and I will be taking a taxi. Be safe." With that Alex headed towards the exit, steady, yet, a slight stagger aided his gait to the door.

"I didn't think that the D.A. could be out with the public like Alex was tonight?" Dontavious questioned.

"It's the new South. It's Friday night. People do them, and others don't say much in return." Cole explained, not really making much sense. Dontavious' confused look on his face gave hints to the statement coming out as weirdly as it had been posed.

"You've had too much to drink man…"

"Not enough after the last few weeks I've had." Cole started to smile. Dontavious wasn't sure if he had had on filters before while looking at him, or was he just a little tipsy, but the combination of his smile and the glimmer of the light against his gray eyes hypnotized Dontavious.

"What's up?" Cole had caught him staring. But he didn't mind.

"Nothing...I was daydreaming or something." Dontavious said trying his best not sound uncomfortable because he was indeed caught staring deeply at Cole, even if it were for just a second. "It's funny how you meet someone and then you see them everywhere afterwards..." Dontavious said changing the subject quickly.

"Yeah, I know what you mean man...So tell me about yourself man."

"What do you want to know?" Dontavious was surprised by the follow-up.

"You seeing anyone? Any army wife running around behind you?"

"No...I...really don't have time. I didn't have time, I mean, with my career, my moving from base to base...and going to Iraq, etc..."

"So when was the last time you got some?" Cole interjected.

"Wow, that's a little personal, don't you think, man?" Dontavious balked at his intrusion. Not only did Cole not know him like that, Cole had stepped on a subject that Dontavious rarely discussed. He was considered a eunuch by common belief. He never had girlfriends, never spoke of a beautiful female who attracted him, nor did he ever comment on the *Sports Illustrated* model, movie starlet, or *Playboy* centerfold when all of his friends would divulge their secret yearnings at lunch and in the locker room. No one ever thought he could have been gay because he didn't fit the proverbial mold. He was considered "A"-sexual and he liked it as such. Hell, he didn't lose his virginity until he was twenty-five, and that was to a prostitute his buddies in the army had bought him while on duty in South Korea.

"Sorry bud, didn't mean to step on any toes..." Cole said, as he took one more sip of his drink.

"No it's cool. I just don't like talking about sex. It's never been my thing."

"Well, if you had what I had the other day...You wouldn't do anything but talk about it. Yes, Lord!" He guffawed. He was done: drunk.

"So I take it that's when yours was?"

"What, when mine was what?" He slurred.

"The last time you had some?"

"Yes, two days ago...one of my old pieces. Nothing too serious, just a breezy I knock down from time to time. I actually met her when I was out with your brother undercover one evening last spring."

"That's cool..." Dontavious said as he tried to search for something else to speak about. Luckily he was saved by his phone ringing. "Give me just a second." He picked up the phone. "Yes....I'll be right there..." He put his cell phone away. "I'm sorry to cut this short Cole, but I got to be going man."

"What's wrong?"

"My sister's been hit by a car." Dontavious said still in shock.

CHAPTER 21

Crawford Long Hospital in its hundred year history had been known for its renowned patient service and care. Located in the heart of Atlanta, the hospital is known as one of the best hospitals in city, as well as one of the premier medical institutions in the country. This night in particular it became the healing bay for Paige Dean. Paige laid sleep from the pain killers she had received an hour before. Marcus sat by her bedside holding her hand. He was still in shock at the events that had happened that led them here.

They left the Sundial Restaurant, rain coming down drenching the asphalt more than two hours prior. It was definitely a relief to the scorching day. About the time of their arrival at the Dean Estate, the rain was gushing from the sky, visibility near impossible. Marcus had gotten a call, and knew that he would have to drop Paige off to actually be able to conduct the *business* properly. She was not pleased and another argument ensued. She scolded him for his secrecy and that he hadn't spent much time with her since they arrived in Atlanta. He reminded her that she asked for space to mourn. She hated the comeback and told him to let her out of the car at the end of the driveway. He insisted that she be dropped off at the front door, but she got out of the car, and proceeded to walk up the drive.

Visibility, as bad as it was, Paige didn't see the red brake lights until it was too late. She tried to dart out of the way, but was clipped by the Mercedes. She was left on the driveway writhing in pain. Marcus came to her aide, and when he saw Jordan stepping out of the car, the look of surprise could have beat any word that could have been said in that moment.

Jordan sat in the waiting room, her hair still wet from being out in the rain, and a blanket over her shoulders shielded the cold of the air conditioner on her wet clothes. She was crying. She thought that she was going to do something good for her son Kevin, and ended up hurting her daughter in the process. She felt guilty for running her daughter over, and bringing more bad press to her family in this difficult time.

"Why were you out there Jordan?" Zechariahs asked, putting his arm around her.

"Kevin told me to come to his grave to rescue him..."

"Do you know how crazy that sounds?" Zechariahs said emphatically.

"I know. I know. This has been so hard for me..."

"And it hasn't been for me? My son died as well Jordan, but you don't see me getting plastered and then getting behind the wheel and running our daughter over!" He was angry, and the blanket of decorum was slowly peeling back. The country boy who he was raised as was about to rear his head, but Malek appeared in the door.

"Dad, I came as soon as I heard. Is Paigey all right?" Malek questioned. Zechariahs came to him.

"Yes, she'll be okay. She broke her leg in three places, and they had to set it with surgery." Zechariahs reassured him.

"What happened?"

"Your mother happened. She was drunk and decided to go for a drive."

"Have we handled the police, etc?"

"Brianna's on top of it."

"Great, we don't need another scandal right now. Our stock prices will definitely take a hit, not to mention your campaign."

"Tell me about it. Thank God for the Swedish acquisition deal or our stock definitely would have taken a hit when Jordan sprawled drunk on the stairs yesterday." Malek hated that Kameron's deal was the one thing that was the cushion for D.A.C. in the time of need.

"I'm still here!" Jordan said as she approached the two trying to clear the air.

"Mom, are you okay?" Malek asked as he hugged her.

"Paigey's the one who got hit."

"Mrs. Dean, I've brought you a change of clothes and we can get you some coffee..." Brianna said as she entered the waiting room.

"Thank you Brianna. I don't know what I would do without you."
Jordan hugged Brianna and the two left for the restroom to get her
changed.

"Her drinking has gotten out of hand dad." Malek soberly said as
his mother was safely down the hallway.

"Kevin's death has sent her spiraling out of control. Thank God it
was only a broken leg. I could only imagine if she was going a little bit
faster or..."

"The good thing is that Paige is okay now."

"What happened to Paige pops?" Dontavious said as he entered.

"Dontavious, Sascha called you too." Malek snarled.

"She's my sister too, Malek... What happened pops? How did Paige
get hit by a car?" They explained what happened to Dontavious and the
extent of his mother's drinking. The reality of Jordan's drinking was clear
and all of the men in her life knew that it had become a serious problem.

"I remember when I was just a teenager, mom used to go on these
binges..." Malek started.

"But they were never like this. They didn't last so long or get this
bad." Dontavious continued.

"I don't know what to do. I understand her pain. But I'm afraid that
if she keeps this up, she'll severely hurt herself, or kill herself."
Zechariahs said as he poured himself a cup of coffee. "She's already hurt
someone else...Paige."

"Dad, she could have killed Paige this evening."

"Malek, don't you think I know this?"

"Pops, she's got to get help. We can't allow her to get worse." Dontavious continued, trying to find a balance in the conversation.

"I brought you some coffee. I know how badly the hospital coffee can be." Mya said as she walked into the waiting room. She had a tray of Starbucks coffee in hand.

Zechariahs came to her and hugged her, taking the coffee from her. "Mya, what are you doing here?"

"Sascha called and thought that I should know. And I thought I should be here for you all."

"You should be home resting." Dontavious said sitting her on the couch.

"I'm fine." Mya reiterated. "How's Paige doing?"

"Well. She just got out of surgery to repair her leg. Doctor's said she should make a full recovery." Zechariahs stated.

"So Jordan hit her? What was she doing driving?"

"She said Kevin asked her to come to his grave." Dontavious said.

"She's taking this badly. She reminds me of my mom. You know she died of an overdose. It started small just like this and then it just escalated."

"We need to do something, dad, and we need to do it now!" Malek said interrupting.

"What do you suggest we do Malek?" Dontavious queried.

"Rehab, one that will finally rid her of her demons. Kevin's death was just a catalyst to push her over the edge." Malek continued.

"She's always had a drink with dinner or when we would go to functions. But it wasn't until after Paige was born that it started and all these years it's just gotten worse." Zechariahs somberly said as he took a sip of his coffee. He remembered the nights of finding his wife in her study, and covering her up with blankets. He remembered wiping up vomit that lay on the bathroom floor adjacent to the toilet that his wife had clearly missed. He had resigned himself with the fact that he was living with an alcoholic and would do everything to keep face to the outside world. It was just now that the reality of the situation was relevant and it wasn't just an embarrassment for Jordan, but for him as well. All of the money and power he had acquired was no help to Jordan in her time of need. "So, rehab, it is?"

"Yes, I think that's the best thing. And you can always spin it in your favor dad. You can make mom an example of what addiction can do to a family..." Malek inserted.

"And you can also show Atlanta that your family is still just as simple and frail just like any other family in Atlanta for the sake of the election, dad." Mya continued.

"Are suggesting rehab Malek because of you fear of falling stock prices and a smear on the campaign or is this a genuine care for our mother's health and well being?"

"Of course I'm thinking about mom's health and well being. What other choice do we have Dontavious? Mom has hit our baby sister because she heard the voice of our dead brother. If that's not an out cry for help, I don't know what the hell is." Malek retorted. He seemed quite offended at the fact that his brother was willing to suggest that he didn't want the best for his mom.

Unknown to the group arguing her fate, Jordan stood on the other side of the door listening to the conversation. The tears had welled in her eyes as she realized the severity of her problem that she honestly didn't believe that she had. She weighed within herself rather or not she should go in and defend herself, but she realized that the jury was out, and her fate was definitely sealed, plea or no plea. Guilt panged her as she sat on the other side of the door. She realized that she could have been the death of her daughter and caused a greater tragedy to the Deans than Kevin's death could have ever caused.

Jordan made her way down the hall where she found her daughter's room. She cautiously stepped into the door, not wanting to see the carnage that she had caused but knowing that she had to at least get a glimpse to ease her curiosity and visions of horrific images that were dancing inside her head. She surely knew that she had killed or maimed her daughter, at the least left her with an eternal reminder of her mother's drinking and irresponsibility.

The door crept open and she came into the room to find Marcus holding her daughter's hand and holding her water up to her that she was drinking through a straw. "Paige, you look wonderful."

"Mom," she started groggily, "What happened? Why am I here?"

"Paige, I'm so sorry." Jordan went to her bedside tears streaming down her face. Marcus hadn't told Paige of the events that had transpired that evening and it would be left up to Jordan to fill her daughter in on every gruesome detail of why Paige lay on a hospital bed. Marcus wasn't there to the end though, because he had to fly back to New York. Well at least that was his excuse to leave the Deans in yet another time of need.

CHAPTER 22

At the same time Malek was debating over his mother's fate, Kameron arrived at the Peachtree Plaza Hotel in downtown Atlanta.

She had come here plenty of nights before, and each night brought her more to her life than she could have ever expected. She remembered coming here during her escort days, where she would be wined and dined, but sex never followed. She narrowly escaped a rape here when a businessman visiting from Russia didn't want just her conversation. She narrowly escaped with the seven hundred dollars she had asked for, and barely her life in tact. But her beauty and street smarts had gotten her out of plenty of pinches, and she had come out of many situations smelling like roses, when she should have had a shit like aroma.

She didn't fear that she would have to make this a short trip in length, seeing as though Malek was at the hospital with his family in yet another tragic turn of events for the Dean family. She stepped out of her car, stilettos hitting the pavement as though she walking the runway to the front door. Her white trench coat helped to ward off the rain that was still pouring out of the sky. Her clutch under her arm, and Kentucky Derby sized white hat was pulled mechanically over her face. Her shades also shielded her identity from those in the hotel lobby. Though she had been here before as a high class escort, she was now a businesswoman whose face would soon be all over Forbes, and a snapshot of her coming to a hotel room without her fiancée would be fodder for the tabloids and be mar to the position she had schemed for all this time.

She stepped onto the elevator. She knew instinctually knew which floor. she had been here recently more than ever. The doors closed once she got on the elevator, and she punched in PH, for the Pent House. The long trip to the top of the cylinder shaped hotel by Westin allowed her to refresh her lip gloss. The ding of the elevator signaled that she had arrived at her floor some five minutes later. She exited the elevator and walked towards the Pent House. She knocked on the door. Seconds passed and the person she came to visit answered. "Hello, how are you?"

"I'm well, and you?" The familiar voice said as she hugged him.

"Great! Everything is coming into focus."

"I told you that it would. Come on in. Take a load off."

"Sure." They walked into his penthouse. They sat at the table. He had just finished his room service and had just a bit of Cabernet left on the table. She made herself at home and poured the rest of the wine for herself.

"By all means, make yourself at home." The familiar voice said to her sarcastically.

"Don't I always?" She giggled as she took the last bit of wine down her throat.

"So, is it taken care of darling?" The familiar voice asked as he sat across from her at the table.

"Everything is all signed sealed and ready to go. He will make his move tomorrow."

"That's great Kameron. All of our hard work will pay off."

"Thorneheart, you know I couldn't have done it without you."

They both laughed. It was indeed Thorneheart Kincade, Zechariahs rival, that Kameron was coming to visit and they were laying the groundwork for something so big that Zechariahs could never see it coming.

CHAPTER 23

Dontavious placed Mya's bags down on the kitchen table. He looked into the expanse of the lavish living room of Kevin and Mya's six bedroom house sitting in Lithonia's most exclusive neighborhood. When driving her up through the gated community he noticed the manicured lawns, tall pines and luxury cars that littered the neighborhood. Lithonia, like much of Atlanta, was a chocolate family's dream. They could have a life that their forefathers had dreamt about, and they didn't have to go to the great city of gold streets in the sky to get it. "You and my brother did well for yourselves."

"I loved this house from the moment I saw it. Kevin and I knew we would be happy here raising a family." Her sigh lamented her sadness. But she continued on to the refrigerator and took out the Brita pitcher and poured water. "Anything I could get you Dontavious?"

"I'm good." Dontavious said taking a load off sitting at the island in the kitchen. "You have really good taste."

"That's all your brother's doing right there. From the color of the carpet, to the color of the walls, he picked them. He had an eye."

"A pretty good one at that." Mya sat down next to Dontavious. She grabbed his hand.

"We spent maybe a month total here together. The rest of the time, we just missed each other like ships in the night. Our careers..."

"You were happy right?"

"Honestly, there was nothing I would have changed."

"Regret is something I can live without, but I seem to have it on a daily basis."

"I try not to let those things interfere. They only make life that much harder to live."

"Mya, you unbelievably still look just the way you did the day I met you over twenty years ago." He said changing the subject.

"I'm as big as this house. I would kill for the body I had back then."

"You're even more beautiful now, than then in my humble opinion. Kevin was a very lucky man."

"I was the lucky one. Your brother was someone special."

"And to think you weren't feeling him at first."

She laughed. "You're right. If I had had my way, you would have been my husband. Remember?"

"A school girl crush." Dontavious said smiling at Mya who was now going to down memory lane. He remembered being on the field, fresh from the laps at the end of football practice. The cheerleaders, who Mya had recently joined, were finishing up their practice as well. Mya and he had caught each other's eyes as she went down to pick up her bag and walked off the field.

"It was the first day I actually talked to you, got turned down and felt like a total loser—the popular jock who wouldn't give me the time of day." Mya continued, ushering him into the memory she so vividly recounted in her mind.

"You were too young."

"I thought you thought I was ugly."

"You've always been fine Mya. And you know this."

"I felt rejected."

"And then my brother came down to the field a few weeks later to tell me that our driver was there to pick me up, and you saw him and..."

"...And I fell instantly in love." She continued his sentence recollecting the day she met and knew she would marry Kevin Z. Dean. She remembered how they first met eyes, like something out of *The Lady and The Tramp* and they were inseparable from that day forth. They experienced first kiss, love and sex together. They were each other's soul mates. Each knew what the other was thinking and could feel each other presence and knew the other's move and whereabouts without a needed phone call.

Only death could have broken their bond, and it had. "And now he's gone. My love story is over."

A single tear ran down her face. Dontavious wiped it away with an awaiting paper towel. "He will live on in our hearts forever. And this child, your child with him, will always be apart of him and live on in another generation." He hugged her.

"Tomorrow's my first day back at work, Dontavious."

"On a Saturday?"

"I felt it would be a good easing back into the situation."

"Well, congratulations..."

"I'm not ready. I can't face the outside world, not without Kevin."

"Kevin would want you to go on Mya."

Mya pondered his last statement in silence. She thought about the world that she was now apart of, alone, earlier than she thought she would be. Now having to raise a child by herself and find a way to deal with all the difficulties of life alone when she thought that she would have help at least until they both were old and gray. "Dontavious," she broke her thoughts, "will you do me a favor?"

"Anything for you."

"Will you stay tonight...hold me 'til I fall asleep? If I am going back to the newsroom tomorrow I need to be fresh and staying here, tossing and turning alone is definitely not going to do it."

"It would be my pleasure sister-in-law."

_____

That was the first night that Mya had gotten a good night's sleep since Kevin's death, and honestly could be said for Dontavious as well.

CHAPTER 24

By morning Paige was checked out of the hospital and was comfortably back at home. Marcus was on a plane back to New York to continue his run on Broadway. They had many unresolved issues before he boarded the plane, but she knew her first priority was to get better and heal properly. Before he left he slipped a filled syringe to her and told her to use it whenever she felt she couldn't handle the pain of physical therapy. He promised that all she would have to do is dial a number on a business card he had given to her, and she would have a much needed supply. She didn't question him, and stated that she loved him. And the way the drug made her feel, she was more in love with him when the pain became too much.

CHAPTER 25

Serene Haven was touted as one of the best rehab centers in the world. Jordan was going to get clean and regain her life that she felt she had lost. Kevin's death brought her to rock bottom. His death in turn would be her turning point as well. Zechariahs and Jordan kissed as she boarded the plane that next morning bound for a rehab that would take her from Atlanta for three months. They avoided the press. She had chosen to take the addiction head on without the comfort of family, friends or the luxuries of life in which she had gotten accustomed.

CHAPTER 26

Malek and Kameron sat across from each other at the dining room table, not saying much. Her wheels were turning, as well as his. They nodded pleasantly at each other through sipping on coffee and eating dry toast. "I hope your mother gets the help that she needs." Kameron stated with a tinge of sarcasm as only she could deliver.

"I do as well." Malek finished his eggs and wiped his mouth. He pushed away from the table and walked out. "I know you were being your normally bitchy self, but thanks for the thought regardless. He stated as the door closed behind him.

CHAPTER 27

Cole woke up sluggishly in his condo that overlooked Turner Field in Downtown Atlanta. The cool air from the vent hit him like a freight train once his trapped body heat from under the blanket was released. He shivered. He walked into the bathroom, where he gargled Listerine to get the "yuck" out of his mouth.

He walked back and his phone that was on the night stand was buzzing. He had three messages. The first was from Alex hoping that he had made it home safely. The second was from Dontavious inquiring the same. The third was from a familiar voice telling him, "Everything is set." He knew what the cryptic message was alluding to and he knew that the rest of the day would be busy, even if it were Saturday.

CHAPTER 28

There was hardly anyone in the office of WSB-TV when Mya entered that Saturday morning. The early morning broadcast had just finished, and preparations for the evening's broadcasts were underway. Those present said their hellos and gave their condolences as they saw Mya as she made her way to her office. She thought that she would be overwhelmed, but surprisingly, being back at work actually snapped her instantly out of the funk that she found herself post Kevin's death.

She walked into her office and it was left just the way she had left it a month prior. She sat in her chair behind her desk. It felt natural. She was glad to be back. She knew Kevin would want her to follow her dreams that she had been going after for years. She was on her path to becoming a national news anchor.

Anchoring a nightly news program was a job she had aspired for since childhood. Seeing the Atlanta news staple Monica Kauffman anchoring the evening news with poise, dedication and various hairdos, she brought to the Channel Two news team in Atlanta, she knew she wanted to be an on-air personality that would bring a sense of truth and realness to the job as did Ms. Kaufman. This was a station and team she was now apart of, in which she could make her strives to reach her goal.

She started as a production assistant here during her undergrad days at Georgia State University. Post graduation she became a morning correspondent building her reel at Channel Two with such news stories as building openings, Christmas shopping at Lennox mall, or any other menial story that was used as fluff between the daily murders, law breakers and grim news that now plagued the growing city. She grew as a reporter and a person.

As the years went by, she was allowed to have more hard hitting stories. Her latest was the city's emerging drug problem and in tangent with her husband, she vowed to find its source and crack down on it. She was not only thinking of her future, but that of the child she would some day carry, her child she was now having with Kevin. And now that she was back at work, she made it her goal now to finish what her husband and she had talked about countless nights over dinner they fit in between busy shifts.

She looked at Kevin's picture and a smile flashed over her face. Coming back to work was the beginning of her acceptance of his death. The baby must have felt her joy because her little one began to move around vigorously. The child knew that its mother was beginning to feel better. It was out of mourning as well.

"Mya, I thought I saw you." Jennifer, the morning anchor, said as she knocked and entered into Mya's office.

"Hey, Jennifer..."

"Barry said you could have taken a few more weeks."

"I needed to come back. I was going crazy in my house."

"I know no amount of cards and flowers could ever fill the void left by Kevin's murder."

"The thoughts and prayers do help. Thanks Jennifer."

"Jennifer, there you are..." The news director Barry said he entered the office. "We're going live in five minutes. Detective Dean's killer has confessed."

"What?" Mya was dumbfounded.

"Mya, what are you doing here?" Barry questioned.

"My husband's killer confessed?" Mya continued.

"Yes, just thirty minutes ago. Rory Tremont walked into the police station and confessed all."

END OF PART I

PART II

CHAPTER 29

"Hell yes, I think he should die! He killed an officer and his wife is pregnant. What about that baby? He ain't goin' have no daddy. There's enough kids out here with no daddies as it is." The caller said to Frank Skee on the popular Atlanta morning radio show on V-103 three months later. Kevin's murderer's sentencing was coming up soon and it was fodder for the morning radio talk shows.

Many debated whether or not his killer, Rory Tremont, deserved the death penalty, and others were enamored by how attractive his killer was and like the one caller said on this particular morning, "Honey, I would let him take my life any day. That boy is finne, chil'." Not since Brian Nichols, the 2004 killer who went on a semi shooting spree and gave the self help book *The Purpose Driven Life* it's popularity, had a murderer been looked at with such ogled eyes in spite of his heinous crimes.

The conjecture of public opinion had not dissipated from the initial hearing and confession, to the sentencing that was to take place some three months later. As the prosecution brought many witnesses to the stand to validate Kevin's life and how precious, and how senseless the act truly was, the defense tried to paint Rory, Kevin's killer, as a mentally unstable young man from a bad neighborhood who had gotten the wrong end of the stick. But the picture that was painted to the judge helped prepare him to not only convict Rory for Kevin's death, but give them permission to give him the greatest penalty: his life for Kevin's.

Mya was listening to this particular broadcast on the radio as she woke to start her morning routine that she kept at a constant during the past three months before the sentencing. She usually woke three hours before she was due at work. She meditated and prayed for God to give her strength. She took a short walk around the neighborhood. She showered and got dressed. She went to Kevin's grave and then arrived at the work. All the while there, she tried to work diligently, but the pangs of what Kevin's killer did and his impending sentencing were gnawing at the back of her head.

The morning of the sentencing, however, she would not go to the courthouse to see the conclusion. She knew that Kevin's killer being sentenced to death wouldn't bring him back. As the sentencing was handed out she sat by the grave, holding her stomach, touching her child, their child together.

CHAPTER 30

A text on his Blackberry that early morning revealed that it was a *JKJ Holding Company* that was the beneficiary of the money that was being stolen from his family's company. Malek was too upset to eat, as he had proof now of blatant stealing being done by someone within his company. His thoughts of betrayal and suspicion were interrupted when Kameron sauntered into the dining room.

Kameron had been gone since six thirty the morning of the sentencing. And when she arrived back at the house that she shared with Malek, she was dressed to the nines. A black dress that hit every curve, a waist-high belt, and a slick pair of red stiletto hills with fishnet pantyhose, is what Malek saw when she sat at the breakfast table and pulled out the *Atlanta-Journal Constitution* to read some three hours later.

"I would think that you were out on the street selling it like you used to. And that would be more explainable to me as to why you were gone when I woke at seven this morning." Malek spat at her.

"Malek, I don't have to explain a damn thing to you!"

"You've gotten real bold over the last three months. I hold the key to your future. So watch your step!"

"Yes suh massah!" She spat back at him sarcastically embodying a slave in the field. "I think I might just kill myself to get away from you and this stupid contract."

"Please by all means do it. Put me out of my misery."

"You won't get rid of that kind of power, not that easily. You love having me on your little leash, being able to control me whenever you want."

"Keep up this behavior, and I will let the leash go!"

"You throw threats at me every time you think I'm out of line. This rolling threat, I'm so used to like the rolling blackouts that come during these humid summers." She knew what he was capable of, but what he didn't know was that she had a plan to take care of his threats and solidify her future for herself.

"Are you going to come to the sentencing today?" Malek asked not missing a beat.

"What makes you think the sentencing would bring me to the courthouse?"

"A public showing of solidarity, Kameron."

"For the press?"

"Among other reasons."

"I have a meeting today."

"It's been canceled. I took the liberty to move it to next week."

"You had no right." Kameron now stared at Malek straight on. The newspaper hit the table as though it were a brick.

"It's my company! I will expect you in the court room at eleven o' clock in the seat right next to me." Malek left. Kameron's mouth hit the floor.

CHAPTER 31

"One more time Paige. Come on." Paige's physical therapist Steven said as he pushed her to her limits that bright and early morning that she was now used to three months later.

"Shit! This hurts!" Paige sputtered out as she did the last sets of lounges on her semi-healed leg.

"You've made a lot of progress Paige. A few more weeks and you'll be back to normal." Steven reiterated to her.

"You're evil!" She said as she sat on the ground, finishing the long and arduous training session. Of course she was joking with him.

"I'm not evil. I'm getting your groove back."

"I'm not fucking Stella, Steven." She laughed as she sat drinking the water that was next to her. Steven and she had began her training sessions a week after she came home from the hospital after her mom ran her over with the car on that fateful rainy night. Three months after her training sessions started, she was gaining her strength in her leg back with physical therapy sessions she had on the grounds of Dean Estate every morning at seven a.m. She was pushed to the limit and the pain was quite unbearable for her. The syringe that Marcus had left for her before he went to New York, and the subsequent refills that she got from his dealer, helped her to make it through the sessions.

"Remember three months ago, you couldn't even sit Indian-Style."

"I remember three months ago I wasn't hit by a car either." Paige's venom was evident, and her seething animosity towards her mother was present, and forgiveness was not on the horizon.

"Apart of the physical healing is dealing with inner emotional as well, Paige." Steven tried to reassure her.

"I don't know if I can forgive her, though. My life could be ruined by this. My agent has all but dropped me. The girl who replaced me is now soaring in the role and getting critical acclaim. And this morning I find out that the show will be closing in a few months. My life seemed to shatter the same day my leg did."

"But your mother is getting help. Your leg will be healed and stronger than ever, and you'll be back on Broadway as soon as you know it."

"From you lips to God's ears." Steven's phone rang. "Go on and get it. Give me a little time to breathe before the next round."

"I'll be back in five."

"Make it ten." She flirtatiously said back. He answered his phone and dismissed himself to toward the back porch that overlooked the massive land the Dean Estate sat on. Paige cautiously looked around before she removed the tiny syringe from her pocket. She pulled her shirt back, and like a seasoned pro she entered it into a venous canal and was once again was in euphoria. This was a pattern. Though she hated her mother for what she had become and how her addiction had led to her accident and pain, Paige was subsequently going down the same pathway.

"All right Paige. That was your break. Let's get you finish so we can get you to the courthouse this morning." Steven said as he approached her. She quickly hid the syringe.

"Yea..."

CHAPTER 32

The light crept into the big bay window of the condo early that morning. The rays touched Dontavious, who hadn't really been able to sleep. He stared at the horizon and the beautiful topography and concrete mass that was now downtown Atlanta that the condo overlooked. He thought about his brother's murderer and how the sentencing would be the closing of the chapter of his family's life that he wished hadn't been started to begin with. He hadn't planned on staying three weeks, let alone three months. He hadn't planned on fibbing to his father either about an early retirement from the Army, and how his father anxiously made him his campaign manager for a campaign that was now picking up steam in the middle of the summer months.

"You tossed and turned all night." A voice said as an arm rested on Dontavious' shoulder.

Dontavious continued to stare out the window in spite of the arm. "I can't believe that it's finally going to be over."

"Me either, babe. This has been a long time coming."

"You really loved my brother didn't you Cole?" Dontavious said as he turned to face the new man of his life.

"He was like a brother to me. I loved him with all of my heart and I just wish I could have protected him."

"It's not your fault, babe. It was an incredibly horrible crime that you couldn't have stopped." He kissed Cole. The two entangled their bodies, keeping the heat they had trapped under the sheets between them. "You are a great detective and an even better friend...and the best boyfriend anyone could ask for."

"Today is our three month anniversary, remember?"

"You remembered? Who would have ever thought I would have found love with my brother's partner, who I could have sworn was straight."

"And vice-versa Mr. Sergeant First Class."

"Don't ask, don't tell." Dontavious playfully said as he kissed Cole.

He remembered back to the fateful day they had come the conclusion of each other's true selves and what that meant to the other. Cole and he had struck up an accord when they had gone to *HALO* that night. Cole had gotten drunk and two had a casual conversation that bordered on flirtation but each one denied and continued on as if the spark wasn't there. When Dontavious was called to the hospital because of Paige's accident, the bud of the longing was left un-plucked and the two couldn't speak on it.

It was two weeks later when Cole invited him to watch a Brave's game from his balcony. Cole hadn't gotten off later than he had expected that evening and about the time of Dontavious' arrival, he had only a towel wrapped around him, from his quick shower that he thought that he could get in before his night's guest would arrive. Dontavious was shocked when Cole opened the door, but was more so intrigued at the hard body that lay underneath the shirt and tie he was accustomed to seeing Cole in when they would run into each other randomly.

After Cole was dressed the two of them bantered about the randomness of life and Dontavious tried his best to avoid eye contact with Cole, who was now in gym shorts and a tank top. They talked about their love of The Braves and how each one had remembered when the team had played in Fulton County Stadium and they practically gave away tickets, even though superstar Hank Aaron was playing and the emergence of new Atlanta hero Dale Murphy was bringing new notoriety to the Braves.

After a few Heinekens, the two found themselves tipsy and laughing at the most obscure things. One thing led to another and the two ended up feeling each other up, playing some poor piss game of "Anything you can do, I can do better." Suffice it to say the two express themselves and stated how much the other found the other attractive and their past relationships with men. By the end of the ninth inning the two were in Cole's bed.

The next three months Dontavious split his time between Cole's place, Mya's and his father's campaign headquarters. Both agreed that they could not be outed, except to each other, and the two were in perfect harmony as long as they were in Cole's condo. No one even knew that the two were lovers and were falling deep in love.

"I hope that motherfucker fries." Cole said jostling Dontavious from his memory.

"He hasn't shown an ounce of remorse. It's like he doesn't feel guilty about killing my brother."

"Seeing that little fucker coming in there with his flashy suits, braids and gold teeth made me ill three months ago, like he's gloating that he's killed an innocent man, all for some stupid money. And the nerve of prosecution painting him as some victim of society...it made me ill..."

"I studied the criminal mind and it's like these people never change. They are and will always be the same."

"It's sad to say but it's so true." Cole said getting out of the bed, his buttocks on display in the fresh day's sunlight.

"I'm lucky to have that sight every morning."

"Naw, babe, I'm the lucky one. My life has been so much better since you've stepped into it." Cole said as he kissed his man.

"Go brush your teeth!" Dontavious said with a laugh. Cole went into the bathroom and began his morning routine. Dontavious' phone rang. It was his father telling him that he wanted to meet him at campaign headquarters in an hour before they would go to the courthouse.

CHAPTER 33

Alex finished his breakfast burrito on top of his desk, as he routinely did: a quick breakfast before he headed to put the "bad" guys away. He looked over work that early morning avoiding spilling salsa on it.

"Will my mijo have his life back to normal after today?" Sascha said as she entered her son's office.

"Ma ma, what are you doing here?"

"The sentencing day of my son's big trial, I've come to congratulate him. Good job mijo."

"Thanks."

"You've come so far. I'm so proud of you."

"Everything I've done, I did it for us, for you to quit being a maid."

"I know mijo, and I'm forever grateful. I wouldn't have all the nice things I have if it weren't for you."

"But you still choose to work as a maid even though you don't have to."

"You've given me a lot mijo, but it was the Deans who took us in when we had nothing. I have loyalty mijo."

"You're still their maid. And now you're his lover!"

"¡Cierre su boca!" She shouted at him. His mother was angry. "I didn't come here to fight with you mijo."

"If he hurts my mother, I will kill him!"

"He's promised me that when Mrs. Dean comes back from rehab, he's asking for a divorce mijo." She reassured him.

"And you will be Senora Dean?" He said unconvincingly.

"Si."

"Ma ma, I hope you know what you're doing."

"I do mijo. Have a good day in court. By the way, I have sad news, I won't be there today in court."

"Por que ma ma? I wanted you..."

"...Lots of errands mijo. But I will make it up to tonight with dinner after, just me and you to celebrate, okay. I'm cooking all of your favorites..."

"Carne Tampiqueña?"

She kissed her son: "Of course Carne Tampiqueña! I do make the best..."

"You do mama." He hugged her back. "You know I only want the best for you. I want you to have everything you want, even a man that loves you and only YOU!"

"Mijo, let it go! Tu madre es una persona adulta. Ella puede cuidar de sí misma."

"I know you're an adult and can handle your situations. I just want you to make the right decisions." Alex pleaded with his mother.

"Trust me mijo. Trust me!" She kissed her son once again. "I'll see you tonight." She hugged him and exited, leaving Alex to his work.

CHAPTER 34

"We are up in the polls by fifteen percent. We are gaining on some key demos that Emory has been lacking." Dontavious said as he presented the weekly report to his father at Dean Campaign Headquarters that morning around nine.

"Well our debate next week should show me the most viable candidate to clean up this mess that Emory has left in this city." Zechariahs said as he got up and refilled his coffee.

"Are you glad that Kevin's killer will be sentenced today?"

"It won't bring Kevin back. But I'm glad we have closure. To know when your mother gets back home she can rest easy. Our son's murderer will be behind bars for a very long time and possibly on his way to the death chamber."

"Have you heard from mom?"

"Serene Haven sent me the weekly update, but no word from your mother herself."

"I guess she wanted to do this her way and away from everything and everyone."

"That's Jordan Campbell-Dean for you."

"It will be a circus down there today. We should get going."

CHAPTER 35

The Fulton County Court House was filled to capacity as the sentencing was read by Judge Franklin Turner, a forty year veteran of the bench. "It is the opinion of this court that such an act of violence against an officer of the law, husband and father should not be ignored. Through the hearing coupled with the confession, the defense tried to paint a victim of environment, as the defense attempted to persuade the jury that a killer could not be rehabilitated. I found you Mr. Rory Jamal Tremont GUILTY of first degree murder. And on this day of sentencing Mr. Tremont, it is the opinion of this court that you are to be sentenced to DEATH BY LETHAL INJECTION for the murder of Detective Kevin Dean. You are to be reprimanded to the Harris Country Correctional facility until the day of your death. God have mercy on your soul Mr. Tremont. That is all."

The courthouse erupted in frenzy. Media outlets began to run tape and cameras started to flash though-out the courthouse. The Dean family began to hug in celebration at the conviction and sentencing of their kindred's murderer. The long three month wait was now over and some semblance of life could move on.

"I can't die for this shit, yo! I didn't do this! You told me I would do time Brenda! Come on B. Tell them I didn't do this shit! Tell them I didn't do this shit, boo. Come on B." Rory said as he was carted away.

Everyone was confused as the defendant was taken away. He hadn't said much during the last three months, even when given the opportunity to be on the stand to testify on his behalf at the initial hearing. And now on the day of his sentencing he was professing his innocence and calling out to some unknown woman that she must give up the evidence of his innocence to save his life.

CHAPTER 36

"It was our pleasure Mrs. Dean. You have made us proud." Jordan's counselor said to her as she was walked to the front door of Serene Haven. She had dreamed of the day when she would walk down the long oak hallway to the front door a healed woman. This treatment center in the Colorado Rockies was a welcomed escape for Jordan and her stay was very accomplished. She was able to deal with demons that she had let fester for years. She finally realized that her money and power couldn't help shield her from the pain that she was masking with alcohol all of these years.

A town car waited for her that breezy afternoon, no remnant of the humidity that she knew she would return to in just a few short hours. She got in a sat.

"You look fabulous Mrs. Dean." Brianna said as she exited the town car and hugged Jordan.

"Brianna, I'm so happy to see you."

"Rehab has done wonders."

"I feel great. I was blind and now I see."

"The clouds are gone?"

"Most of them Brianna. I know it will not be clear skies and rainbows always, but I now know how to deal with the stormy days. And I'm so happy you don't even know the half of it."

"You look happy."

"I'm ready to get back to Atlanta. I'm ready to see my family. I'm ready to go back to my life. I'm ready to finishing planning the biggest party that Atlanta has ever seen."

"And we're happy that you are coming back."

"Does anyone know I'm on my way home?"

"No one per your instructions Mrs. Dean."

"Good. I want to surprise everyone. I feel like I've been blind for years."

"And Mrs. Dean, there is plenty to see too. I have so much to fill you in on." Brianna informed her kindly with gossipy undertones.

"Good. I've been lying dormant for nearly three decades, Brianna. Letting those around me do whatever they want. But it's time for Atlanta to know that Jordan Campbell-Dean is back!"

They entered the town car and were on the next flight back to Atlanta without telling a soul. Jordan was on her way back to Atlanta to reclaim the life that was slipping from her grips for nearly thirty years.

CHAPTER 37

It was a week after the sentencing when she would finally open the box. "Kevin Dean" is what it read in black bold sharpie marker. She had stared at it, the plain cardboard box, daily for close to two months. She had received it from the precinct with Kevin's belongings one month to the day after he was killed. As though Kevin was calling her to this immanent object, Mya was strongly drawn to the remnants of what was left of his professional life that sat on her office floor in a corner for months. Kevin's murderer had been sentenced to death, and that chapter was finally closed. So the appropriate thing, she thought, was to finally open it.

The box was heavy, but she lifted it ever so carefully to her desktop. The baby began to squirm, and she rubbed her belly to calm it down. She took the letter opener from her desk and slit the tape that was sealing the folds together. She opened cautiously, not knowing what emotion would surface. She looked down into the box, as though it was a cave, only seeing objects and not what they were. She stepped back for a few moments, not continuing. It was a bit overwhelming. She gave herself a pep talk to continue. This was almost as bad as the night she viewed Kevin's body in the casket at the funeral home. But she knew that she had to move forward.

She reached in and pulled out the first thing that she could recognize and it was their wedding photo. It seemed like ages ago. She and Kevin looked so young. Hell, they were only eighteen and nineteen, too young. She remembered the lavish affair at the Dean Estate the summer after they had graduated college. She hated the audaciousness of the wedding, but once she saw Kevin, all that went away. She was so happy to finally be Mrs. Kevin Dean. They felt they had their whole life ahead of them and that nothing would stop them. Their dreams would come true—she a national news anchor and he a top notch detective. Now it seemed her dreams were shattered that Kevin no longer was there. And she didn't think she would ever get used to the fact.

She placed the picture on the desk and grabbed for a few more framed pictures, an award, and a plaque, one of many that lined the bottom of the box. Her husband had touched a lot of lives. He was considered by many a rare commodity in the city of Atlanta where corruption and politics reigned. Each one she hadn't seen in a while, and some she had not. Her husband was modest, and he would only keep his recognition at his place of work. He dared not bring them home to clutter the house. He was just that kind of a person. He did what he had to, Mya thought, because it was the right thing to do. He didn't expect anything in return and he was all the better for it.

After sifting through awards, Mya came across a few notes and cards from people who were touched by her husband's dedication and hard work. She sat down as she inspected the large volumes of cards, notes and letters that were written so diligently to this man who was a transformational figure. He was a person who knew that by touching one life, that all of humanity could possibly be changed. She read through the stack for what seemed like an hour and each account of her husband's generosity and tenacity enveloped her soul and realized just how much of an impact this man, her husband, had on those who he came in contact with.

She placed each letter, note and card back in their holder and looked in the box once again to see what would be yielded. She came across a worn leather bound notebook. She had no clue what this was and what she saw when she opened it, she was amused and not surprised at all. She discovered a journal of sorts that laid out Kevin's day in pros form. He described every detail, what person he was seeing and what was going to be done throughout the day. This not only showed his thoroughness, but also his honesty. He was transparent and prided himself in that fact.

She skimmed through as though she was in Borders or Barnes and Nobles looking through a new novel for purchase. She skipped from one day to another. He had lunch meetings with her in detail. He talked about going to doctor's appointments with her. He laid out goals for the week and what meetings he would have with politicians and other officials throughout the day. He had days when he would hoop with the boys at Run and Shoot, as well as the quiet evenings at home he had planned with his wife. She sifted through until coming across the day he was killed. She was cautious, but she wanted to continue.

"*May 10. This is the fourth month of investigations and still no leads. I am beginning to think it's going to take longer to find the source of these drugs coming into the city. But we must be getting closer because of the calls I have been receiving. Honestly, I fear for my life. I get threatening calls from inmates and other blocked calls demanding I stop being such a 'do gooder.' A few calls won't stop me, though. I have my meeting with Rory later this afternoon. He has some information...*"

Mya put the journal down, mouth agape. She couldn't believe what she had just read. Her husband, she discovered, was meeting with his confessed killer.

CHAPTER 38

"You really should join me." Zechariahs said as he spooned the tomato soup.

"I have too much to do. Besides I hate tomato soup." Sascha said as she kissed his forehead.

"That's right. Well, I will see you later on, right?"

"I don't know Z..."

"Oh, okay. No promises but, I would like to see you."

"When will you ask for the divorce?"

"It's complicated. As soon as Jordan is back..."

"As soon I get back, what Zechariahs?" Jordan said as she entered the room.

"Jordan, what are you doing back here?"

"Well hello to you too!" Jordan said with a devilishly smile.

"Welcome back Mrs. Dean." Sascha said with surprise, as she had no idea that the manor's first lady would be returning so soon. Though she was happy that his wife had returned, it would be put her closer to his "divorce" and her eventually happiness with Zechariahs that she had been pining for.

"Thank you Sascha. At least some body is happy to see me return." She hugged her. "So do I get a hug from my husband?"

"I'm happy you're back. But aren't you supposed to be in..."

"I went the intense detox route. I'm finished. I'm clean. I can be your wife again, and a mother to our children."

"I will go prepare your room Mrs. Dean." Sascha said grabbing the small piece of luggage that Jordan held.

"Thank you Sascha. But I think I'll be moving back to our bedroom." Sascha exited with bag in hand. "I'm so happy to be back home." Jordan looked around the room as though she had never seen in before. She walked over to Zechariahs and put her arms around him as she sat on his lap, something she hadn't done in thirty years. "I'm so sorry Zechariahs." She kissed him.

"For what?"

"I know these last few years have been hell with my addiction. The program really helped open my eyes. I missed my family. I missed living my life. And thank you for being there for me in the worst of times."

"I'm your husband." He was looking at a clean and sober Jordan who he had not seen in years. She _was_ reborn. Her whole aura had changed. It was like she had transported herself back to the year that they met, and he liked what he saw. No longer did he see the mean drunk woman she had turned into. He looked into her eyes, no longer clouded by murky depths of despair drudge in alcohol and bitterness. They were now vibrant, full of color and he could see life once again in them. Three months was all it took for his wife to return home the woman she once was.

"I love you Zech."

"With all my heart, I love you too Jordan."

Sascha hadn't gone upstairs. She heard the whole exchange just beyond the kitchen door, as she had done so many nights before. She was now privy to the man she had grown to love declaring his love for a wife she thought would never return to reclaim him.

CHAPTER 39

After her morning rehab session Paige discovered that she had run out of the drug. Withdrawals were beginning to set in when she finally called the drug dealer and agreed to meet him near Piedmont Park. She got behind the wheel of the Benz sweating profusely. She had no clue her mother was back, or that she was making significant progress with her treatment. All she cared about was the drug that she needed coursing through her veins.

CHAPTER 40

Grant Park was adjacent to Zoo Atlanta and it was always a good spot for Malek to sit and ponder life before a busy day. These days were rare for him since assuming the role of C.E.O. of D.A.C. but today he felt would be a perfect time for a retreat. He was pondering the JKJ Holding fiasco and had scheduled an appointment with Alex to see what could be done in order to cover his ass on the legal front. He dare not bring it to his own legal department from fear that they would go inform his father. That meeting wouldn't be until later on this morning.

So, his early morning was spent on his favorite bench in Grant Park overlooking the children's play area. He took out his Wall Street Journal and read the morning figures, but allowed himself to be distracted by the children playing on the playground. Sliding down slides, swinging on swings and gliding from bar to bar on the monkey bars, he imagined that he would soon be watching his own child at this very park.

He had always wanted children as long as he could remember. He could imagine a little Malek that he could mold into his own little person, and make him as spoiled and arrogant as he. He imagined a little girl that would be his little princess that could never do any wrong in his eyes. He was in his thirties, and wanted to get on this task as soon as possible, but with Kameron, he wasn't sure if he wanted to procreate with her. He could only imagine the life he would have with her. But she was more beautiful than any other woman he had laid eyes on, and knew that they would make some beautiful children.

His ponderings and imaginings were brought to an end upon inspection of his blackberry. The time had arrived for him to go meet with Alex to see if he can rectify the situation.

"And how long have you known of this holding company?" Alex inquired looking over the paper work handed to him by Malek at their meeting.

"I recently discovered it. A large amount of money had been siphoned from my family's company and I was finally able to find the source."

"A *JKJ Holding Company* in The Caymans?"

"Apparently it was established some three years ago. And the money was wired to that account a few times in smaller increments."

"You look like you have a smart embezzler."

"Aren't they all smart?"

"Yeah, just trying to make this less awkward." They had a laugh to cut the tension of the already stressed moment.

"Isn't there any way of needling the bank to find the person wiring the money to that account? I've been trying on my end, and it's almost impossible." Malek sounded worried.

"The Caymans have strict extradition laws. That includes criminals, and finances alike."

"There isn't anything your office could do?"

"My Atlanta office can't trump internal laws Malek."

"So, where does that leave me?" Malek inquired.

"I might be able to work something out. But I can't make any promises."

"And if we do find the culprit?"

"Automatic jail sentence plus a fine that will leave them in debt beyond what they ever stole from you."

"Thank you for your help Alex."

"What's family for?" Alex replied.

Malek exited. His mission for that morning was complete.

CHAPTER 41

"I didn't mean to eat so much. I'm so tired now." Dontavious said as he pushed the plate away from him at the Soto-Soto restaurant, which was now his favorite spot to eat.

"Don't worry we'll work it off later." Cole said as he finished his last bite. He smiled.

"Will that be all Mr. Dean?" Joshua, the young effeminate sever from months earlier, said as he picked up the empty plate of his now favorite weekly customer.

"Yes, thank you Joshua. And as always the food and service was excellent."

"Thank you. I try my best." Joshua said as he dismissed himself to get the check.

"I wish I could have the balls." Cole said finishing his juice.

"For what?"

"To sashay like he does." Cole said with a guffaw.

"To each his own."

"My daddy would kicked my ass."

"Mine too." Dontavious said with a slight smirk. His cell phone rang. He looked down. The number, unknown, displayed it's origins of Oregon on his cell phone. He was perplexed. "Sorry, I have to take this."

"No problem. I have to go to the restroom anyway." Cole excused himself from the table.

"Hello." Dontavious answered the phone.

"Hey stranger." A familiar voice said on the other end.

"How did you get this number?"

"You know I've always had my ways."

"I'm done with you..."

"We need to talk...I'm in Atlanta now!"

"I have nothing to say to you!" Dontavious tried to keep his composure in the busy lunch time rush of the restaurant.

"I know a spot...meet me at..." The conversation trailed on for a few more minutes as Dontavious gathered the information from this person who he didn't think he would ever hear from again.

As Cole left the restroom he ran into their server Joshua, who stared him up and down in the corner by the restrooms. "So is that him?" Joshua said condescendingly.

"Great service Joshua. I'm impressed. Who would have thought you were THE Joshua Dontavious has been raving about."

"You know my service is impeccable in and outside of the bedroom, Coleman."

"Keep your fucking voice down."

"That's right you're still pretending to be in the closet, even though everyone knows that Mr. Detective gets down with the get down."

"Joshua, stop being such a damn queen. We didn't work out, get over it!"

"What does he give you that I couldn't?" Joshua inquired.

"He's a man Joshua."

"Remember our little trips we took to Savannah and all the freaky shit..."

"Shut the fuck up!"

"You know you still want this. Here's the check. Make sure my tip's great!"

"It was great seeing you." Cole spat at him veraciously. He made his way over to the table. He placed a hundred dollar bill in the receipt holder and placed it at the edge of the table. "The bill's taken care of. Ready?"

"Yeah. I got a quick unexpected meeting. I might be late this eve."

"Everything okay?"

"Just routine campaign stuff...Alls good."

The two left. Joshua picked up the receipt holder and saw the hundred. He was left a sixty dollar tip. He smiled. His phone buzzed in his pocket. He stepped to the back and saw that there was a message waiting on him.

CHAPTER 42

Zechariahs combed through each fact meticulously...not a sound. Flipping one page to another of the thirty-five page report Malek gave him—every asset and expenditure that his twenty eight year old company held. He was more ruthless with his company than the stockholders, *WALL STREET JOURNAL* and *FORBES* could ever be. Zechariahs and Malek did this monthly to discuss the company that he had ceded to his son almost a year prior. He was happy with the progress of it and the new direction that it was taking.

Malek hated that his father micromanaged him, but he knew it was a needed annoyance to keep him on top of his game. But this month was different. He wasn't as confident in his numbers and the forecast from the previous months. He wasn't even aware of the problem until a week before this meeting, and he knew that if he didn't correct it that his father would have his ass on a plate. Zechariahs had entrusted his baby to the only child who would take up the family business. And Malek knew that if he kept up the good work that he could sustain his father's love and admiration, something that he had strived for since childhood, with little success.

"Gains in the North West sector, I'm surprised." Zechariahs said as he put down his glasses on the table of the restaurant.

"I'm trying to make gains as much as can. I saw some fat there, and I cut it."

"A fresh pair of eyes always does the trick. Great job. Everything looks in order."

"I'm glad that I can make you proud pop." Malek said nervously.

"I meant to tell you, your mother arrived in town this morning."

"How's she doing?" Malek questioned.

"She's back to her old self." Zechariahs smiled.

"Great investment if I say so."

"With your mother doing better; D.A.C improving by leaps and bounds; and me gaining in the polls, I do believe that the Dean Family is coming out of this mar."

"The shit storm does seem to be dwindling." He chimed in.

"Hate to cut this short but your brother has meetings set up for me this afternoon." He held his hand out. Malek shook it, which was expected. Zechariahs left.

Malek picked up his phone and dialed a number frantically. He spoke: "It worked. Great job crunching those numbers...The Northwest sector? Really? Wow, I guess you had to do what you had to. Now we need to find that money before he knows anything." He hung up the phone.

CHAPTER 43

The middle of the busy *Atlantic Station* open air shopping mall seemed like an unusual place for two old acquaintances to reconnect without any suspicion, but it was perfect as Dontavious discovered when he came to have a meeting with his mysterious caller from the phone. He looked around for evacuation routes if needed.

He sat in the court yard that sat adjacent to the cinema. Each person that walked by made his heart pump harder and the nervousness was increasing by the moment. Two years nearly passed since the last time they came in contact. How was he found? And what was wanted? Questions racked in his mind and Dontavious tried his hardest to not look or act as nervous as the felt on the inside. His hands were sweaty and the thoughts of leaving crept up more often than not. He was on the verge of abandoning ship when he heard a voice from behind him.

"Dontavious..."

He turned and faced The Private who was standing right behind him. "How did you find me?" Dontavious inquired.

"I saw you in a campaign photo for your father and..." The Private said with a whisper almost. The Private was nervous as well.

"What made you think I wanted to see you after how you dismantled my life?"

"It wasn't my fault!"

"What?"

"The accusations, the trial, the bargain, they all weren't my fault."

"You said that I forced you to have relations with me from fear of you losing your job, your rank, and your livelihood. How is that not your fault?"

"Your lawyer told me to."

"You are talking stupid now Percy!" He was looking The Private right in the eyes.

He remembered when he first met Private Percy Collins on his first day of boot camp with the rest of the new recruits five years prior. Dontavious was his commanding officer and they instantly had a rapport. Percy was a strapping young man of about eighteen. He stood five-nine and the caramel skin tone complimented his hazel eyes perfectly. He had always been an A-sexual person, Dontavious, but looking at Percy on the field dressed in his greens and the sweat glistening off of his forehead clouded his head with thoughts that had never been there before. He had played sports and been through basic with men who looked twice as good as Percy, in his opinion and had better physiques, but it was something about him that made him do a double take.

It wasn't long before the two became intimate and Percy had agreed to keep their secret just that: between the two of them. But Percy started to want more than sex, and Dontavious wasn't too comfortable with it. So after he returned from Iraq, he gently let Percy go. Percy was furious. Next thing he knew he was facing a Court Martial.

"I'm serious. I was approached by your lawyer Lawrence Franklin. I didn't mean for it to come to what it did."

"If this is true, why didn't you say anything then?"

"The military was the only choice I had. If I lost that, then I would have nothing. And my parents didn't know about me. I felt that was the only choice I had..."

"So you destroy my life instead?"

"I cared for you. I didn't want this!"

"You had a funny way of showing it."

"Didn't I mean something to you?" Percy asked.

"I can't honestly answer that right now." Dontavious was hurt, but deep down he knew he had hurt him when he told him that he no longer wanted to be with him. "I got to go!" Dontavious said turning and walking away.

"I will recant my story and you can have your job back." Percy said in a last ditch effort to salvage what he once meant to Dontavious.

Tempted Dontavious continued walking. But seeds were planted in his mind. What he had known was now put into question and the past that he seemed to have gotten over was now staring him in the face and it wasn't as simple as he had made it.

CHAPTER 44

Everyone at the police station was very welcoming to Mya. She was there to see Cole. Maybe he knew something about the journal that she found in Kevin's belongings. She was escorted into the office that her husband had shared with Cole for so many years. She looked around and saw that a void was indeed present.

Cole was just as decorated as her husband, if not more indicated by awards that lined the bookshelf, as well as his desk. Pictures also lined as desk along with the awards. Among pictures of his family and co workers there was also a picture of he and Kevin's after intramural basketball team that played weekly at *Run and Shoot*. As evident from this particular picture, they were League Champions that year. She recognized Kevin's face immediate in the back row of the picture. This was the same picture that was in the box at her office. But she didn't really pay much attention to it. Kevin seemed so happy doing a sport he had dreamed of playing professionally but never could.

She picked up the picture. She scanned it. Each man in the picture was very handsome, but not as handsome as her husband. Each guy looked as though they were on Michael Jordan's *Dream Team* during the Barcelona Olympics and they had won a Gold medal and not a rinky-dink trophy made of plastic. She looked at the picture a little bit closer and discovered...

"Hey Mya." Cole said as he surprised her. She turned around and dropped the picture on the desk. "I'm sorry for scaring you."

Startled she said, "I hope I'm not interrupting."

"No. What do I owe the pleasure of this surprise?"

"I was hoping you could give me some information."

"Sure, I'll try. What's this about?"

"The department sent me some of Kevin's belongings back in May. I just went through the box today. Photos, awards, etc..."

"I hope it wasn't out of line."

"No. I'm glad I received it. It's just that I found a journal in his belongings."

"I didn't know he kept a journal." He was honestly surprised.

"I didn't either. It was run of the mill stuff—a blog in the most archaic form. Very humdrum stuff...But I came across the date of May tenth..."

"The day the he was shot?"

"Yeah. He said he had a meeting with Rory Tremont, his accused killer, that day."

"I didn't know anything about that..."

"Are you sure you don't remember him saying anything about a meeting that afternoon?"

"I'm sure. We were partners, but he didn't tell me everything." Cole said skirting the issue. "Mya, I really hate to cut this short, but I really must be going. I forgot I have to be to the mayor's office by three."

"Thank you for your help, though."

"I'm sorry I couldn't have been more of a help."

"My mind is just running a million miles... I need to be resting, anyway. This little one is wearing me out. By the way are you and Dontavious coming over for dinner tomorrow?"

"We wouldn't miss our weekly gathering for anything. And thank you, Mya."

"For what?"

"For being so supportive. You know you're the only one that knows."

"I don't judge. I'm just happy that you all are happy. You were my husband's closet friend, confidant and partner." She hugged him. "Well, I'll see you tomorrow." She exited the office, shutting the door behind her.

"Kevin had a journal! Why didn't we know this?!!" Cole sternly said into his phone. "I'll see you shortly."

Mya drove. Her mind wouldn't stop racing. She couldn't forget the image of the basketball picture. Amongst the eight players of the team was her husband's killer Rory Tremont standing next to him smiling. Not only was her husband meeting him the day he was killed, he played on the same team as her husband on a weekly basis. He was friends with his killer.

CHAPTER 45

"Actually, Mrs. Dean, he just left for a meeting in Alpharetta. He should be back later on this afternoon." Malek's secretary said to Jordan waiting to see her son.

"Well, I'll just leave him a note."

"That shouldn't be a problem, ma'am."

"I won't disturb anything I promise. And I'll be on my way."

"By the way, I must say Mrs. Dean that you are looking great."

"I thank you dear." She walked into his office and closed the door. She hadn't been to the office building in almost three years. Malek had made her husband's office into his own. She felt a moment of nostalgia. This was the place where Zechariahs had toiled away for years providing for their family. And now her son, who had always wanted to be like his father, was doing just that in this place, that was made for him to do so. It was without a doubt a full circle moment where the generational baton had been passed.

She went to the desk and sat down to write the note to her son. She wanted to tell him face to face that she was back from rehab. She also wanted to thank him for putting his foot down and making her get the help that she needed.

The door opened and then slammed! "Malek, what the hell do you think you're doing..." Kameron said rushing into the office. She didn't realize that Malek wasn't there, and she didn't even stop to listen to his secretary who tried to inform him he wasn't in the office.

"Is that how you enter every room?" Jordan looked at her. She was disgusted. "Young lady have some couth!" She dropped the pen and the pad on the desk.

"Mrs. Dean, when did you get back?" Kameron was none too pleased and very surprised to see Jordan back in Atlanta.

"This morning. My, don't you clean up well."

"Thank you."

"I didn't mean it as a compliment, darling."

"I'm glad to see you're back and doing okay." She said biting.

"Stop lying. Honey, you wish I never came back." Jordan came face to face with her. "Let me save you the trouble of creating small talk. When I met you I was inebriated. I thought you were trash. Don't think just because I'm sober that I think any more of you. Actually through clearer eyes I see that you not even up to par with what I did think of you."

"You have looked down upon me since the day I met you, with your 'no' at that Christmas party. I've tried everything I know to be nice and it's not working. You still look at me as some classless gold digger. What is your problem?"

"Kameron, my family owned a house near Savannah. It had a huge porch. The summers were good and long. But they were humid. So humid in fact that we spent much of the day laid out doing nothing from fear of a heat stroke. Everything was perfect except for the mosquitoes and the gnats. They were just awful. I hated them."

"What does this have to do with anything, Mrs. Dean?"

"You're mother didn't tell you not to interrupt a grown person when they are speaking? Well, let me wrap it up for you, ye of little patience! You're just like those gnats, Kameron. You buzz around and buzz around annoying the living mess out of me. I was able to rid myself of those pests back in Savannah, and I will rid myself of you. I don't think you belong in my family."

"Well, Malek chose me. I'm not going any where Mrs. Dean. So get used to seeing my face at every function, dinner and gathering at the Dean estate because I will be there."

"Not if I have anything to say about it! You and I both know Malek can't think straight when it comes to you. He has all this brain and only uses one of his members to do the thinking when it comes to you! But honey, let me tell you, mama has a stronger hold than some girl who learned a few tricks from her days on the street!"

"My mother told me I didn't have to take no disrespect from any one. Not even a bitch with money like you!"

"Kameron, consider this your notice! You will never be a Dean. So enjoy everything you have now! Like sands through the hour glass so are the days of your life, and they are running out fairly quickly." With that Jordan took her clutch and excited the office, closing the door behind her.

Kameron was filled with anger and let out a scream that would have cracked glass. She instantly felt dizzy. She braced herself on the desk and breathed deeply to compose herself. She hated what Malek was doing to her, blackmailing her into staying with him. But she hated his mother even more for torturing her for no good reason, other than that of just mere trivial hate. "Bitch!" She said to herself.

Kameron stepped into her office after finally composing herself and sat behind her desk. She saw that she had a voicemail. She retrieved the messages. Minutes later she dropped the receiver on the desk. Her face was pale as a ghost. "This can't be."

CHAPTER 46

Zechariahs sat on the back porch of the mansion smoking a cigar. The tough decisions he had to make were racking his brain, most notably, the decision to be with his mistress or his newly returned wife. He thought the choice would be easy, and it turned out that it was not. Jordan hadn't been a wife to him in almost three decades. Sascha was there for him physically and emotionally, helping him through some tough times, lately the death of his youngest son. And she never wavered in her devotion, not only to him, but to his family as well. He had it all figured out. He was going to tell his wife that he wanted a divorce when she returned from rehab. He was planning to divide his assets, which he knew he had to do. He hoped for a quick divorce so that he could finally move on with the woman he truly cared for: Sascha. This was the plan until Jordan showed back up unexpectedly that morning.

Seeing his wife sober was like looking back in time. She was just as beautiful as she when he met her. All those bad years went out of the window as she sauntered into the dining room with that beautiful smile he had missed so much. She was the love of his life and the mother of his children. It took him back to the first time that he had met her some forty years prior. She had a special place in his heart then, and she returned to that exact spot by coming back sober and repentant about the pain and discord that she had caused the family all of these years.

"Mr. Dean, put that cigar out!" Sascha said entering the porch.

"Sascha, don't you have anything else to do besides taking an old man's habit away?" He said jokingly.

"I want you to be around to be much older. That's why I'm so hard on you."

"You're so good to me Sascha." He put the cigar out on the sole of his foot. "That's why this is killing me so much."

She knew what was on the horizon. She wanted to soften the blow for herself: "Mrs. Dean's back. I was just as surprised as you."

"I know. She's my wife. And I don't mean to hurt you. But I would be doing my family and myself a disservice if..."

"I know Mr. Dean. I was silly to think that you would ever leave her for me, the maid."

"Don't do that. I love you! But..."

"You love her and she had your children."

"So you understand?"

"I understand that my husband died too young. I understand that I was a single mother barely making it. I understand that I loved a man for thirty years who could never give it back to me fully. I understand that you will always love her, mijo. And you should understand that I can not stay your maid. Mr. Dean I quit."

"Sascha don't go!"

"I have to. I have way too much pride to stay after being rejected another time. Be well mijo. Be well." She kissed him. She walked into the house to pack her belongings. She had been at this house for thirty years. And she was finally going to leave it and never look back. She had been promised for years that he would leave Jordan, and she finally had to make his decision for him. She didn't need this job, but her obligation to the family that took her and her son in when she was at her lowest kept her in their grace. With the rejection of her lover, it would show her that she had paid her debt back to the Deans and then some.

Upon Jordan's query as to what happened to Sascha and why she quit, Zechariahs told her that Sascha wanted to retire. When Jordan insisted upon going to her and urge her to come back and work for the family, Zechariahs insisted that she let her be. Jordan did as was asked and continued to put her life together, including looking for a new executive of the manor.

CHAPTER 47

Jordan and Brianna had a late lunch at STRAITS, Atlanta Entertainer Ludacris' restaurant, in Midtown Atlanta that afternoon. Their main discussion was about the gala that was being thrown in a month. Jordan was quite pleased at the progress that Brianna had made while she was away at rehab.

She wasn't too surprised by the quality of work that she had done, seeing as though she had helped plan the event some years before as well. This year was going to be different and more luxurious than years prior, and with Zechariahs close to being the mayor of Atlanta, the Deans had to show off to the city that they were ready to take the reigns as Atlanta's first family.

"I don't know if I could have pulled this off without you." Jordan said sipping her tonic water.

"It's my pleasure Mrs. Dean. I've learned from the best."

"We make a hell of a team. I wish that son of mine would have picked you as his companion than that tramp Kameron."

"Well, rumor has it that she got that position on her back."

"That's no rumor, dear. That is a fact." She laughed. "She has to go."

"Good luck with that contract she has."

"What contract do you speak of?" She inquired the now tipsy Brianna.

"Oh, Mrs. Dean I'm surprised I haven't told you. Your son has his whore on payroll..." A smile crept over her face as she clued Jordan in on the details of Malek and Kameron's deal, which no one outside of the two of them knew about, or so they thought.

CHAPTER 48

"Malek, I'm so proud of what you've become. Love mom." Malek read the note that his mother left for him on his desk. He smiled. He put the letter down. He sifted through the various other papers and folders left on his desk. At that moment he received a call on his cell: "You've found it? When will I know specifics... Get back at me as soon as you know anything concrete." He put the phone away. A knock on the door jarred him from his frazzled state. "Come in."

"Hey, bro, I hope I'm not interrupting." Dontavious said entering the office.

"I am a little busy. Just got back from a day long meeting."

"It will only take a minute, Malek."

"Make it fast, Dontavious." He spat at his brother.

"I need the company's contributions' list for the press release that I'm putting together as well..."

"Human resources can help you out with that and the other things as well. I'm too busy for little things like that!"

"What is your problem, man?"

"I am busy and you are bothering me with small things that can be easily handled by human resources, even my secretary if you chose to ask her."

"I don't mean just today, bro. I mean in general. Ever since I came back for Kevin's funeral and chose to stay in Atlanta, you've been given me shade. What have I done to you to deserve that treatment?"

"Dontavious are you really asking me this now? I told you that I'm busy. If you want to have a counseling session to figure out what my tone indicates and what predicates your worry of something being wrong, please by all means schedule it with the family therapist we have on speed dial, make an appointment and let my secretary know, and I'll try my best to be there if my schedule allows me to be there so that we can hash this out. If that is all, please leave, I have a lot of work to catch up on!"

"Malek, I have done nothing to you! I have been trying for three months to reconnect with my brother, and you have not made that easy. You keep acting like some bitch! Why don't you be a man and tell me what's up. And I'll drop it!"

"You and Kevin abandoned this business and this family. I work hard as hell to get in pop's good graces to keep the Dean name alive and well in the business world. I finally earn his respect and my position with hard work and dedication. And what the fuck do you do? You come back home as some prodigal son after twenty years. They lay out the fat of the land for you. You're his campaign manager. You are welcomed back with no incident. And now I'm fighting for my position yet again!"

"Your insecurities are not my fault!"

"They've always been your fault. 'Come on tubby' you used to say. 'Stop studying and get out and play.' 'You want a girlfriend' don't you?' You remember you used to say those things to me?"

"I don't know what reality you are living in, but I didn't mean harm by those things. We were kids then. Almost thirty years ago. We are grown. Get over it!"

"That's easy for you to say. You had easy. I had to work twice as hard."

"I hated school. I hated to study and no one ever said I was the bright student. You were. Always have been. I wanted to be you. You made it seem so easy. And I always looked up to you Malek."

"That still doesn't change the past, or the future. Dontavious, please leave my office."

"Malek, I'm trying..."

"Not hard enough. Good bye Dontavious."

Dontavious tried to speak but his pride and emotions wouldn't let him. He turned around and left the office. Malek never thought he would feel like this again, but every emotion of childhood resurfaced. He was still that hurt little boy. No amount of education, status or awards could make the hurt of nearly thirty years go away.

CHAPTER 49

Visiting hours lasted until six p.m. It was almost five p.m. when Mya arrived at the Harris County Correctional Facility. Traffic was hell on I-75 as it always was at that time of the day. She walked in and flashed her press badge and asked to see Warden Barber, her godfather who she knew could get her to see Rory Tremont amidst the influx of press outlets that now ascended upon the Facility.

She was escorted into the warden's office and she was greeted with a hug by the husky man of sixty. Warden Jacques Barber was a friend who had known her deceased father since their years at Clarke Atlanta University. "How are you doing Jacques?"

"I'm well Mya. I heard that you were expecting. You're due any day now."

"No, this is just a big baby." She laughed as she touched her belly.

"It's so great to see you. How's everything going? Since Kevin's murder and all?"

"Well as can be expected."

"I can reassure you that Mr. Tremont is not getting any special treatments here while he awaits the death penalty."

"I'm glad to hear it. I wanted to know if it was possible for me to speak with him."

"I'm sorry only his lawyer and close family are allowed in to see him."

"But Jacques I need to see him. I discovered he and my husband were friends. He knew him well according to a journal I found in his belongings."

"Is that right?"

"Yes, and I need to understand what and how, and why he did this to my husband. It doesn't make sense. Please, for my own well being, Jacques?"

Thinking, Jacques spoke: "I can't do anything today because he's already in lock down. But I can get you in to see him tomorrow. Is that okay?"

"That would be great, thank you." She hugged him.

"He's already had two visitors today. I don't want him to think he's a celebrity or nothing. No special treatment or nothing, you know."

"So just his lawyer and close family, huh?"

"Yeah, today was his lawyer and his wife."

"Wife? I didn't know he was married. She never even came to the trail."

"Yeah, wife. Her name is Brenda. Very attractive. He must be killing himself being in prison with someone like that waiting at home."

"Another favor Jacques..."

"I'll see what I can do."

"Can I get her information to call her? Maybe we can meet and discuss this tragedy."

"I can't..."

"Come on, for your Goddaughter."

"All right." He went to the sign in sheet and took down the visitor's information on a sheet of paper and gave it to her. "Here you go. Don't tell anyone I did that for you. And if she asks, just say that you have connections.

"I promise. Thanks Jacques. And it was great seeing you again." She hugged him.

"You take care of yourself and that child. And I'll set up that visit for you tomorrow." The phone rang.

"Go on and take it. Have a good one." She left the office and headed to her car.

Jacques answered the phone. "None at all? I'll let my men know." He hung up the phone. He dialed an extension and spoke into the receiver yet again: "From this day forward Rory Tremont is to have no guests." He hung up the phone. He feared disappointing his goddaughter with the news he was just given.

Mya couldn't wait until she got to the car to dial the number that was given to her. It rang twice before she got a voicemail recording: "You've reached Kameron Hanes. I am not available..." Mya nearly dropped the phone. She had called Kameron's phone, Malek's fiancée. She was even more confused now.

CHAPTER 50

Kameron ignored the call to her cell phone, turned it off and placed it in her purse as she entered the convalescent home. She drove around all day thinking about the news that she had gotten on her voicemail earlier in the day. She knew this was the only place where she could get some real thinking done. She walked up the nurse's stand. "How's she doing?"

"Responding very nicely to her new meds," the nurse responded, knowing exactly why she was there.

"I'm glad to hear that. I know it's late, but may I still visit her?"

"Sure Miss Hanes."

"Thank you." Kameron walked down the sterile hallway of the convalescent home to the familiar room that she visited at least twice a week. This month, however, her visits were very few. She looked at the name tag, "Janika Hanes." She pushed the door and entered the room. Everything was still the same as she remembered it from previous visits. Balloons, flowers and cards coated every inch. The incessant beeping of machines was still prevalent. The shades were drawn, and very little light escaped within. The gentle hum of the television added ambiance.

She saw her, lying in the bed, still looking the same, in her present slumber that she hadn't awaken from in nearly seven years. Her hair had grown, and was nearly past her shoulders. Kameron pulled up the chair that was adjacent to the bed and sat down. She grabbed the woman's hand

and kissed it. "Mom, I'm so sorry I haven't come in a while. I've been busy." Tears rolled down her cheeks. Kam still couldn't believe such a vibrant woman was now in a coma devoid of life. She was barely alive and a shell of her former self. "You know me better than I know myself. What have I gotten myself into?" Kameron continued. She was at confession, and her soul she wanted to be free. "The doctor called me today and told me that I am pregnant. I'm not ready to be a mother."

"Girl, what the hell have you gotten yourself into?" Her mother's voice said to her.

"Ma, I thought I could play the game without being caught up!"

"Playing with fire can only burn you! I told you that since you were a little girl!"

"I know! But I was doing this for you both."

"Child, your brother and I would have been okay without you scheming and conniving to get this life YOU desperately wanted. How're you going to lose yourself trying to chase after something that doesn't belong to you? Girl what God's got for you is for you! Don't be taking nothing that don't belong to you! Yo mama didn't raise no fool!!!"

"Ma, I know. But what should I do now?"

"Your father put me through a world of hell because I wanted what he could offer me. Fuck his wife, his children and anything else he had."

"I know ma." Kameron said trying to interrupt her mother.

"When he decided he was done with me, I was left to raise you and your brother by myself, two jobs and no sleep. I had cigarettes, coffee and the grace of God helping me through those hard times." Her mother continued.

"Ma, I'm not you!"

"Yes you are. Just as ambitious and stupid as me. God, your brother didn't give me a lick of problems, but oh, you baby girl gave me a world of hurt. Leave that boy alone. Leave Malek alone! Make your own path. You have a child to think about now, girl! You ain't just got yourself now!"

"I know ma. I know…" Tears were now streaming down Kameron's face. She looked at the bed. Her mother was still unconscious, still comatose. The whole conversation she had just had with her was something that she had wished her mother was telling her at that moment. But her mother couldn't counsel her like she had hoped. She missed her mother and the bond that they shared.

"I called you four times last week and you never returned any of my phone calls." He said as he entered the room.

"I'm sorry I haven't been here, Joshua. I've been busy." She turned around to face him.

"I'm busy at Soto-Soto working my ass off each day, and I have school too. I still find time to come and see our mother."

"Who's paying for that education Joshua? It's because of what I do that you are able to go to Morehouse debt free and stress free."

"I know big sis. I am grateful too. But our mother had a bad reaction to some medication they gave her last week and was throwing up all over the place and they called me."

"But the nurse said that she was doing okay." Kameron said with concern.

"Now she is. They needed permission to make the adjustments. You weren't available."

"I'm so sorry mom." She kissed her mom's hand. "I'm going to try and do better Joshua, I promise."

"How're things going in corporate America anyway?"

"I just landed a huge account in Switzerland. I'm making strides."

"I guess you have to make the best out of the contract situation."

"You always seem to catch me as I am confessing all at the alter of our mother, don't you." She chided her brother.

"Well, you shouldn't be so loud." He laughed and hugged her. The tension was broken. "I'm not going to say anything big sis. We are fam. The only fam we got besides this beautiful lady in this bed!"

"Well at least I have you little brother if I don't have anyone else." She hugged him in return.

"You will never believe who I ran into at the restaurant the other day." Joshua baited her.

228.

"Who?"

"Cole."

"I told you I saw him at the funeral of Kevin looking all butch. If I didn't know his tea from you Joshua, I would never have guessed that man was a fag."

"But real tea is that you won't believe who he is dating, now big sis."

"I'm intrigued." She perked up.

"As you should be. Does Dontavious Dean ring a bell?"

"Malek's older brother?" She was taken aback.

"I think so." Joshua finished his last piece of gossip: "From Cole's lips, he is twice the man I could ever be." He laughed it off.

"Malek's brother is dating Cole? Hmm, this just brightened my humdrum day." Kameron's wheels begin turning. She was up to something and it was not good.

CHAPTER 51

"...So for now thousands are now without power in the Sandy Springs area. And many of the residents hope that it will at least return by the morning commute. For eyewitness news, this is Mya Kim-Dean for Channel Two-Eye Witness news..." Mya said as she signed off from a live feed that she was called in last minute for the eleven p.m. broadcast. She rarely did live feeds any more, but she was happy to be back at work and it was a perfect distraction. She was tired, and couldn't wait to get home to fall asleep.

She said goodbye to her producer and cameraman and headed to her car to go home. It wasn't until she got back to her car and sat down in the seat that she remembered what had happened earlier that day: the business at the prison and getting a hold of Rory's wife, who just so happened to be Kameron. *How did Kameron fit into all of this, and why would she be visiting Rory at all?* Mya was trying to rack her brain for a possible connection, but those thoughts were taken over once more by a phone call she received. It was Zechariahs. He asked her to come to the hospital, there was an emergency.

CHAPTER 52

It was almost midnight when Zechariahs got the call himself. It had taken the nurses that long because of lack of her identification. Records from her previous stay at the hospital positively identified her and Zechariahs was called. Subsequently the family was informed and the Deans held vigil in the waiting room until they heard any new news as to why Paige was in the hospital. It was a little bit after one a.m. before they heard any news.

"Is she's going to be okay?" Jordan said cradled in Zechariahs' arms.

"She's a fighter. Just like her mother." Zechariahs reassured her.

The doctor entered the room. Dontavious and Malek gathered with their parents to hear what Paige's prognosis was. "Mr. and Mrs. Dean I have some news for you."

"How is she?" Jordan asked exasperatedly.

"Your daughter overdosed. We did a toxin screen on her and discovered copious amounts of the drug Praveline in her system."

"What's that?" Dontavious inquired.

"It's a ravenous hallucinogen. It severely weakens brain activity and muscle reaction and is normally very deadly. Paige was very lucky that she was found when she was."

"How long until we can see her?" Zechariahs said.

"Another thirty minutes she should be prepped. But only one visitor at a time is allowed."

"Thank you doctor." Malek said. The doctor left.

"Drugs?" Dontavious questioned.

"The same drug that Kevin was investigating." Mya said as her wheels began to turn.

"It's my fault." Jordan chimed in.

"Why would you say that mom?" Malek questioned.

"She was taking that drug to ease the pain of the rehab of her leg." Jordan continued.

"You don't know why she was taking it." Dontavious said rubbing her back, trying to comfort her.

"Yeah, we don't know why she was taking those drugs. We've all but forgotten about Paigey since the accident three months ago. It's not your fault mom. It's our entire family's fault. We assumed she was okay in rehab and just let her be." Malek showed rarely seen compassion. It was merely to make himself look good to trump his brother's concern.

"I'll go get some coffee while we wait. Anything for you Jordan?" Zechariahs said.

"I'm okay Zech. I'll just wait here until they're ready for me to see her." Jordan said sitting.

"I'll go with you dad. This baby needs something. And I'll bring something back for you Jordan you need your strength." Mya said.

"Thank you darling." Mya and Zechariahs exited. "Malek, that's what a real woman looks like."

"Don't start mama." Malek said as he exited the waited room, Jordan followed.

"Thank you so much for being here." Dontavious said as he approached Cole who was gazing out the window into the starry night.

"Anything for you?" Cole asked.

"No, nothing. My sister was on the same drug that you and Kevin were investigating."

"Ironic isn't it?"

"I'm glad she's going to be okay."

"Me too babe." He placed his hand on his shoulder, unseen by anyone, at least everyone except Kameron who entered at that precise moment. She had a slight chuckle to herself. But she was taken out of that moment by a heavy hand on her shoulder.

"What the..." She said as she turned around. It was Malek. He was furious.

"Where have you been? I've been calling for hours."

"I come when you call me? Just like the little bitch I am, right?" Kameron said snidely.

"Precisely."

"Is Paige going to be okay?" She said as to dodge more questions about her whereabouts.

"Doctor said she should make a full recovery."

"That's good. Well, if that's all, I think I'll be on my way."

"Malek, your mother said that she needed to see you on the veranda." Mya said as she reentered the waiting room with a Rice Crispy Treat and Chamomile tea.

"Kameron, don't go anywhere I have something I need to speak to you about!" Malek barked as he exited into the veranda overlooking the city.

"You've gotten twice as big since the last time I saw you Mya." Kameron tried making conversation, making the moment less awkward, or so she thought.

"This child must be a giant. It's getting so big so quickly."

"I see." In that moment the gravity of her new found pregnancy was apparent and she envisioned herself just as pronounced as Mya, and what a new life in her body meant to her and her future. "And how many months are you?"

"Six months. It's almost over."

"Well good luck with the rest of it."

"Thank you."

"Mya," Kameron continued as the thoughts hit her, "may I ask you something?"

"Sure."

"You've been apart of this family for years. When do they finally except you?" Kameron almost seemed genuine.

"I've learned over the last ten years that The Deans have power, wealth, and respect. But what they want from us who enter their world is transparency. They want to know your true motives." Mya said with almost accusatory undertones. She was about to jump in with her questions about the day's events but was cut off by Kameron.

"Thanks for the advice. Tell Malek if you see him I had to go. Thank you again." The future sister-in-laws left it at that as Kameron excused herself, not waiting for Malek, as he had instructed.

Mya wanted to continue but it was too late, as Kameron exited quickly. She spotted Dontavious and Cole by the window and approached. "Hey my favorite two people in the world."

"You look tired." Dontavious said with concern.

"I've been up since six and have been busy all day." Mya said explaining herself.

"Well being tired isn't good for the baby, is it?" Cole said, giving her belly a pat. His phone rang. He excused himself.

"So, what have you been doing all day? I haven't heard from you once?" Dontavious inquired as he sat her down.

"Well I went to Harris County to see if I could interview Rory Tremont and I had a live feed tonight. I'm exhausted."

"How did the interview go?"

"He was on lock down and I have to wait until tomorrow, or is it later on today...so tired."

"Isn't that wound too fresh?"

"I found a photo of Kevin's after work basketball team. Rory Tremont was a teammate of his."

"They knew each other personally?" Dontavious was intrigued.

"Yeah. Cole was on that team as well."

"Cole never said they knew each other."

"There's a lot about this whole thing that just doesn't add up." Mya's phone rang. She answered. "Hello." The phone call wasn't but a few minutes long, but her face told of its contents. "Thank you Jacques." She hung up the phone disappointed.

"What was that about and this late?"

"It was my connection at the prison. He's been trying to get my all evening. Apparently I can't interview Rory today or any other day. His visiting privileges have been revoked."

"Why?"

"No particular reason given. Something's not right Dontavious." Mya said with concern.

Cole's phone call was from Kameron asking him to meet her downstairs in front of the hospital. When he arrived Kameron was standing grinning like a Cheshire Cat. "Spit the canary out Kam." He said. She laughed.

"You dumped my brother for Dontavious?"

"What're you talking about?" He feigned ignorance.

"I saw Joshua today. He told me all about you and my future brother-in-law." He grabbed her by the arm, and carried her away to a corner, as to not let anyone hear what she was saying. "Let go of me!" She pushed him away.

"Keep that to yourself. No one knows about me and I plan to keep it that way!"

"Who you fuck is none of my business, but what I do know now can make our deal with our boss that much more profitable for me."

"What you and *he* have worked out is none of my concern."

"I don't think you want this getting out! When you were with my little underage brother, he could have been hurt, but now I have no ties, so I can kill two birds with one stone!"

"Who do you think set this up!? Our boss did!!!" Cole blurted out, almost a last ditch effort to save his own ass.

"Are you serious?" Kameron knew of duplicity, but didn't realize it reached these heights.

"I would advise you to stick to the plan and do your part. Have a good one. My man is waiting for me." He entered into the hospital.

Kameron was taken aback. This thing she had gotten into had just gotten more complicated.

On the balcony overlooking the city Jordan couldn't stop the tears that were flowing. Malek comforted her best he could, but he was not used to seeing his mother in this condition. Even with her notorious binges, she never broke down, well not in his presence. "Have I failed as a mother?" Jordan asked in all sincerity.

"No. You are a great mom."

"Dontavious didn't come home for almost two decades. You are saddled with some tramp you won't get rid of. Paige is on drugs and Kevin's dead. I have failed."

"Mom, we are grown people. We make our own decisions. There're not your doing. And Kevin's murder was a senseless act of violence. You can't blame yourself."

"I can't help but to blame myself." He cradled her.

Inside the waiting room Cole returned and found Mya and Dontavious huddled by the window talking. Mya let him in on what was happening. What Mya didn't know was that this was the last thing she should have done.

Preoccupied with his daughter's condition and his inevitable media blitz later on that day to explain her condition, Zechariahs almost didn't hear the faint voice that was in the hallway that early morning as he returned to the waiting room. He turned and saw a frail fair-complexioned black woman in a wheel chair. She wore a scarf and flowered robe. An orderly pushed her. "Excuse me?" He said upon seeing who had called his name. He wasn't sure if he was just hearing things.

"You are Zechariahs Dean aren't you?," the melody of Southern days gone by sifted out of her mouth with ease as she asked him what she already knew to be true and that he was Zechariahs Dean.

"I am."

"Your face is all over the newspapers and such. I'm very proud of what you're going to do for the city when you're elected."

"Well thank you for your support." Zechariahs wasn't too wrapped up in his problems to acknowledge a supporter.

"Anyone who can get that corrupt bastard Emory out of office, I say the better."

"Thank you again Miss...what's your name?"

"I'm not surprised you don't recognize me."

"Should I?"

"Well I'll reintroduce myself. I'm Olive Westport. But when we met over forty years ago, I was Olive Annex." Zechariahs' mouth dropped. This was definitely a blast from the past.

CHAPTER 53

In the three months he was gone from Atlanta, Marcus was trying to make ends meet. He was avoiding loan sharks and various other people who he owed money. He was balancing all this with his nightly performances on Broadway. But the increasing amount of debt and his lack of access to Paige's dwindling account made him more leery of his future wellbeing in general.

The night of Paige's overdose he got a call. Zechariahs informed him that she was in the hospital, a call he didn't get until the wee hours of the morning. He knew he was responsible for turning her to the drugs to numb the pain, and he knew that he would have to get to Atlanta as soon as he could to try and make it right with his supplier before the news leaked that it was indeed the drug that he had given her was the one that caused her bodily harm.

He was on the next plane to Atlanta. He would arrive early morning and go straight to his dealer's house. How would he break the news of the loss in income and drugs? He would have to figure this out. He had a three hour plane ride in order to do so.

CHAPTER 54

"Honey, I've been meaning to ask you..." Dontavious broke the silence of the bedroom at three that morning.

"I told you babe, it was just a misunderstanding." Cole explained.

"That is strange that she thought Rory played on your after-work basket ball team. That you know him personally has to be a mistake." Dontavious was mulling over the suspicions that Mya revealed to them.

"Then why are you still questioning it?"

"Mya is usually on top of her stuff. Why would she..." Cole put his hand on top of his mouth, kissed him so that he couldn't speak. Cole then got up and walked over to the desk and rummaged through the drawers. "Why are you doing?"

"I'm getting the picture to show you."

"You don't have to..." Dontavious said, secretly wanting to see proof of what Cole was saying to him was true.

"Here you go." He handed him the picture. All of the guys from the basketball league were present in the frame. On this picture standing next to Kevin, though, was not Rory, as it was in the photo that Mya saw at Cole's office. It was a new person, someone that Cole had photo-shopped in only two hours before to cover his tracks knowing that his lover would have further questions when they arrived home. It's amazing what technology can do and how fast it can help cover an ass that was indeed going to be exposed.

Cole would have a meeting in the morning with his boss and he would have to tell Kameron the latest developments, they were indeed working together.

CHAPTER 55

The early morning sun was peering through her window. Mya looked at the lap top. Though, she was exhausted, her brain was going a million miles per hour and there was no way she could have had a good night's rest. Her connections at the Atlanta Journal-Constitution and WSB-TV allowed her access to a database of articles and pictures that would aide her in her search. Even with all of those resources at her disposal, the connection to Rory and Kameron still seemed far fetched, and the results that she was finding online expressed those same sentiments exactly. She did search after search and still there was nothing that she could come up with.

She put every possible entry into the search engine with each one of their names and a combination of both. Still after three hours staring at the screen she was lost. She didn't know where to go and couldn't even find a connection to either one of their lives. More current pictures and articles were slim to none and she felt that her current suspicions were not valid. It wasn't until she expanded her search by a few years that she came across an article that she could use:

> "*Janika Hanes, assistant to Senator Thornheart Kincade, was injured severely at the Kincade Estate in McDonough, Georgia yesterday. The accidental shooting is still under*

> *investigation. Her daughter and son wait vigil by their*
>
> *mother's bedside waiting on word from investigators ... "*

She read the article that was dated some seven years prior. The article was accompanied by a family picture of the single mother. To her surprise she saw Janika, her son, and a younger Kameron. It didn't have any connection to her current connection she was looking for. But she found it quite interesting that there was a connection to someone so powerful within Kameron's family.

An email alert that pop-up on the screen alerted her that she had new mail and she proceeded to check it. To her surprise she saw Rory's bio of sorts and she was surprised by its findings. Rory had been a diligent worker for Dean Architecture and Construction for the past three years. This was a fact that was left out of the information that the media was given about the now convicted cop killer. Mya's brain was working overtime as she became more confused. Not only was her husband's killer on the same basketball team as he, Rory also worked for her husband's family's company. His connection to her husband was too uncanny and she knew that this was becoming a little too eerie.

Mya tried connecting the dots but these dots seemed too far apart and they just didn't make any sense. The next logical step, Mya thought, was that the connection between the two of them could be their D.A.C. ties and the work environment could have bred the ending result of her husband's untimely death.

In that moment a phone call came. She was quite surprised because it was early. Who it was on the end was someone she never expected.

CHAPTER 56

That early morning he saw his mom sitting in the chair—staring out the window as she had every morning for the last couple of weeks. She didn't say anything. Her heart was definitely broken. He went over to her, offered her something to eat and to drink, and both she refused. "Mama, you have to eat something." He said to her day in and day out. She refused. He knew what ailed her, but he dare not say it aloud. One part of him knew this would happen, and his mother would be hurt by the affair she had with Zechariahs. But the other part of him wanted his mother to find some kind of happiness, even if it were with a married man. He knew Zechariahs was never going to leave Jordan for his mother Sascha. But he dare not tell her that. She had so little to live for in this world and had so many disappointments, but this one he felt would change his mother indefinitely.

He left her staring out of the window as he did day in and day out. He looked at her as he backed out of the driveway on his way to work. When he returned home he knew she would be right there. Was his mother waiting for her lover to return to her? Or was she just staring at the void in the sky trying to figure out the void in her life? Either way he felt her obsession was quite unhealthy for her.

CHAPTER 57

Dontavious was running interceptions left and right with media outlets calling into the headquarters the next morning. He fielded many questions about the hospitalizations of his sister and what that meant for his father's campaign. He thought that the press release that he put together would help with onslaught of callers, but it only baited the sharks that were swimming. The Southern political spin machine was in overload and Dontavious didn't know what to make of this newest setback in this busied campaign that his father was running, successfully, but very arduous as it inched closer to election day. But his father was no where to be found that morning.

Zechariahs had sent word to Dontavious to set up a press conference in time for the midday news broadcast, but he didn't realize his father wouldn't be there all morning to prep. But like a good son and a diligent campaign manager, Dontavious prepped notes for his father, even though there would be no time for preparation on his father's side. He attempted to call his father once again unsuccessfully.

"Where's Mr. Dean?" Brianna said as she hung up the phone.

"I wish I knew. His phone went straight to voice mail."

"You think he's at the hospital?"

"That's where he was this morning when he called me."

"He'll be here by noon." She reassured him.

"I would hate to see his campaign falter because of a missed conference of this magnitude."

"Everything'll work out you'll see."

"Thank you again for coming to help me with these calls."

"It was the least I could do. And besides your mom didn't want me at the hospital and the things I must do for the ball can't be done until after noon."

"Well thank you. You do so much for this family."

"Your family has done so much for me. Trust me I'm getting the better end of this stick."

Dontavious rubbed the back of his neck. "I haven't slept in almost two days. First Paigey, and now this. I'm wearing myself out."

"Hey, sit here and relax. Let me rub your neck for you." Brianna said sitting him down in the chair. It was only the two of them in the big office and she wanted to take advantage of the situation. He didn't move as she slid her supple fingers around his neck and began to rub. She had dreamed of this moment from the first time she laid eyes on him via a picture Jordan had tucked in her daily calendar. And when she saw that he looked better than the picture the day he arrived for the funeral, she couldn't wait to get her hands on him. She had everything that she wanted in life, but she lacked a man, and she felt Dontavious could be that man for her. "So Mr. Dean, do you have a date for the Harvest Ball?"

"I haven't really thought about it with the debates and such."

"Why don't you go with me?"

"Um, aren't you going to be busy with the planning and running around?" Dontavious said tying to skirt the issue.

"There's always a time for a dance, right?"

"I guess you're right." Dontavious felt uneasy now in his situation.

"So it's a date then?"

"Sure." The phone rang, thank God, and he answered it, releasing himself from her therapeutic hold. "Dean Campaign headquarters," he answered the phone. "No, we will not be making any statements until noon today during our press conference."

Brianna saw the man of her dreams answering that phone. But what she didn't know was that Dontavious dreams were not of her, not even of women.

Outside, unknown to either one of them a pair of eyes were watching them. Everything they said and did. Those eyes would stay on them for the rest of the day, unseen by anyone.

CHAPTER 58

Zechariahs looked at the clock on the wall. He had been in Olive's room for almost six hours. They were talking about old times and how good life was and how simple it all was back some forty years prior when they had met. What was ironic about their current states was that Olive was the one who initially had an eye for Zechariahs.

They met in 1965 when Olive and Jordan were the best of friends. Olive and her family moved to Atlanta when she was thirteen, four years prior for her father's job at *The Atlanta Journal*, and she would come to Jordan's plantation in order to escape the hustle and bustle of Atlanta's face pace. Olive was more so the innocent one, and Jordan the instigator, but together they had many scandalous summers but none like that summer that they had met Zechariahs. It was a summer of love, romance, sex and switching of potential mates.

It started off as any other for the girls: The *Jack and Jill* Cotillion took place at the local Mason hall to jumpstart the summer. It was a local get together and tradition where lighter skinned blacks came to meet other lighter skinned blacks and fraternize. Jordan met her suitor Emory Westport that summer at that particular event and she had fallen head over hills. He was more dashing than anyone she had ever met before. She felt like Scarlet O'Hara in *Gone with the Wind*, a book she had loved since childhood, and a film she now adored even in reruns on the local television station. She felt that her Rhett Butler was there to sweep her off her feet, and he came in the form of Emory. Not all was well in the Campbell household that summer as Olive began to pine for the handsome Mr. Westport, whose family was the namesake of a small Southern town not far from Savannah. He was also the product of intermixing and had the best of both worlds wrapped in his butterscotch hue. It was a natural that he would be able to charm his way to being mayor of Atlanta some forty five years later. Emory began to steal Jordan away, leaving Olive to her own advances, neither caring about their previous summer plans. It wasn't until the emergence of Zechariahs on the plantation some two weeks later that the Olive had a distraction.

Zechariahs came to work for the plantation through a series of events. His adventure started with a routine trip to Savannah that he took to work at the local Farmer's Market. Zechariahs loved his escapes to Savannah from Statesboro, some forty miles South of the city every chance he got. His family was sharecroppers and he hated the life they led: always working hard and never getting ahead. He spent many nights on the farm sketching on a pad different buildings and structures by candle light and hoped that one day they would get him away from the poverty around him.

On this particular trip to Savannah he saved Jordan's father from being mowed down by an escaped truck at the farmer's market. Her father was so grateful that he hired him at the plantation as a farm hand and promised that he would take care of his education if he chose to go to college. Zechariahs didn't care what the job was as long as it wasn't in Statesboro.

He worked hard daily and rarely did anything fun. The sketching was relegated to twice a week near the end of the day after work was complete. It was on one of those random sketching days that he met Olive. She was walking the land by herself to escape the love fest that was Jordan and Emory. She bumped into Zech as he sketched and they began to talk. He ended up sketching her, and by the end of the evening, as the sun went down they were locked in an embrace. From that day forth she would come to watch Zech sketch every evening that he would sketch, and a month later, they were hot and heavy.

Jordan and Emory had an argument one random day in July regarding 4th of July plans. Jordan went for a stroll on the land and sat by her favorite tree to think. From behind Olive and Jordan must have looked alike, because Zech came behind her and embraced her. She was so scared that she nearly tackled Zechariahs. When he realized that it wasn't Olive, he profusely apologized and stated his mistake. Some where between his apology and helping her off the ground, Jordan was intrigued by this dark stranger she didn't know was a border on her land. She had never seen a dark man so handsome. She honestly never looked at a darker man in that way in her life. She was in the school of the paper bag test, and he definitely would not pass with flying colors. But his soft spoken demeanor and beautiful visage helped her look pass their definite color differences. Everyday afterwards she would find a way to sneak down to see Zechariahs as he worked and would have the vapors just watching him lift the bails of hay and his other chores that paid for his boarding on the plantation.

Her thoughts turned to Zechariahs and further away from Emory, while Olive and Zech were getting hot and heavy. Emory went his own way by mid summer, leaving Jordan alone and pining for the young farm head. By the time Jordan was officially single, Zechariahs was caught between the two of them emotionally. After toying with who he was more attracted to more, he finally gave into his feelings for Jordan and made love to her. For weeks their affair was covert, until Olive caught them having sex by the oak tree, after seeing her sneak out the house one late evening. Olive was so upset and betrayed that she rang Emory to drive her back to Atlanta and their destinies were carved out forever. Jordan would be with Zechariahs and Emory would be with Olive.

"So how long have you been in here?" Zechariahs said jarring her from her remembrance by touching her hand.

"A few weeks." She said uneasily.

"And the tumor?"

"Inoperable."

"Has Emory even come to see you?"

"Who really comes to see their first ex wife who couldn't give him children?"

"You two share a past. We all share a past. He at least owes you a visit."

"He owes me nothing, just like you don't nor Jordan. The past is the past."

"Is there anything I can do for you Olive?"

"No, I'm going to let life run its course. It's been a good one for the most part."

"I really hate to leave you, but I have a conference to go prepare for."

"Please. I've taken too much of your time as it is."

"It was time well spent, to reconnect with an old friend...love..."

"That was years ago, Zech. We were kids then."

"Right...Kids... I have to be back to visit my daughter later on this eve. Would it be okay if I stopped by?" He kissed her hand, showing her more affection than she had had in years.

"I would very much so like that."

"Well, 'til later." He kissed her cheek. He left her.

She picked up the journal that was next to her bed. She flipped through the copious amounts of filled pages and found a blank one. She wrote very diligently finishing where she had started days earlier:

"By writing this confession I know that my part in this whole thing can exonerate my soul before I leave this earth forever. But it was his doing that all of this has taken place. His days of controlling this city must end. I have detailed everything and please take this as truth. I swear by it... Olive Annex-Westport."

She closed the book and placed it back on the table. It was done.

"Ms. Annex, time for your medication." The nurse said as he entered.

"Thank you. By the way, could you bring me an envelope that can fit this and some stamps when you get the chance?"

"It would be my pleasure." He administered her drugs and she was out like a light.

CHAPTER 59

Malek was at his desk that next morning. He was three weeks into his new investigation, and he hoped that it would eventually pay off. Finding out who owned *JKJ Holdings* was his first priority. He hadn't stopped perusing leads after leads until the night before when he was called to the hospital because of his little sister. By the next morning his sister would be okay and he was diligent in his pursuits.

He was becoming increasingly upset at the fact that close to a billion dollars had be siphoned from D.A.C. and it had happened months after he had taken control of the company from his father. If Zechariahs were to find out about the catastrophe there was no telling of what kind of actions would be taken. But he was more upset at the fact that he was disappointing his father and violating the trust that he had instilled in him when he had made him C.E.O.

At that moment Malek received an email notice on his desktop—subject: *The New Season at the Alliance Theatre*. In a time such as these, he would have normally dismissed the email, but this morning he needed a distraction and what better distraction than his love of the theatre and its up coming season. He opened the email and to his surprised he saw a banner: "*Anastasia* starring Russian actress Olga Perastrova."

On the advertisement for the show was a young lady that looked strikingly familiar. He looked closer. This was the woman, he knew, who met with him and Kameron during the Swedish deal and introduced herself as Ursela Olsson the owner of the company that D.A.C. would buy in a very lucrative deal acquiring many thousands of acres in Western Europe. If this Ursela was really an actress, what was going on, and what kind of deal was put into play?

At that moment, a knock came on the door. It was his investigator, who assured him that this lead would pan out and he would get closer to the money trail that would find the one who had been taking the money from the company. The investigator handed him the envelope. Malek opened it and saw picture after picture of a cloaked person sending the wire transfer. Hoodie, black garb, and gloves, in winter no doubt, aided the person's disguise against being found out.

"Is that all you could find?"

"I narrowed down the location..."

"That's not good enough!!!" Malek barked.

"I have a source there at that location. With any luck I can get a name by tomorrow morning."

"Make it as fast as possible! Do you know what's at stake man?"

"Yes sir."

"Well get on top of it." With that the investigator was dismissed.

Malek sat back in his chair. He picked up the phone and dialed a number.

He was going to meet with the Russian actress.

CHAPTER 60

"Are you serious?" Kameron said as she was just given the news that she had feared.

"Heard it with my own ears. Mya has started to put the pieces together. And she started with the most notable one." Cole said as he sipped on his tea. They both were in the office of Thorneheart Kincade that bright and early morning. Cole couldn't wait to inform Thorneheart of what Mya told him the night before about Kameron being "married" to Rory and visiting him.

"What the hell were you doing down there? That trash needs to stay behind bars so that we can finish this plan."

"I miss him Thorneheart. He's the love of my life."

"You will have him soon enough. Just stick to the plan! Both of you do what you have to do."

"So, what next? How do we keep her from doing more snooping?"

"Don't worry I have that taken care of."

"She's pregnant. You're not going to hurt her?" Cole worriedly inquired.

"You're not going to harm the baby?" Kameron added.

"Of course not. But I will make her scared enough to realize that her nose shouldn't be where it doesn't belong!" Thorneheart said as a grin came across his face.

"Glad I'm on your side Thorneheart." Cole said knowing that he wasn't feeling Thorneheart's wrath. "Well, I got to get going. I'm supposed to meet Dontavious at his press conference by noon."

"Are you falling for him Cole?" Kameron asked trying her best to rub in what she already knew.

"Don't be crazy. I was paid to do a job Kameron. Unlike you, I don't get involved with my targets." With that Cole left the office. He had no idea what Thorneheart had up his sleeve, nor did he want to know. But unbeknownst to him or Kameron, he was beginning to have feeling for Dontavious, deeper than he could possibly realize and those feelings would be tested in the coming days and weeks.

"I'm scared. We've worked too hard for all of this to blow up in our faces." Kameron said as the door shut behind Cole.

"Phase three has been enacted and we will have everything we have worked so hard for. You trust me don't you?"

"What daughter doesn't trust her father?" She hugged Thorneheart. This man she had found out was her father some twenty years after her mother started working for him as his assistant. He didn't know that she and Joshua were his kin until right after Janika was shot at the Kincade estate. It was laid out in her living will for everyone to see.

"How's your mother doing?"

"She's still in a coma. I'm still not over your wife for shooting her."

"Betty was a jealous bitch! I didn't think she would have had the guts to harm anyone except herself with that gunshot!"

"Well, she did. Well, I have to get to the office before Malek gets suspicious."

"I can't wait until you can hand that fucker his balls on a plate, my dear. Those Deans have gotten too big for their britches! The nerve of him putting my darling daughter under contract to be in his bed."

"It won't be long according to you daddy."

"I do love it when you call me that." She kissed him on the cheek and exited the office.

Thorneheart picked up the phone and dialed. "Yes, there are a few problems that I need for you to take care of..." Thorneheart put a plan into motion in order to continue his treachery. He was not going to stop until he had everything that he wanted—to hell with anyone who got in his way.

Cole sat in his car thinking about what had just transpired in Thoreheart's office. He couldn't believe that he had gotten this deep in this thing that was originally just about the money to supplement his menial detective salary. He didn't have a trust fund like his partner and needed to make ends meet on his luxurious lifestyle he created for himself. But what he didn't count on was the direction in which this thing was headed. He picked up his phone and dialed.

"I need to know what you want to do about Thorneheart. He's getting way out of control!" He stayed on the phone discussing his current concerns.

CHAPTER 61

She sat in the hospital room for almost twelve hours before going to the cafeteria for something to eat. She sat for another two before she went to get coffee. Jordan sat vigil by her daughter's side listening to the machines beep and her daughter breathing in and out.

Alone with her thoughts, she started to remember the day in which they met. It was a cold day in February, the 24th actually, that daughter was placed in mother's arms. This was Jordan's special gift. After three boys she was glad to look in the eyes of someone who she would always understand. Her tiny hands, ten digits, feet, ten toes, all so perfect as she suckled Jordan's thumb. She petted her hair, so soft, and in place, God himself attached each hair flawlessly. She was beautiful, and her bright skin was red, as evident of her trip down the birth canal. She was almost too perfect, and Jordan felt guilty for it, like she or Zechariahs didn't deserve it.

She thought further back to about ten months before Paige's birth. The fights that were happening between she and her husband, and the lack of communication between the two, were always a part of the Dean household none stop. She couldn't believe that her husband's newest ambition was driving them apart, a company he wouldn't have had if it weren't for her and wealth. They were becoming wealthier, but the consequences of not having her husband present were beginning to take its toll on the pampered princess that Jordan was. In true Jordan fashion she sought comfort in her past love Emory, while he was still married to her old friend Olive. It all started off very innocently in Jordan's defense, but she was still aware of what she was getting herself into.

Emory and she saw each other out one day during a function for her charity. From that initial reconnection, dinners ensued after work. Dinners turned into walks in Piedmont Park talking about the past. Eventually they got bold enough to make love in the Dean home. She knew Zechariahs' schedule and wouldn't fear him catching them. What she didn't count on was the ever-present Sascha who she knew would never sell her out, or so she thought.

Three months later Jordan discovered that she was indeed pregnant with her fourth child. This child she couldn't say for certain if it was her husband's or not. She couldn't say for sure because after one of their many heated arguments they made love on the boardroom table at D.A.C. when she confronted him about decreasing her role with the company she helped found. Now she had the predicament: her lover and her husband could be the father of her new child. When she found out it was a daughter, she dare not abort it. This would be her secret and she prayed that this child would be perfect in every way, despite her scandalous behavior.

The incessant beeping jarred Jordan from her dwelling on the past and her mistakes. Jordan looked at her daughter, now a grown woman at twenty-four years of age, laying the hospital bed. Paige, a new victim of an addiction, one that she hoped would not mirror her own that she had for close to thirty years. Truth be told, it was because of Jordan's guilt about Paige's paternity and trying to escape her life that she even turned to pills and alcohol to begin with.

It was eleven that morning that Paige's beautiful eyes were open. "What am I doing in the hospital again?"

"Paigey, you overdosed on that damn drug. What were you thinking? You could've killed yourself."

She was ashamed that her mom and family now knew her secret, but what else could she do but admit why: "I just needed a fix."

"How long have you been taking those drugs?"

Reluctantly she continued: "A few months maybe." Paige finally realized that gravity of the situation once she looked down and saw the i.v. in her arm.

"Why take drugs? I've suffered from my addiction for over twenty years. You saw what it did to me!"

"I started taking those drugs to numb the pain. And rehab and pressure from my agents to get back in the Broadway game in New York, the pressure, all of it was, is maddening!"

"We're here for you!"

"Now you are! But what about those three months you were gone to rehab? What about the fact that everyone is so knee deep in scandals and lies and cover ups that they can't even see that one of their love ones needs help! I need help mom and no one was there for me when I needed it!" Paige said with tears streaming down her face. She had finally let out what was bothering her. She was no longer numb. The pain was biting: for her and her mother.

"I'm so sorry baby."

"Your sorries won't take back the fact that you ran me over!"

"I'm so sorry?"

"I need to be alone!" Paige was resolute in her decision. She wanted solace.

If that's what you want." Jordan got up against her instincts and left her daughter alone.

CHAPTER 62

"Drugs have been affecting this city for years now and now they have hit close to home with the overdose of my daughter Paige on the new designer drug *PRAVELINE*. Our city's current regime has done nothing to end this war that is being waged in the city. If anything that my latest family tragedy has taught me is that change must be brought to his city immediately, and we must all want it to come in November. I promise that out of this tragedy will come hope, not only for my family, but this city as a whole. Thank you." Zechariahs finished his news conference with the corral of press asking him many follow-up questions. He answered and he and his son Dontavious disappeared into campaign headquarters.

The press conference lasted close to the fifteen minutes, and he hoped that he had answered all the questions that were on the minds of those concerned. "You were speaking from your heart dad."

"This has got to end! My daughter's life was almost ended by those damn drugs. Kevin was killed investigating their origins."

"What's next?" Dontavious signed off on paper work and continued to the office.

"We have the debate with Emory to get ready for."

"I will have your notes soon."

"That's why I hired you. Thanks son."

"How're Paige and mom?"

"Paige was still unconscious when I left the hospital this morning, and your mother was in her own world."

"It will all get better pops."

"I do hope." Zechariahs was stuck. He was finally at a moment in his life that he had no control of what was going on around him. Unlike D.A.C. or his campaign, he had no control of what his children did not the path that any of their lives would take.

CHAPTER 63

Kameron had been in the office for a few hours before a knock
came on her door. Not surprisingly she was a little jumpy as she asked the
person to enter. It was Mya. Somehow she was not surprised in the wake
of her newest revelation that Cole gave her that morning. "Mya, what
brings you down here?"

"I just had to ask you a quick question. Hope I'm not interrupting."

"Go ahead, always time for the one person in the Dean family that
actually speaks to me." She laughed.

"Thanks. I was wondering if you had any dealings with Rory
Tremont when he worked here?"

She thought about the nights of steamy sex on her desk and in the
mailroom with the aforementioned Rory. She remembered lulling him
into confessing to a crime he was not responsible for just so that she
could help with the big picture. She remembered him in that jail cell a few
days before when she had a visit with him to help keep his spirits up
while the plan continued to run its course. "I wasn't aware that he even
worked here until I saw it on the news. Sorry." She lied.

"He never delivered your mail or anything? No previous contact in
the cafeteria or anything?"

"Mya I hate to sound callous, but you're looking for answers where
there aren't any."

"I hope I didn't come off accusatory? That wasn't my intent." She lied.

"That's okay. But your husband's killer has been found. Just let it go." Kameron said trying to quail the situation. "I have a meeting to get to. You can show yourself out can't you?"

"Of course. Thanks and I do apologize if I offended you."

"You didn't. Have a good one." She excused herself. She thought that she had weathered that particular storm. "Charmaine, could you show Mrs. Dean out please?" Kameron said to her secretary as she passed her desk.

"I sure will." Charmaine said with the greatest of disdain for a boss she felt didn't deserve her position. Kameron continued down the hallway and Charmaine disappeared into the office. She knocked on the door, and it startled Mya who was looking around the office.

"Mrs. Dean, anything else I can help you out with?" Charmaine inquired.

"As a matter of fact, could you tell me about a co-worker of yours from the mailroom, Rory Tremont."

"Oh, his fine ass! Anything you want to know! Name it!"

"So you knew him personally?"

"Yes, and so did Miss Kameron too. She thought she was being sooo slick and sneaky..."

"What do you mean?" Mya inquired.

Charmaine gleefully revealed all that she knew to Mya. Everything that Charmaine told her only confirmed her suspicions.

CHAPTER 64

Emory and Thorneheart had lunch at the exclusive Executive Club downtown. It was what any wealthy gentleman in Atlanta could want their escape to be. The finest wines, cigars and beautiful waitresses waiting hand and foot is what awaited its most exclusive members, which the two were definitely apart of, and had been for years. They had a mid-afternoon swim and sat poolside shroud in plush terry-cloth robes and garnering each a freshly clipped Cuban cigar.

"A great idea I must say." Emory said inhaling the smoke from the cigar, leaving just a trace of ash.

"It's been a very long morning..." Thorneheart said taking one final stretch.

"The nosey widow?"

"She's the least of my thoughts, don't worry." Thoreheart reassured him.

"No harm will come to the child?"

"Of course not. I'm not an animal."

"Glad to hear that my friend."

"Is everything being taken care of on your end?" Thorneheart turned to him. He wanted answers and he wanted them immediately.

"I will definitely have this election locked down."

"Not if Zechariahs has more press conferences like he had today."
He was looking at him with idiomatic glare.

"No one knows the drug's source."

"But they do know that you're not doing a damn thing about *JEM*."

"All will be taken care of trust me. I have everything under control." Emory said with confidence.

"You better. My plans have been laid. We've come too far to turn around my friend."

CHAPTER 65

Five-thirty and dress rehearsal was about to start in an hour and a half. The opening of *Anastasia The Musical* was only a few days away. She finished applying her makeup and wig. Her microphone was put in place and she began to put on her dress over her corset She did her warms ups which usually consisted of the flubbering of the lips, chanting and other various vocal warm ups to make her voice as limber as her body. She would take the stage at the top of the show and have no break until intermission and then again when her character died at the end of the last act. At almost three hours in length the new work would take its toll daily on her voice and she wanted to be prepared. After her ritualistic beginning of the day she stared into the mirror getting herself mentally prepared for the show.

She was ready to take the stage in her first starring role since leaving college some seven years prior. Before then she was a struggling actress who barely made ends meet in the New York Theatre community. She got encouragement from friends to audition for the work shop of a new work by a recent Tony winner about the last days of the famous missing Russian Princess Anastasia. She jumped at the chance to portray such a known figured as well get to use her Russian ancestry and accent which she felt was hindering her with other roles in the New York theatre scene.

To her surprise and delight she booked the show and would be doing an original run at the Alliance Theatre in Atlanta. But to her disappointment, she wouldn't get paid until the show actually started its run. She worried how she would pay her bills living in a new city, and furthermore survive until running into an older gentleman named Mr. Kincade at Piedmont Park some five months prior. She was there walking and clearing her head when she ran into Thorneheart, as she later would find out his first name, by accident. They began to talk and one thing led to another and a deal was struck.

"Olga, all you have to do is say what I write for you and you will get fifteen-thousand dollars." She remembered Thorheart saying to her. It wouldn't be anything too difficult or lascivious. What she was doing for this stranger was exactly what she had gone to school for. She was allowed room for improvisation, but primarily as long as the basics were hit, she would be okay. She was told to put on a Swedish accent and her character's name would be Ursela.

The initial meeting lasted about an hour. The follow-up was a few more hours. The meetings in tangent with the rehearsal schedule would be very tiring, but they would all be worth it once the check cleared for fifteen-thousand dollars. After two weeks her job was done and she had the money in her account.

She thought that was the end of it until that day before one of her last dress rehearsals when she got a knock on her dressing room door. It was the gentleman that she met with in those meetings in which she played the character of the Swede Ursela Olsson. Malek was there for answers and he demanded them from the actress. This was definitely a distraction for the actress about to take the stage.

CHAPTER 66

"Mya, you there?" Dontavious said. He was on the phone with her some thirty seconds prior to hearing the crash. Dontavious' voice was so tiny in the big scheme of things that evening. When she came to she could barely hear it in her Bluetooth as the sounds of the sirens almost drowned it out.

Almost five hours later Mya walked into her house. She was thoroughly checked out by medical officials and mama and baby were doing fine. She was a victim of a hit and run driver on Interstate-400 that sent her careening into the divider. It was a miracle that she escaped with barely a bruise. She didn't know what to think about the whole ordeal until the sirens were coming and she was aware of the accident finally.

The last thing she remembered was being on the phone with Dontavious, and she was trying to inform him of what Kameron's secretary told her about Kameron and Rory's torrid affair, but a car sideswiped her, leaving her nearly unconscious. Dontavious was waiting in her kitchen.

"What the hell happened to you?" He questioned her as she walked into the kitchen, startling her. He was happy to see her alive and well.

"I was a victim of a hit and run on 400." Mya said taking a load off at the kitchen counter.

"Are you okay? The baby?" He continued.

"Everyone's fine. Just a little jostled is all." Mya said relieving Dontavious' worries.

"I didn't know where to go. I called you repeatedly and then I came over here thinking we might have just been cut off."

"Well thank you for worrying."

"Of course. Can I get you anything?" Dontavious continued.

"I'm okay."

"What was so urgent you called me out of my meeting?"

"I went to see Kameron and she flat out denied being entangled with Rory."

"I thought we resolved this. It was a horrible misunderstanding. Why are you still going crazy about it?" Dontavious wondered.

"I thought I may have overstepped too until her secretary told me some dirt on her and Rory. Apparently they were seeing each other anytime that they could."

"How do you know it's not just hearsay?"

"She had proof. The secretary had receipts of hotel stays, et al. Days missing including the day she went to the prison to visit Rory." Mya continued trying to plead her case. "You have to believe me."

"And what reason would this secretary have to tell you these things?"

"She's tired of Kameron getting away with things."

"Or could it be jealousy on her part for not climbing the corporate ladder faster and a combination of you being paranoid."

"I know what I saw in that basketball photo and what I heard when I called that phone number of Rory's wife. Rory is connected to my husband and Kameron. And I feel that if we find that connection, we can find out the truth behind Kevin's murder."

"Cole showed me that picture last night. It was clearly not Rory in that photo."

"It's clear as day, look." She took the photo out of her briefcase that was on the counter. She pointed at the photo showing him all the guys on the team including Rory who was prominently next to Kevin.

"Where did you get this?" Dontavious looked puzzled.

"This is the photo I was telling you about. The one in Cole's office. I had a copy made."

"This is the only one from that year?"

"Yep, Cole has an exact copy." Mya stated.

"That's not possible." Dontavious said confusingly.

"It is. See the date. This was the same photo."

"The one Cole showed me last night didn't have Rory on it. It was some other guy entirely different." He was now flummoxed at the revelation that he no longer knew what was going on before him.

"What's going on here is very strange Dontavious. And I'm sorry to say that you're the only one I can trust right now; especially after what I learned from my friend at the coroner's office as well."

"You've been busy. Why did go to the coroner's office?"

"I asked my friend down there pull the files, when he had a moment and he called me bright and early this morning. You won't believe..." She was cut off at that moment by her cell phone ringing. She picked it up. She listened for a second and slammed it down on the counter. "Who was that?" Dontavious was worried.

"Someone saying, 'next time you won't make it out alive'."

"Is there a number?"

"Blocked!!! I'm scared Dontavious. Someone knows I'm getting too close to the truth."

"Is this really worth your life, the baby's?"

"Yes, this baby deserves to know who killed its father and why."

CHAPTER 67

Cole sat in the interrogation room for close to twenty minutes before Rory entered shackled from head to toe.

"You summoned me?" Cole said sarcastically as he watched his former friend being sat in front of him.

"Nigga, I'm ret' to go, man."

"We just need a few more weeks. You going to have to be patient man."

"Ain't no pussy worth dis' shit right here!"

"Just give us a few weeks. Evidence will be found, your conviction overturned, and you will be with that "pussy" you so rightly deserve."

"Right, right...and be here wit' some faggots tryin' to get my ass. No thanks. Been through dis' shit 'fore. I want out! Tell yo' boss man this shit gots to end tonight!"

"You ain't got no choice, dog."

What you mean, shawty?"

"You owe us. Kevin got you that job and that put you onto Kameron. After this you will get a million dollars and go to the Bahamas or wherever the fuck you want to go. Just give it time!"

"Ain't goin' happen like that nigga. I want out now! I want my money. I want my bitch! I want out now!!!" Rory became indignant. He felt he had the upper hand.

"Look here you little shit you sit put. You do as you told."

"Fuck you nigga!"

"Ain't you got a faggot in here to do that for you?" Cole laughed. Rory tried to jump at him for his remark, to kill him, but his shackles prevented him.

"You bets be glad I'm locked up fucker." The venom was seething from the once placated Rory, who was now fed up with his treatment and superfluous nature in this whole scheme. He felt that he was getting the raw end of this deal and wanted more. Three million dollars and Kameron wouldn't validate him any longer.

"Calm down," Cole said getting up heading towards the door. "You don't have that long left."

"Yo, shawty, yo' jump shot is as week as yo' truth tellin', man."

"You will believe whatever I tell you. You ain't got no other choice." Cole signaled for the guard to come to escort him out of the room. He was ready to go.

"Yes I do. I heard some reporter was 'round these parts looking to holla at me!"

"Don't worry about that. It was shut down before she found out anything."

"Oh, yea? Bet she want to know 'bout my letters."

"What letters?" Cole turned around from his exit.

"I been writin' some letters since I got to dis place. They at my home boy Loke's pad in Decatur. If dis shit don't go down like it spose' to, nigga goin' sing like canary, my nigga. Well my letters will."

"Motherfucker," Cole charged toward and grabbed him by his shirt. "You don't know who you fuckin' with."

"No my nigga, yo' ass don't know who you fuckin' wit."

Cole dropped his hold on Rory. "Guard let me out!" Cole screamed at the door. He turned back to Rory who was grinning from ear to ear. He had penetrated Cole's ego. "That was a big mistake."

"Got t' cover my ass, shawty." The scowl resumed.

Cole left the prison and he dialed his connection. Rory, the pawn, would have to be sacrificed.

CHAPTER 68

Balloons and flowers covered the face of her visitor that mid afternoon. She assumed it was her father as she spoke, "Daddy you went overboard."

"Nothing's too much for my baby." Marcus said revealing his face to Paige who sat in the hospital bed reading the latest *US WEEKLY* to pass the time.

"Marcus, what are you doing here?" Paige was happy to see her man, but she was also torn because she was angry with him. He hadn't been back to see her since he left for New York some three months prior, and she was even more angered as she remembered that he was the one that hooked her on her vice.

"I got a call from your father. I came as soon as I could." He put the flowers and balloons down on the table and walked over to her. He attempted to hug her, but she pushed him away. "What's that about?"

"Marcus, three months, really?" Paige was letting him have it.

"I was working babe. The show is going wonderfully. And they are even talking *TONY*."

"No phone calls, no emails, no nothing. This is an age of technology where communication should be easy. I didn't ask for a carrier pigeon Marcus. A quick hello would suffice." She laid into him.

"I'm sorry babe. 'What about tears when you're happy?'" Marcus tried getting in good with her by quoting lyrics from the musical *The Color Purple*. He knew a slight smile and a sweet word would melt her heart.

"Marcus, I'm in this place because of those damn drugs. You did this to me."

"But what about wings when I fall?" He continued with his serenade.

"Marcus, I am so lost right now."

"I want you to be a story for me, that I can believe it forever." Marcus continued as he placed his hand on her cheek."

"Marcus..." She tried to continue.

"What about love?" He finished placing a nice soft kiss on her lips. She was silent. She had missed him so. No amount of anger could tear her from this moment. Her man was back. With him by her side she felt that she could go on.

"Marcus, I never can stay mad at you."

"I'm so sorry you got hooked babe. That wasn't what I intended. And that I wasn't here for you. Do you forgive me?"

"Please be there for me. I need help and I don't want to go alone." Paige pleaded with the man of her dreams, or she thought he was.

"Babe, I'm for you. I promise we will get through this together." He hugged her. She was lost once again in Marcus' charm and lies.

CHAPTER 69

"Mr. Dean is here to see you." Emory's secretary said over the intercom that afternoon.

"Send him in Dorreen." Emory returned. Zechariahs entered.

"I'm surprised you wanted to see me." Zechariahs quipped as he entered the mahogany castle that was Emory's mayoral office.

"I didn't. Thought since you came all this way, I could extend the courtesy. I'm still Southern Zech." Emory continued his paper work that lined his desk.

"Well, thank you for your courtesy. I would bow, but I would fear its triteness."

"It's amazing you didn't even know that word when I met you some forty years ago when you were the hired help. It's amazing what a vocab and a Hugo Boss suit will do for you. But class can't be bought Zechariahs. You do realize that right?"

"And neither can decency and morals." Zechariahs spat in contempt. Zechariahs took a seat facing Emory. They were now eye level.

"I heard your press conference today. You sounded like some over the top Barack Obama with less rhetorical skills and a sense of entitlement." Emory laughed at his joke. "But you're playing in the big leagues now. Don't get eaten alive."

"I've never backed back from a challenge. You should know that by now."

"Your transcendent American story is commendable, but unlike future President Obama, you will not have my seat."

"This mahogany sarcophagus will not be yours for much longer."

"This is what public forum debates are for not my office. So if this is all you've come to say, then please excuse yourself. I, as the mayor, have things to do."

"This was just a distraction actually. I've come to tell you that your ex wife is dying at Crawford Long, and you really should make it a point to see her before she passes. You at least owe her that much for the hell that you put that poor woman through." Zechariahs threw his past in his face, this he could only do in this office and wouldn't dare to do it in the debate that was scheduled.

"Which one?" Emory said smugly and honestly, because he had had three wives since his first wife.

"The only that really should count, Olive."

"Well, I'll have flowers sent. What room is she in?" He honestly got his pen pressed against his notepad expecting a response from Zechariahs.

"You're an ass, and I hope that you get everything you put out and more." Zechariahs was disgusted at Emory. He got up and proceeded to exit.

"Have a good one. See you at the debate." Zechariahs exited.

Emory hadn't heard the name Olive in almost twenty years. She didn't ask for alimony, nor did she require anything from their nearly thirty years together. When they broke, it was clean and Emory had moved on with his life. And now some decades later her name had surfaced and he learned that she was dying. He felt remorse for not being there for her. After all they were friends first, lovers and then partners in crime in this thing called life. He hated the fact that she couldn't give him children, but he thought his love for her could overlook those things, but years with no heir to call his own lead to anger and resentment towards her, which lead him back to Jordan's bed and a quick divorce from Olive afterwards.

On the other hand Emory was quite happy that she was getting closer to taking her last breaths. During their years of marriage she knew where the "bodies" were buried and was, for the part, there for all of his scandalous dealings. This included his entanglements with Thornehart earlier on his career in city council and the connection to the drugs that were running rampant in Atlanta. He wanted to see if the news was true. Was Olive dying and how great would that be for him? He wouldn't have to worry about his past resurfacing and hopefully she would take his secrets to her grave.

Emory was on his way to the hospital to see Olive. Meanwhile Olive's packaged that she mailed out earlier was on its way to a destination that would threatened Emory's very life. He would wish that he was on his death bed as she.

CHAPTER 70

"I started working for the Deans thirty years ago: mother, father, and two little boys. I had a son and they were all like brothers. The secrets that the family had, I kept them all of these years. Now I have no reason to hold on to them..." Sascha was sitting at the dining room table writing in her diary. She was sitting there from when Alex arrived home that day. He didn't care what she was doing, as long as long as she wasn't staring at the window into a void.

"Hey ma-ma." He kissed her fat cheek.

"Hola mijo. Something to eat for you? I cooked today?"

"What's gotten into you?" Alex was surprised at his mother's one-eighty.

"As they say, life goes on." She smiled, the first time in weeks.

"I'm glad ma-ma. And si, soy muerto de hambre."

CHAPTER 71

Jordan sat in the massive dining room at the Dean Estate alone that evening eating. She was alone with her thoughts and had been all day. The sun set and she continued to think about the state of her life and what a mess she had arrived back to after she returned from rehab. The only bright spot was her annual Harvest Ball that was nearing. She looked forward to the glitz and glamour that she would bring to Atlanta once again. But even her thoughts of grandeur were no competition for the guilt that she felt.

Honestly she thought about taking a drink to numb the pain, but what would that accomplish? She thought back to her rehab and what she had learned about herself. She had to face her problems. She couldn't hide from them, because if she did she would be in the same sorry state of affairs she was in for the last twenty years. Her orange juice and hearty meal kept her at bay. She heard the rustling of her husband as he entered the dining room.

"I've been looking all over this house for you and here you are." Zechariahs sat next to her, gave her kiss.

"All these years and I just took a sober look at this house today for first time since it was built: my own personal tour." Jordan continued mid-bite.

"And what do your sober eyes tell you about my beautiful architecture and design?" Zechariahs asked pleasantly.

"It's huge. Too big. What were we thinking?" She said with a laugh.

"I wanted my queen to have her castle." Zechariahs picked up a fork and proceeded to pick off her plate.

"Have we lost sight of what is really important Zech?"

"Meaning?" Zechariahs asked.

"When we first got married I was the rich one. I wanted materialistic things left and right."

He interrupted: "And I could barely afford a stamp, let alone anything you desired." He laughed.

"Right. But you told me that you would love me no matter what, and I believed you. So we lived in nice apartment in downtown College Park, no extravagances and were happy."

"I remember lying on the floor, we didn't even have a bed, and listening to the planes going by above us. Lulling us to sleep, each night they would." Zechariahs added to the memory.

"And then Dontavious and then Malek was born. You said your son would have the world. You started working harder, selling designs left and right and booking jobs and then with daddy's help you opened D.A.C."

"Jordan, money was pouring in and we upgraded to a bigger house, cars, stuff and then Kevin came..."

"Our boys...your boys..." She added, they were still eating, smiling, taking in the memories. "Then we had hired Sascha and we moved into our Dunwoody residence."

"I was working all the time." Zechariahs stated.

"And we fell out of sorts with each other. It's amazing how simple can become complicated so very quickly." She continued. "And then Paige came complicating it even more. I turned to drugs and booze to fill the void. Zech, why do I miss the sounds of planes, children running and boys fighting? I miss Sascha and her Mexican food and advice. I miss our family and lives from back then." Jordan lamented.

"It's not all bad is it? We can afford anything that we want, Jordan."

"We can, but at the cost of what really matters?"

"What's got you like this?"

"Being home, being sober, losing Kevin, almost losing Paige one of those or a combination of all has got me drifting."

"You want the last asparagus?" Zechariahs asked Jordan.

"No, you can have the rest of my food." Jordan joked.

"You were just playing with it anyway. Who cooked it?"

"I did." Jordan smiled. Zechariahs threw her a look of confusion. "Okay, I ordered in from Soto Soto."

"I thought so."

"Thank you Zechariahs." Jordan was heartfelt.

"For what? Eating your 'cooking?'" Zech joked.

"For choosing me."

"I don't follow?"

"I'm not stupid. Sascha left because you chose me."

"What do you mean?" Zechariahs was caught, what else could he say.

"I've known for years you two were in love or in lust or whatever you call it. You needed her because I was not there for you. But I thank you for coming back to me once I got it together. I didn't deserve it at all."

"We've been through too much babe for me to leave you. You are making an effort. I had to see where this road could go."

"I love you Zechariahs Dontavious Malek Dean."

"You are my world Jordan." They kissed.

For that moment their world was perfect. They could hear planes. Kids were playing and the boys were fighting.

CHAPTER 72

Marcus lulled Paige to sleep before he left the hospital that night. If he had known that would be the last time he would see her, he may have stayed longer. But he was about to meet his destiny.

Marcus Tillsdale was what every parent would want their daughter to marry. He was attractive, smart, relatively successful and very respectful. He wasn't honest though. He had never been. He got his first job on the Great White way through fibs. He even met Paige under false circumstances. Marcus was desperate to be something more than he was. Paige's money was not enough, though. His salary was not enough. He wanted more and would do anything to get it. Here he was in the beginning of his career on Broadway, a position many artist would kill for, and he was supplementing his down time with drug dealing. He wasn't a run of the mill dealer, though. He was selling the most toxic drugs that had hit the country since Crack Cocaine of the seventies and Methamphetamines of the eighties and early nineties: Praveline a.k.a *JEM*.

When Marcus saw its affects first hand, he knew that he wanted to be apart of its power. His roommate had the substance some five years prior, and could go for days without sleeping, eating, and looked like he had just awakened from a nap, all refreshed and not a care in the world. But as the high came down, the crystals took their hold and began to destroy the psyche of the user. All the good times and euphoria were now lashes of dark demons and warlocks of shadows plaguing the brain. Thoughts of suicide, murderous attempts and a host of other non natural desires would surface that would drive the user right back to the drug to escape the actual realities of their lives. This desire would keep the addict coming back for more at a higher rate.

He found a source through a series of connections he acquired through his dead roommate. One person led to another until he got connected to a source in Atlanta who could get him a supply from the main source. He made millions and spent millions. It was his lavish spending that lead to him spending the drug money and owing his supplier. It wasn't his initial plan to take money from Paige. But he knew that she was coming into millions in her trust, and could hook her on a drug that would distract her from what he needed to do to cover his own ass. It was a two fold effort. The higher she got, the better she became at her craft, and he could do whatever with her money and she would never know it.

It was kismet that he had found, not only an heiress he could steal from without persecution, but she had a direct link to the Atlanta social circle from which his supplier was apart. When Paige's brother died, he wanted to finally go to Atlanta and get close to the heart of the operation that was pulling him in just as addictively as his clientele was getting hooked to the drug itself.

The night he met Paige at the restaurant, the night in which she was hit by the car, he met with a high official who was enamored by Marcus' charm as was everyone who met him, and was glad to have such a valued salesman in his presence. But once further investigation of Marcus came to light months later, his boss was non-too pleased and Marcus had a lot of explaining to do. One was why were many of the payments late and why and how Paige Dean got addicted to the drug. Marcus tried to explain the situation but his days would be numbered.

On this night in particular he left that hospital, got in the car awaiting him and headed to a secret location the message told him that he would come to that evening. He didn't know what to expect, and many thoughts entered his mind. His car stopped in front of a warehouse and he walked into a clandestine setup with little light and echoes of his voice calling for someone to show up. "Anyone here? I was told to come here at ten p.m."

"You're right on time." A voice called to him out of the darkness.

"So, what's this about?"

"You think you don't have to pay!"

"I told the boss that the money would be here. I just needed time."

"Where's our supply." The voice inquired.

"It's gone. It goes like hot cakes in the NYC."

"Then why don't you have the fucking money?" The voice stunned him.

"Just tied up is all."

"Not a good excuse." A shot rang out, leveling Marcus to the ground holding his abdomen from where he had just been shot. He screamed in agony, pleading for his life. His assailant was not too merciful as he plugged him three more times, sending a resounding final thud to the temple, killing him.

A huge brick wall of a man came and took Marcus' dead body away.

The killer exited the warehouse and dialed a number before entering the car. "Yeah, taken care of." He hung up the phone and dialed another number and spoke: "Hey, I need you now...What do you mean, who is this? It's Cole. Have the door open! I'm on my way."

Cole Denavar had killed Marcus. But it wasn't anything he hadn't done before. He, like Marcus, was covering his ass and trying his best to become something more than he was. But unlike Marcus, he felt, he was going to do it. He wanted more. He would do whatever it took to get it, including murder again.

CHAPTER 73

Malek's understanding was waxing. His desperation to find the missing money was intensifying. The investigation led to a series of cryptic photos of unidentifiable assailants who were depositing the money his father had worked so hard for into overseas accounts. They were stealing from his family, and even more so were marring his tenure as CEO of D.A.C. He hated the latter the worse because he had worked so hard. And now through a series of weird coincidences he ran into a Russian actress who was paid by Thornheart Kincade to pose as the owner of a Swedish company his company had just purchased with the insistence of his forced-fiancée.

What did Kameron have to do with this? Was she actually the mastermind behind it all, or was she, just as he and the Russian actress, the victim of an old man's desire to stick it to a one time rival. He couldn't figure it out and tried his best to put the pieces together without much luck. It was that moment that Kameron walked into the bedroom from being out. "How did you find out about the Swedish deal?"

"And hello to you too Malek." Kameron called back. She was not having it. She had had a very long day.

"I'm serious. Where did you learn about the Swedish deal?"

"Can I have a few minutes please? I'm tired."

"Answer me now Kameron. I need to know!" Malek was determined to get an answer out of her. She had never seen him this terse. She knew she would have to give into his questioning.

"Okay," She reluctantly began her explanation, "I found out from a former john."

"Was it Thorneheart Kincade?"

Kameron wasn't taken aback by the accusation. She continued: "No, it was one of my johns from Florida. Why would you say Thorneheart Kincade? He's a senator right?"

"I have reason to believe that Thorneheart set up the Swedish deal in order to launder money from my father's company."

"How crazy does that sound Malek?" Kameron tried to be evasive, yet concerned as possible. Hearing it from Malek made it sound more preposterous, but the sad truth was that it was that detailed and twisted. Only her father could have come up with something so dastardly.

"I met with the actress who posed as the owner that we met with, who helped him pull it off. Crazy or not, it's true! So, what do you know Kameron?"

Kameron was not surprised at the line of questioning. She had been informed by Thorneheart that Malek had met with the actress and that he knew all, but not her involvement. What she was surprised about was how upfront he was being about the whole ordeal and that he was putting all of his cards on the table. She was more intrigued at the fact that he was vulnerable and strong at the same time. "I bet I don't know as much as you know. I researched the company. It seemed legit. I ran it by legal. I went through the proper channels," she continued to lie, "and then I presented it to the board. That's the extent of what I know about the deal, Malek."

"I have to plug this hole. We are taking on more water daily from this deal and I need it stopped A.S.A.P."

"That's not possible," She tried to stop him. "What is done is done. Those funds have been allocated. We still own a huge company in Western Europe."

"It's all a bogus. I've stopped the transition, or at least what I could."

She didn't get upset. She sat down on the bed and stared out of the bay window overlooking the vast land their mansion overlooked. She knew what she had to do in order to stay here and she knew the hell that she had gone through to acquire it. But was this really all worth it, she thought. She had to make Malek believe that she didn't know anything about what was happening, to keep the lie up. And she continued, making herself out to be the victim, even though it was Malek that was in those shoes.

"I was only trying to impress you, show you that I knew I can handle my job. And now this revelation about the deal being a setup, I feel badly. If I would have known Malek..."

"We've all been duped."

"I'm sorry Malek."

"I want to blame you, but I can't. This rivalry with my pops and Thornheart goes back years. But I can't believe he went this far." He was angry for not seeing this before now.

"So, what happens next?"

"Don't worry about that. I got it under control."

Kameron feared what that meant. She needed to warn her father, but couldn't break her cover of being the novice in the situation also claiming to be a victim of this whole scheme. She would have to wait until Malek had fallen asleep or at the very least in the morning when she could talk to him. Malek sat on the bed. She rubbed his back. She had to play the role of the devoted fiancé. Malek couldn't find out anything more, especially her involvement. But unbeknownst to her, he would soon know everything.

CHAPTER 74

A storm had rolled into the city. Thunder was rumbling and lighting was crashing. Mya sat in front of her computer with Dontavious over her shoulder. They had been sitting there for hours combing over articles and other evidence and lastly, reports from the coroner that had been hidden until recently.

They were getting closer to the truth and everything was becoming more convoluted. They were becoming more tired, but kept pressing on despite the fatigue. It almost seemed like a lost cause until the coroner report. They didn't trust Cole and Dontavious knew that he wouldn't ever reveal the truth. When they saw the facts, they knew that what they had feared was true. They knew Kevin's killer was someone other than Rory but who?

"There's no way he could have done this!" Mya exclaimed.

"Why wasn't this evidence brought up at trail?" Dontavious was trying to figure it out, but everything seemed almost too unreal to believe.

"He claimed his guilt. There was no reason to look into it."

"This is deeper than we thought." Mya continued reading over the material.

"What do you mean?"

"Look at the last line from the coroner's report."

"Traces of the drug Praveline, a.k.a JEM," Dontavious continued to read, "were found under victim's fingernails…"

"Kevin would never have come in contact with that drug without gloves. Especially if Kevin had that drug in evidence lockup or found it. That's policy."

"Is there a way it could have gotten under there even if he had them on?"

"Not likely. Dontavious I fear that this drug has got something to do with his death. It wasn't a random homicide."

"He was getting too close to the truth about the drug and they killed my brother." He said out loud what Mya didn't want to say or even believe.

CHAPTER 75

Rory had been in jail before. He had survived lonely nights, awful days of monotony for close to ten years. It was for a crime he committed at eighteen. He knew what he did was wrong and through years of counseling, mediation and self forgiving, he was able to come a general consensus that he was paying for his misdeeds and lost most of his twenties because of it. When he got out he knew he would never return under any circumstances. He knew that it was not a place that felt he belonged and couldn't survive again. He would not be a statistic of the returning convict. He would turn his life around. But here he was sitting in a solitary cell listening to the rain and paying for a crime he knew he didn't even commit.

Why did he agree to take the fall for a crime so horrible? Love was the reason. He thought he loved Kameron and would do anything for her. When she told him what she wanted him to do, he was too distracted by her in her teddy and she doing things he had only dreamed. But once the effects of her loving wore off, he began to wonder if this could really be worth it. She explained to him the reward at the end of the day, and he couldn't help but jump at the chance, to not only be rich, but have the woman of his dreams by his side.

Sitting there he ran the events of the proposal over in his head. All he had to do was confess to the murder of Kevin Dean. He would go to prison and then be released on bail. He would get found guilty, sentenced to life in prison. When evidence of the crime would come out weeks later, he would be released. He would explain that he confessed under duress and perjury would only garner him a few community service hours and a he would be in another country before the fine could even be leveled. It all sounded good on paper, but now he it was going on four months that he was sitting in this cell and couldn't wait to escape his prison.

He had set up his own "get out of jail free" card with his letters he wrote and sent to his friend. He had given him instructions to send them to the victim's wife if he wasn't out of jail in the time frame agreed upon with Thorneheart. As the weeks turned into months, he felt that he would need to use this to accelerate his freedom and finally get everything he felt he deserved. And with Cole's visit and his threats being overlooked, he knew he had to take his future in his hands.

This night in particular, a rap came on the cell door. Lights out was at nine p.m. and his awakening came, what felt like hours afterwards. In reality it was only thirty minutes after lights out. Smitty, a guard he had gotten close to, came into his cell. He stabbed him with a syringe that knocked him out immediately. He was dragged from his cell.

By ten p.m. Rory was killed. His body was returned to the cell where it would be found early the next day during line up. No one would know of his death for a few weeks. The cover-up began. But Rory's last words would reach Mya the next day.

CHAPTER 76

Joshua sat on the edge of the bed just able to catch his breath. They were going at it hard and strong for a good hour. Close to midnight they were done. He was exhausted. He hadn't had a night like this in almost four years—at least since the last time they were in Savannah. He did find it quite strange that he had received a call from him. The shower turned off. He knew that his lover was done bathing.

Cole entered clean and fresh with just a towel wrapped around his waist: "Thanks Josh."

"Anytime...just leave the money on the nightstand." He said disgustingly.

"Why does it have to be all that?"

"Your man couldn't have handled that for you?"

"You do something to me Joshua like he can't."

"Yes, helping you forget your misdeeds and such."

"It's not even like that."

"Tell that to someone who doesn't know you Cole." He sauntered over to the pile of clothes and presented Cole with his pants. "Put this on before you catch a cold." He was compassionate. He still loved him. This hurt him.

"It's summer. That's almost impossible."

"No time to be funny. You need to go!"

"You're kicking me out?"

"You've done what you came to do."

"Well it was fun while it lasted?"

"For you maybe. I should have never opened that door."

"Tell me you didn't enjoy yourself." Cole put on his clothing as he prepared to leave.

"It was good as always, but I didn't have your heart." Joshua was hurt that he was used.

"Dontavious has that. Sorry."

"He doesn't know you like I do." Joshua approached him and straightened his tie.

"We are the past." Cole slipped on his shoes and headed to the door.

"Couldn't tell it by tonight's activities in my room."

"Well, it missed you. Good night Josh." He went to kiss him goodnight, and Joshua turned his head. Cole left. He was on his way home to jump in the bed with Dontavious.

Joshua felt badly for what had happened. He had Cole in his bed. But now he was all alone.

CHAPTER 77

It was almost midnight and Dontavious couldn't sleep. His mind was going a million miles per hour with the information he had learned earlier. It wouldn't have mattered if he had gone to sleep, because Cole hadn't arrived back at the loft. He was more relieved that he hadn't showed up at home seeing as though he had too many questions, and he was urged by Mya not to get the answers he so wanted.

How was his man connected to this thing? He knew Cole—at least he thought he did. He wouldn't have been involved with Kevin's murder, he thought. He thought about the fact that they were partners at the police station for years. They had gone through the academy together some years before and gone through detective training together as well, and how Cole rightly respected him and made mention every chance he got.

When Mya first had approached him about a bigger cover-up, he wanted to believe that it was just her hormones or grief getting in the way of logistics and the actuality of the situation, but as evidence began to present itself, Dontavious was becoming keenly aware that there might just be something more lying underneath the murder of his brother after all. But was his man involved? And if his man was involved, what did he have to gain from killing his partner and best friend? Dontavious' brain was going a million miles per hour.

It was almost two in the morning before Cole snuggled up next to Dontavious. He had so many questions, including whose eau de toilet did he have on? It wasn't his normal fragrance.

CHAPTER 78

The rain was coming down harder. Emory sat and watched the puddles form on the pavement outside of his penthouse. He swallowed the Hennessey quickly. It was his fourth glass in two hours, and he was drunk. Every sip he tried to ignore the guilt. But he couldn't. He constantly replayed the events of the latter part of the day, and wished that they would go away, but they wouldn't. He thought that this was what he wanted. He thought that with it done, he could move on and not have to look back at the things from his past and other things that were holding him back.

He had set in motion the execution of Marcus and then Rory. This was different, though. This was more personal. He had done it himself. He went there. He closed the door and looked at her laying there. He rubbed his hands against her hair. He looked at her breathing in and out. He knew it wouldn't be long until she took her very last breaths even if it weren't at his hands. He went to the i.v. and inserted a hypodermic needle with potassium chloride. She was dead instantly.

He was out of the room before the nightly check up and back at his house. He had killed his ex wife Olive with no interruptions and her rapid state of decay would be the catalyst for lack of investigations into how she died. But his guilt would eat him alive more than any murder conviction could ever.

If his guilt over her death wasn't enough, he had a visitor that evening. It was someone who he thought he would never see again.

END OF PART II

PART III

CHAPTER 79

It was two weeks after she was murdered by Emory that her body was laid to rest. The funeral was held at Ebenezer Baptist Church, a church which started the career of Dr. Martin Luther King, Jr. It was an intimate ceremony, but those who were there represented all walks of life and the people she came in contact with. Her brothers were there, old friends from her days as mayor's wife, as well as her ex-husband Emory, who sat front row with his new wife.

After the funeral everyone adjourned to a small reception at the Margaret Mitchell house, the famous house of the author of "Gone with the Wind." Everyone in their various groups huddled and talked about what an amazing woman Olive was. "She would have been very proud of the way she was sent off. She didn't deserve to go so soon." Jordan noted to Zechariahs.

"She was our friend for so long. I feel badly I didn't know she was sick until I did."

"She was my best friend for close to forty years. I feel horribly" Jordan lamented.

"She lived a great life. She will be missed." Emory said as he approached with his new wife on his arm.

"Emory, you have some balls. New wife, old wife's funeral, and no tact I see." Zechariahs said with contempt.

"We both had moved on with our lives, if you must know. I'm only here to give my respects."

"Enough you two, this is about Olive, not about you all." Jordan said trying to quail the situation.

"You're right, honey. Let's go get some punch. Have a good one Emory." Zechariahs said as he and Jordan exited into the other room.

"Couldn't wait until the debate I see." Thorneheart said as he glided over.

"Honey," he said to his new bride, "go get me some water. I'm parched." The young wife did as was asked and disappeared. "I can't stand that smug son-of-a bitch!" Emory continued with venom.

"He's been a thorn in my side for years. And I can't wait to bring him to his knees."

"Neither can I."

"Are you ready for the debate?" Thorneheart asked.

"As ready as I can be."

"Not acceptable. I need you to knock him off his moral pedestal. You need to let the voters know that you are the best choice, regardless of your questionable morals, character and choices."

"I was elected before without you. I certainly can handle it now!"

"You better! If he is elected mayor we are all screwed. You included!" Thorneheart drove the point home with a hand on the shoulder. "All of this planning and plotting will not be in vein, you hear me."

"I have too much to lose." Emory said soberly.

"We both do."

"Well the wifey is trying to get my attention. We'll be talking soon."

"Yes, we will. And by the way I am going forward. The pictures will be published."

"I told you I could win this election without playing dirty. That's his son."

"So?"

"Have a heart old man." He thought about his words, and chose them very carefully, as not to give any power away. "Let's make a deal. If I don't do well at the debates, then publish them, but give me some credit in doing well in this election."

"Your numbers say other wise."

"Votes count, not polls." Emory responded. He was annoyed.

"Okay, but they will be published if you don't hit the mark."

"Deal. Have a great one!" He left to join his wife. Emory was worried that Thornheart was getting way out of control. This just proved that he was getting consumed, and not in a good way.

Thorneheart was on his way to exit when a touch on his shoulder stopped him. It was Malek. He was staring him right in the eye. "Malek, your father and mother are in the other room last I saw them."

"I'm here to speak with you Thorneheart."

"What do I owe this pleasure?"

"I know about Olga Perastrova."

Without a beat he continued. "I know not what you speak of. I'm a very busy person. Please contact my office if you need to speak about matters, personal or otherwise."

"I did and you are always busy."

"It is an election year, son. I am busy."

"Play stupid if you want to, but your ass is going to be mine before you know it!"

"Malek I have no time for idle threats. Have a great one Mr. Dean." He tried to leave, Malek grabbed him.

"You old fuck, when I finally get proof in black and white that is was you who has been stealing from my company, I'm going to nail your ass to the wall. You hear me!" People's conversations quieted as they tried to see what was going on with the two. The two were center ring.

"People are beginning to stare. Malek calm down. We will talk about this later. This is not the place. As a matter of fact, talk to your fiancée. She might have answers for you." He disappeared. Malek was dumbfounded. What did Thorneheart mean to ask Kameron?

CHAPTER 80

Alex couldn't believe what he was reading. It was a signed and sealed confession from Olive of her involvement with the drug trafficking through the city of Atlanta. And she had implicated her ex husband Emory as the main culprit. She laid out how her ex-husband brought the original drugs into the city from Savannah and how they had made millions off of them. She detailed everything on her death bed confession that she sent to his office.

But Olive was dead. Her funeral was earlier in the day. There was no way that this document could serve as primary evidence or a basis for any charges being drawn against Emory, seeing as though she wasn't there to confirm that it was indeed she that had written the document. But what he did have was a basis for an investigation into ending the drugs that were running rampant in the city. Could the mayor of Atlanta be behind the drugs? How far did this whole thing stretch and else would be involved? All of these thoughts entered his mind as he read and reread the confession that had come by courier some hours before.

In this moment it proved to be ironic for Alex, seeing as though it was fast approaching the fourth month anniversary of Kevin Dean's murder. He and Kevin had worked tireless nights combing evidence, overlooked details of filed reports and trying to find the beginning of this infestation that was killing many people in Atlanta, namely children. He was getting the beginning of the thread that would lead to a bigger tapestry of drugs that was becoming more out of control. He wished Kevin was here to give him this package and the two could go and look for evidence and take back the city that they both loved for its richness in culture and family ties it had for the both of them.

Kevin was not only a great co-worker and leader in fighting for justice in the city. He was also like a brother. They had been practically raised together. When Alex came back from Boston to take the position as Assistant District Attorney, he found that the two of them would be working side by side in the legal arena in Atlanta. They were both more than excited to touch basis with each other and become family once again. Little did he know the star detective would die some years after they begun to work together. The thought saddened him, not because Kevin was no longer there, but because the family he once thought he knew was no longer. His mother was hurt by Zechariahs, and he tried with all of his might not to try and seek revenge for this grievance done to his mother for only being guilty of loving a man who could never love her back.

A knock came on his door and Mya entered. "Alex, I hope I'm not interrupting."

"No, come on in Mya. I was just thinking about Kevin."

"Four months tomorrow." Mya lamented.

"I know. It doesn't seem real."

"I still think he'll be coming home at any moment."

"Or he will walk into my office." He continued. "What brings you here?"

"I had no where else to go."

"Are you in some kind of trouble?"

"No, well, I don't think I am."

"What do you mean?" He was worried. He wanted her to continue. "If there's anything that I can do."

"I have been investigating Kevin's murder."

"We closed that case. Rory Tremont confessed and was found guilty. He's waiting to die by lethal injection. Baring an appeal, he will pay for murdering your husband, my friend."

"No, he didn't kill my husband. I have proof."

"He confessed Mya."

"He perjured himself. He's covering up for someone else."

"What brought you to this conclusion?" Alex was more intrigued.

"Have you seen the coroner's report?"

"I looked over it. But nothing looked out of the ordinary." He knew he hadn't looked over it as thoroughly as he should have, seeing as though he had a lot on his plate. He was dealing with the continuing drug investigation and the constant problem of his mother and her tawdry affair with Mr. Dean.

"Look at the sixth page." She opened up the page and showed it to him.

After reading he responded. "I didn't notice this. Drug residue was under his nails."

"Exactly. He was killed some where near the drugs. It was under his nails and in his lungs. I conclude that my husband was killed near that drug and taken to the place where he was discovered. There is more. Read."

Alex continued to read and find evidence that was not there upon his initial reading of the report some four months prior. He assumed Rory's admission of guilt wouldn't need a required probing, but this new reading made him feel guilt for not doing all he could to prosecute Rory. "The same slug found in him, the bullet, is Atlanta police department issued."

"I know. How did Rory get a gun that was police issued?"

"And Kevin's gun wasn't fired. That I remembered from my initial evidence."

"So, Rory either got a gun from an officer, or it was someone in the department that killed my husband."

"Do you realize the charges that you are leveling?"

"Yes. And someone else knows I'm getting close to the truth as well."

"What do you mean?" Alex questioned.

"I was run off the road the other day, followed by a cryptic phone call saying I needed to back off the trail."

"I didn't know. Why wasn't it in any of the news outlets?"

"I work for the media outlets. I can suppress things if I need to."

"Friends in high places are always good. Do you need protection?"

"I need you to do me a favor. I have a lead."

"Anything to find my brother's killer."

"Can you figure out why Emory Westport, our great mayor, would want my husband dead?"

"Why Mayor Westport?"

"I know that my husband and he met days before he was murdered."

"How do you know that?"

She reached in her bag and pulled out her husband's journal. "There's also this. My husband kept a detailed journal of his days. I learned from reading it that he and Rory were friends and they played basketball together nights at *Run and Shoot*. I also learned he met with Emory to discuss the drug problem of this city. It's all here." She handed over to him.

"This is crazy. It's funny you should mention this. I just got some alarming evidence from our mayor's dead ex-wife. Apparently Emory is involved in this drug cartel and *JEM* sweeping this city."

The both of them were closer to the truth than they had realized.

CHAPTER 81

Paige sat in the parlor at the Dean Estate. She had been home for two days after her overdose. Her recovery wasn't the only thing on her mind, though. She was worried about Marcus and how he had disappeared almost a week prior. He told her that he was going to take care of some business when he left her that night at the hospital and hadn't returned. His disappearance worried her to no end and she sent her mother to talk to Cole to see if he had any information that would lead to his whereabouts, at the very least put a missing person's search out for him.

Her mother returned home. Jordan was shroud in black, as she had just returned from the funeral of her dear friend Olive. She had an envelope in hand, and Paige was very anxious when she returned to ask her what she had discovered. "Where's dad?"

"At the office. He and Dontavious are getting ready for the debate tomorrow. How did you do today?"

"It was difficult, but I made it."

"Your color is coming back a little bit more." She said, looking into her daughters deep sincere eyes.

"One day at a time. I'm not going to lie and say I didn't crave JEM." Paige said with sincerity.

"Drugs: I never thought my daughter would fall prey to this demon."

"You think I wanted this?"

"I'm so glad that you were pulled back when you were." She hugged her daughter. She felt a longing inside her, like there was a void that was still there. She was on the road to recovery, but there was something more that she felt that she needed. "I learned in rehab that you are and will always be an addict. There's nothing you can do except live."

"I read the pamphlet ma." She said snidely.

"What is up with the attitude Paigey?" Jordan inquired from her daughter.

"I'm worried about Marcus. He still hasn't called. Did you hear anything from Cole? Has he put out a Missing Person's Alert?"

"Paige, there is no need to put out an alert." Cole said entering in the room. He had envelope in hand and more secrets in tow. How was he going to spin this?

"Marcus hasn't been seen in almost week, Cole. I called our friends in New York and they haven't heard from him since he came here to be with me. Where could he be?"

"Let Coleman talk darling." Jordan said rubbing her daughter's back.

Cole braced himself. He was about to spill untruths. It was something he had definitely planned since murdering her boyfriend. When Jordan called him the morning before and asked him to investigate Marcus' disappearance for Paige, he figured it out. And this is what he said, "Marcus bought a plane ticket to Barbados and left almost a week ago."

"Why would he leave without saying bye?" Paige was confused.

"I can come up with a few million reasons why." Jordan interjected.

"What are you talking about?" Paige inquired.

"Look at this." She handed her a piece of paper.

"What's this?" She was confused.

"Your trust fund account statement. When was the last time you check it?" Jordan inquired as she tried to make her daughter understand.

"It's been a while. I haven't had to..."

"Did Marcus have access to this account?"

"Of course. He is my man. I trust him..."

"To help himself to whatever he needs?" Jordan continued her statement.

"Are you accusing Marcus of stealing from me Ma?" Paige wondered. Cole was intrigued. His lie could be the truth.

"Your account has been pilfered. Look at this!" She handed her the statement. "Almost eight million, gone in three years time!"

"This can't be real." Paige said not believing the love of her life could steal from her. But to her chagrin she sat there looking at a statement of massive withdrawals from her trust fund. Her father had set up that account and it was to be her nest egg for her whole life. This was the account in which she could take non-paying or low paying gigs and be able to handle the lifestyle in which she had grown accustomed. Now in front of her was a balance of her account stating that she was robbed blind and the man of her dreams had done it.

"It's very real. Figures don't lie my darling." Jordan ostentatiously stated.

"So, he stole my money and now he's in Barbados some where living off the hog? I know Marcus and he wouldn't do this."

"Apparently you don't know him. Stolen money and plane tickets also don't lie Paige." Cole dug the knife in deeper. He solidified his lie. "I have to be going. If I find any more info I'll surely pass it on to you."

"Thank you again Coleman." Jordan stated.

"No problem, glad that I could be of help." He exited.

Paige sat looking out the window. Tears welled and her unbelief was swelling inside her as well. The man that she loved had been revealed to her. She was now trying her best to make sense out of all of it. The sad part is that she couldn't. She couldn't even begin to rationalize what was going on in her world.

Jordan came to her and put her hand on her shoulder. Paige let the tears fall and she began to openly weep like a two year old who had just scrapped her knee. She was in pain. It wasn't just the physical pain of the accidental overdose or the stomach pumping that ensued. What was hurting her now was her trust being snatched from her. She was no longer in control. Her mother saw it. She knew this pain so well and could empathize.

CHAPTER 82

It was early afternoon when Emory returned to his office and found Alex. He was sitting in his seat with legs crossed and was quite surprised.

"Close the door and have a seat Mr. Mayor." Alex commanded.

"Alexander, did I forget a meeting?" Emory asked.

"No, I have information you are not going to like." Emory came into the office, closing the door behind him. He sat across from Alex, as though he knew this was moment that the other shoe was going to drop.

"You look so stern. What's going on?" Emory tried to chuckle and make light of the situation, but it was impossible...this was serious.

"Your dead ex wife was pretty busy as she lay dying."

"It's such a tragedy that she died from such a debilitating disease."

"It is. But she sure made sure that you were taken care of before she died."

"Do you have a copy of her will or something?"

"Even more damning, a sign and sealed deathbed confession." Alex was standing. He handed Emory the forty page confession that Olive hammered out before she expired at the hands of Emory a week prior to this moment. Emory was stunned as he flipped through the pages. He didn't know this existed, hell he didn't know she would be so vindictive. Catholics have priest, so he thought, and Olive had a pen and paper.

"You believe all of this?"

"Do I have much of a choice Emory? This is not some run of the mill made up story. Details are so succinct. Events that have taken place coincide with things on the books. Her confession is sound. Now my question is what do you think I should do?"

"She's a dead woman, Alex. She hated me for leaving her, and this is just a product of her wild, morphine induced imagination."

"Or is this a blueprint to take a mayor down who has been running a drug cartel for years under the nose of my D.A. office and that of the Atlanta P.D.?"

"Alex, we can work this out. No one has to know about this confession." He was holding up the pages. He was desperate. He thought that the secrets that he kept were buried with Olive, and that definitely wasn't the case as this signed and sealed confession was evident of. "What do I have to do to make this go away?"

"So it's true you are the one behind *JEM* coming to this city—for killing millions of our citizens?"

"This isn't what it was supposed to be."

"Then explain it to me. There's no rational reason for it to this."

"What choice do I have?" Emory was cowering, trying to discover options out of thin air. He was a rat backed into a corner with nothing else to do but attack.

"I'm starting further investigation into these allegations. In the meantime, I will need you to gather with your secretary, and whatever PR people you have, and tender your resignation from the office of mayor."

"Are you serious?"

"Dead ass!" Alex was resolute in his decision, and he felt that this was what could begin to rectify the pain that had taken place. He moved closer to the door, backing his way out of the office. "And you can keep that copy of Olive's confession, believe me there are more copies."

He backed into the door. The door popped open fairly quickly, knocking Alex to the ground, unconscious. It was if it were a gift from heaven, or in Emory's case, directly from hell. Alex was knocked out cold on the floor, prostrate, and at Emory's volition.

"Oh, my God, I didn't mean to do that. I busted in because your secretary wasn't here." A voice said. Emory looked up from the floor and looked at the person who had inadvertently saved him.

"It's not a problem at all Percy. But I am going to need one more thing before I let you go back to your life."

"Haven't I done enough?"

"Just help me take him some place special, and you're off the hook."

The two of them began the last stage of the plan and Alex knowing the truth was just a minor hurdle in which they would have to deal with.

CHAPTER 83

The museum was perfectly set for the ball. Everything that Jordan had planned was in place. Brianna was going down the checklist and to the letter. Everything was working to make this the grandest ball Atlanta had seen in a while. Jordan wanted to overcompensate. She knew the mouths would be talking about the family's scandals, and she needed something to distract, and the ball definitely would do that.

"Everything looks in order Mrs. Dean. You've created a ball fit for royalty." Brianna said entering with the museum curator Liam.

"The Deans are royalty—Atlanta royalty that is." Jordan said looking over the centerpieces gracing the table. She didn't miss a beat.

"So everything looks okay for you Mrs. Dean?" Liam said seeking final approval for the job he and his staff had spent days on.

"I definitely need the gobies facing the staircase a bit more. Want to make the guest feel like movie stars. But other than that, you've done an excellent job."

"Thank you Mrs. Dean. I must be going now. You have a good one. And see you tomorrow evening." Liam shook her hand and made his way to finish the last minute preps.

"You seem distracted Mrs. Dean?" Brianna came behind her.

"A lot on my mind, the ball, Paige and the debate tonight."

"Is she doing okay?" Brianna inquired.

"She's doing better. One day at a time they say."

"Any word from Marcus, the horrible boyfriend?"

"In Barbados with her money, according to Cole."

"I'm sorry to hear that."

"People have always and will always use the Deans for something. We just have to weed them out. I'm just sorry Paige had to learn the hard way."

"As long as Jordan Campbell-Dean is at the helm, everything will be okay."

"I know that for sure." Jordan concluded. "Can you handle the rest of the details for me? I have to meet Zech at the studio for the debate."

"No problem Mrs. Dean. And you get some rest tonight. We have a huge day tomorrow." Brianna said hugging her.

"And I hope that gown I bought for you is a flawless as I hope."

"I'm going to look like Cinderella. Thank you." She hugged her once again. "Dontavious will love me in it."

"Yes he will. You have a great one." She exited and left Brianna to complete the last details of the ball.

CHAPTER 84

"By definition insanity is doing something the same and expecting different results. And that's what we will be doing Atlanta if we elect Emory Westport back to office as mayor once again. Give me the chance to right the wrongs and make this city one that we can believe in and call home again." Dontavious led the applause at the end of the debate between his father and Emory. Zechariahs was in rare form this particular evening as he knocked down each question posed with precision and grace. He was so eloquent that Emory himself was quite thrown and couldn't quite regain a footing he thought he would automatically have being the incumbent. But this was Zechariahs' to win, and win, he was on his way to doing.

If anyone knew what Emory was going through that particular eve, they wouldn't have questioned his failure to meet such an auspicious occasion. He had a lot on his mind. He buried his ex wife Olive a few days before. A woman, who he had once loved, was now dead at his hands. He had ordered the death of Marcus, and then Rory. His world was closing in on him, and he was trying his best to keep his composure, but it was unraveling by the day. And on top of all this he was holding Alex captive at the warehouse until he could figure out what to do with him.

The thunderous applause ended the debate. The two shook hands. The moderator, Monica Kaufman, gave her sign off, and it was officially over. The two of them went to their respective corners where their supporters shook their hands and it gave way to small talk.

"Dad, that was amazing. You nailed him to the wall and took him to task." Dontavious said coming behind his father.

"It was time. I think we have a decent chance."

"More than decent pops. We got this."

"You did wonderfully Zech. I'm so proud." Jordan said hugging her husband.

"Dad, you were amazing." Paige clutched on to her father. Dontavious hugged his father joining in on the celebration.

Emory snuck out of the studio, tail between his legs, trying to avoid all attention on the disaster that was that night's debate. He entered his town car, only to be surprised by another passenger.

"You seemed distracted tonight." Thornehart said letting the ash from his cigar hit the floor.

"Watch where that ash goes Thorneheart."

"Ash is the last thing you should be worried about Emory. You looked like a bumbling fool tonight!"

"I have a lot on my mind. And most of it was caused by you!"

"Excuses aren't going to help win the election. I need you as mayor Emory to help finish this!" Thorneheart was livid. He wanted to drive home the point to Emory.

"I know what the fuck I have to do Thorneheart. I'm not some kid without a clue." He was becoming more irate.

"And I know what I must do as well sir. The pictures and information will hit the media by morning!"

"You can't do that. I promised him that I wouldn't if he helped me move Alex. And I can win this election without the smear."

"You have no chance on winning this election. John McCain has a better chance against President Obama."

"I can't go back on my word. I promised him that I wouldn't release the info. And right now I have to feel good about myself in the mar of shit and scandal you've put me in."

"Are you referring to that faggot Percy!"

"Percy's your son! You set him up. It was the least I could do. I promised him."

"You don't have that power. Emory, this is now in **my** hands. You have no more control. I see you have too many obligations and too many secrets weighing down your judgment. I will get you this election. I will get the drugs transferred and the overseas accounts will be filled. You will be retired soon. You will have everything you've ever wanted. But I will do it under my discretion. Get some rest because the shit is literally about to hit the fan sir." He scooted out of the town car leaving Emory in his wake.

Emory was once again backed into a corner. How was he going to get out of this one? He needed another Percy to get him out of the situation. He picked up his phone and dialed Cole. He needed some last minute reinforcement to make this all go away.

CHAPTER 85

Dontavious pulled up the City Café a little after ten thirty p.m. When he answered the phone just a shy twenty minutes before, he thought it was going to be Cole telling him that he was on his way home. It wasn't Cole though. It was the Private Percy, who begged him to meet him a reasonably public place to talk. Dontavious initially thought against the idea, but what would he do, just sit at home and wait for Cole to saunter him smelling of someone else's smell as he had recently? He decided to meet the Private and satisfy a curiosity that was welling inside him since their meeting a few months prior.

He walked into the brightly dimmed restaurant. It looked like the middle of the day the way the fluorescent lights were bouncing off every surface of the place. He looked around and finally spotted Percy who sat in the corner eating eggs, hash and drinking coffee, black. Dontavious surveyed the room, and upon seeing that the restaurant was sparsely populated, headed towards him and sat.

"Hey, man. Thanks for coming." Percy sounded surprised.

"I told you I would come if I could. I found some time."

"Thanks, man. Do you want anything to eat?" Percy said graciously to his one time love.

"No, I'm good. Why did you call me down here man?"

"Cut straight to the chase." Percy wasn't dumbfounded seeing as though Dontavious shot straight from the hip any occasion, including their initial meeting for sex.

"You know it. So, what's up Percy?" He insisted.

"Remember when we met at Atlantic Station, and I told you that it wasn't my fault that I went under oath and said those things."

"It's partially the reason why I showed up tonight. What is your beef?"

"I have to come clean. This was all a setup by my father."

"What are you talking about?"

"I was insecure when I entered the army. I went home on one of leaves and met with my biological father. He said he knew all about me. My mother told him everything. He said he would forgive me for being gay if I did something for him. He said he would put me on a base with you. I was to befriend you and sleep with you. And then I was to turn you in and make you lose your rank and everything."

"What the hell are you talking about? Do you know how crazy and unfounded that sounds?"

"I know. He told me it was just part of his plan. I had to do it, or I could lose everything myself if I didn't."

"This seems so farfetched Percy. Why are you doing this? What is done is done! My life has been dismantled by your lies. I have moved on, and so should you little boy." He got up to leave. But he couldn't leave without the most important piece of this weird puzzle. And how it would fit in, he didn't know, but he had to know. "Who is your father Percy?"

"Thorneheart Kincade is my father." Percy didn't want to admit that this man was the one who gave him life.

"The Senator?"

"Yes." Percy confirmed.

"Why Percy would your father go through all of this planning and plotting just to take little ol' me down?" Dontavious was stuck. He thought back to the day that his father and he had that initial lunch some months before. He remembered the story of his father and Thornheart being rivals for the *Atlanta Renewal Project* as he was told at his favorite restaurant Sotto Sotto. He couldn't believe that this man, who was once a business rival of his father, would concoct a plan so devious and underhanded to bring down every branch of his family tree, including him.

"JEM!"

"Jem what?"

"The drug. It all has to do with that drug. And everything that I know only makes this all sound even more crazy and even more convoluted." Dontavious sat. He was in for a long night of the truth.

CHAPTER 86

Cole walked to Thorneheart's suite at the Peachtree Plaza hotel and knocked three times. When Thorneheart opened the door, he was wearing a robe and was ready for bed. It was nearly midnight after all.

"What do I owe the pleasure Mr. Denavar? Come on in." Cole entered. Thorneheart closed the door behind him.

"Emory sent me."

"Are you his errand boy now?" Thorneheart laughed.

"Coleman Denavar is no one's errand boy. He sent me to ask you to not release that information."

"How did I know you were going to say that?"

"Come on, Thorneheart, it won't hurt anything. Besides we've rigged the election anyhow."

"We are not playing by Geneva convention rules, Coleman. I believe in not just defeat, but total annihilation. That means Zechariahs will go down and all of his family included. Even that faggot of a son of his!"

"That is the ..."

"What? The man you love? Come on! Don't tell me you've fallen for him. It was your assignment, just like my son Percy, to get close to Dontavious, the prized Dean son. Just like my daughter was to take down Malek, you all were to chip away at the Dean men and take it all away.

And the little Marcus boy, the one Emory had killed, did a damn good job with that daughter Paige, good timing. Man, this is amazing...And I'm so close! So, don't fuck this up Cole..." Thorneheart started to breathe deeply. He couldn't catch his breath.

"You've fallen off the deep end old man. Take a breath!"

"It's not just about money and power Cole. It's about destroying this motherfucker Zechariahs Dean..." He fell on the floor. Thornheart was having a heart attack. He was clutching his chest, and barely able to breathe. "Help me, call 9-1-1! Please. Help, Coleman."

"You can't fuck this up for us Thorneheart. We've worked too hard for this as well."

He left Thorneheart on the floor gasping for air, locking the door behind him. It was the next morning before anyone discovered he was dead. He was found by the maid early the next day after he didn't answer the door. The headline on the newspaper the next day read: "Senator found dead in hotel suite."

CHAPTER 87

Kameron held her mother's hand. Something she had done every time she felt her world crashing in on her. This day was no different as she learned of the death of father. She was shocked and saddened when she heard the news, and she knew she could find solace in the comfort of her mother's serine room. Josh joined her later on that day as she held her mother's hand and wept openly for a man who she only found out was her father some six years prior.

This would be the only place in which she could weep openly for her and Josh's father because no one knew their connection and she wanted to keep it that way. What racked inside her now were the thoughts of the plan her father had and how it would now play out. She had done her part, but she wasn't sure if she would be protected now that her father was no longer in the mix. She would call Cole to meet with her to discuss the future. She wanted her life to be secured as well as her baby that only her and her mother knew about.

CHAPTER 88

Emory was having champagne on the patio of his mansion when Cole arrived. It was early morning, and Cole was quite surprised to find him indulging so early in the morning.

"Champagne? It's ten a.m." Cole took a glass and poured himself a flute of the bubbly, polishing off the bottle.

"It's a celebration. That old fart is dead. His secrets are going in the ground with him." Emory laughed as he took one finally gulp finishing his third glass.

"He looked so helpless as he asked me to call 9-1-1. I'm glad that I didn't have to shoot him." Cole sipped. He was amused at himself.

"The shipment of JEM should be coming in later on tonight. The warehouse and workers are prepared. So I need you on alert."

"Not a problem boss. And what should I do about Mr. D.A.?"

"I will figure that out. But I think Alex is more of a value to me alive than dead." Emory concluded. He popped the cork on a new bottle of champagne. "More champagne?"

"Of course." He emptied his glass' contents down his throat and prepared for another. Emory poured.

"Have you caught up with the Rory's friend who he supposedly sent these confession letters to?"

"His name is Darnell Parker. His friends call him Loke. He lives in Decatur. I'll be going to see him later.

"We need to trim all loose ends. It's almost time for us to get paid. Nothing needs to be in our way.

"Here's to the lap of luxury!" They clanged glasses.

CHAPTER 89

"The senator's body will lie in state at the Capitol Building. Viewing will began this evening. For Channel Two eye witness news, this is Mya Kim-Dean." Mya signed off from her live feed from the Capital Building in the heart of the city. Her cameraman packed up the equipment and she walked to her car. She found Dontavious leaning against it.

"You're still working?" Dontavious remarked as he patted her ever-growing belly.

"I still have two more months. And my doctor said I'm okay." Mya was getting tired of people questioning her health, but was happy someone cared.

"Even after the hit and run?"

"Yep, even after the hit and run Dontavious." She assured him. "So, what was so important that you needed to see me?" She continued.

"I spoke with Percy last evening." He tried to make sure that no one was around.

"I thought you weren't going to see him again."

"He said he needed to talk. And talk he did."

"What did he want?" She questioned.

"He told me that his father was responsible for what happened to me and that it was apart of some bigger plot to take down my family. And something to do with JEM."

"That sounds convoluted. Sounds like someone trying to worm their way back into your life by any and all means." Mya was just as confused as he was.

"You won't believe who his father is, was."

"Who?"

"Thorneheart Kincade."

"That man had sperm that wouldn't quit." She laughed.

"What do you mean?" Dontavious was out of touch.

She went on to explain to him how she had just discovered that Kameron was Thornheart's child by the comatose Janika Hanes. "I didn't catch the connection until after I read the article. I didn't even realize the relevance until just now."

"What does this all mean?" Dontavious inquired.

"If what you say is true, Thorneheart's hands are all over this city and they have infiltrated your family for something bigger than you could ever know. Maybe it was he that had something to do with Kevin's death. I need to give Alex a call." She dialed his number on her cell phone.

"So, the meeting with him the other day was beneficial?" He inquired.

"Very." Her face changed.

"What's wrong?"

"His phone went straight to voice mail." Mya answered.

"And?"

"The mailbox was full. That never happens."

"Maybe he's just busy. You know with the senator's death, there are a lot of things that the D.A. has to take care of..."

"I guess you're right."

"Hey, I get to get going, mom wants to see me before the ball tonight."

"I must start getting ready, as well. Haven't been home in almost a day, have mail backed up, and I still have to figure out how to get this belly in my gown."

"I'll see you tonight, then."

"Of course."

"Please stay safe. We are close to finding my brother's killer. I feel it."

"I do hope so, so that he can finally rest in peace." They hugged and they went on their way.

CHAPTER 90

He found Loke on the back porch in the tenement he called a home on Decatur's west side. The place looked as though Section-8 wouldn't touch it. He was smoking marijuana and doing nothing with the early evening that the long day had given him. He had a long day at work at the mechanic shop, a job he barely got with his previous convictions. He was the stereotype to the letter, even down to the three baby's mothers, six kids and not a dime in child support. He was everything Bill Cosby hated, and many black males unwillingly and unknowingly became through bad decisions and an unforgiving penal code. So, at the end of his long day at work, he loved a nice joint, some beer and the time alone on his back porch.

"Yo, you Loke?" Cole asked as he approached the porch. Loke had spotted him as he pulled up, didn't know what to think, and he braced his glock he always kept on his person.

"Who wants to know?"

"I'm a friend of your boy Rory."

"How I know you legit?" Loke didn't like this one bit. *How did this guy find him? And now he saying he knows Rory.* He was confused and braced to protect himself at all cost.

"Me and Rory spent time together in Henry County, shawty." Cole lied, trying on the vernacular of the Southern homeboy he had grown accustomed to living in Little John's hood.

"Everyone 'dat watch the news know Rory spending time down there! I need more."

"Aiight, he fucking some bitch who made him take the rap. How about that?" Cole knew Loke would know that and instantly he let his guard down.

"I'm Loke, what's good?" Loke stood up to face Cole.

"Yo, Rory told me about them letters you holding for him. He getting out tomorrow. Needed me to bring them to him to the prison before he get out to let that cop Cole know what's up and that he serious." Cole tried to explain to him as not to arouse suspicions.

"Can't do that man. You should know that." The ex con stated.

"Why not?" Cole questioned.

"Rory told me to send them letters already, like last week, shawty." Loke held onto his glock once again. His suspicions were aroused. If he really knew Rory, he would have known about the letters being mailed.

"Oh, for reals. That nigga told me to come get them from you. Damn, where he sent them, shawty?"

"The place he say."

"Come on man. Tell me! You know how that foo gets. Know shawty was in jail for six months for a crime he didn't commit."

"What the fuck you want, shawty?!" He made a motion toward the gun he held in his waist band."

"The letters, man. Rory told me to come get them."

"Told you they gone. Anyone that know Rory know he told me to send them a few weeks ago."

Cole didn't expect this guy to be so intuitive, and was trying his hardest to get the info out of him without raising any more reservations. It was become very hard. "Hope you ain't send the originals to Mayor Westport." Loke's interests were even more peaked. Cole had mentioned the dirty detective. He also mentioned the girl who Rory was taking the rap for. And now he was mentioning the dirty dealing mayor who the letters implicitly named as the ring leader behind the whole plot.

"No, he got a copy, just like that detective's wife, the reporter." Loke's guard was once again dropped.

"So, you still got the originals?"

"No, shawty...I just told you that shit!!" Loke's high was waning and his patience as well.

"So, who got them, shawty?"

"In a safe place," Loke candidly revealed.

"So, can Rory get to them tomorrow when he get out?"

"Hell yeah, they at his place waiting for him to return, shawty."

"That's what's up. You should have told me that to begin wit, shawty. We didn't need the back and forth. You feel me?"

"Fo' sho! Just had to make sure you legit. Aiight man, bout to go lay it down. Tired as hell. Glad I could help you out, man."

"No thank you, glad I could help our boy Rory out. He has helped me so much being in prison." Cole said with a smirk.

"I didn't catch the name, shawty." He held out his hand to give him dap.

"Oh, my bad. I'm Cole. Detective Cole Denavar." Loke's face was ashen as he realized who this new "friend" was. He tried going for his gun to kill the guy who had set up his friend, but it was too late as Cole's bullet from his silenced gun penetrated his abdomen. Loke was dead. No one was around. No one could vouch for what happened. He called it in once he planted evidence. There's no way that anyone would know what happened. The weed, in conjunction with the JEM he placed in Loke's pocket, would be enough to allow him to get away with murder once again.

CHAPTER 91

It was nearly five in the afternoon. Mya found herself in Malek's office. She knew she had to tell her brother-in-law what information she found out about his soon to be wife, even though the two of them were not on the best of terms. When Malek came into the office he was quite surprised by her intrusion.

"I didn't come here to pick a fight I promise." Mya assured him, allowing Malek not to get tense or defensive.

"Well, it is my turf and I would win." Malek tried cracking a joke, unsuccessfully, though. But Mya chuckled a bit. "So what brings you here?"

"I found some information out about your fiancée."

"Have you been speaking to my mother lately?" He said with a slight smile. He knew Jordan and Mya were really close.

"No, I've been investigating your brother's death."

"Those sound like two different subjects."

"Not as much as you think." Mya revealed.

"So, tell me, what do you know Mya?"

"Your brother was possibly set up by the late Senator Thorneheart Kincade."

"That man Rory Tremont admitted to killing Kevin. How you figure the Senator had anything to do with it?"

"That's what I'm still trying to figure out."

"What does any of this have to do with Kameron?" Malek was becoming impatient and short with her.

"Kameron is Thorneheart's daughter." Mya let the cat out of the bag.

"How do you know?" Malek was not surprised by this revelation, seeing as though Thorneheart asked him to ask his fiancée about the missing money from his company.

"I discovered that her mother was Thorneheart's assistant for years. They had two kids together. Her mother was shot by Thorneheart's dead wife. And now she is in a coma. She has been for close to ten years. She's in a facility near Marrietta." She handed him the information in a folder.

Malek knew that Kameron had frequented this facility once he had a detective tail her, but never knew why. With his new information about the money laundering at his disposal and this new information, he put the pieces together. He was no fool and his intelligence only allowed the thoughts that he didn't want to have about the woman he was paying to be in his bed. He was quite impressed by the woman who he had thought he was taking advantage of. All Malek could say was, "Thank you."

"You're welcome. I hope I wasn't out of line."

"Thank you for your consideration."

"I have to be on my way. Got to get ready for the exclusive Harvest Ball."

354.

"Me too. See you tonight." They awkwardly hugged. She went to exit. He debated his next step, but proceeded, "And Mya I'm sorry about what happened in the past. I was young, jealous and stupid."

"It's the past. Life's too short. Kevin's death taught me that. All's forgiven." She walked out of the office.

CHAPTER 92

White dinner jacket, bow tie, and manicured to the hilt, Zechariahs was the picture of perfection. It was seven p.m. on the dot and his wife had instructed to him to be dressed and ready when the clocked chimed that time. He was dressed, looking as elegantly as his money allowed him. And now he waited for his wife to ascend the steps. It was only an hour before her yearly event would take place. They had to be there early to make sure everything was in place.

Paige ascended the stairs first. Her Dolce and Gabbana cocktail dress fit her perfectly. Matched by six inch hills, the silver dress perfectly masked the rough time she had just had in life. She held her clutch underneath her arm and she sauntered down the thirty or so steps. She had cropped off her hair and her pop star Rhianna inspired hairdo got her father's attention right away.

"Wow, baby girl your hair."

"You like?" She was unsure of her father's reaction.

"I love it. What made you do it?"

"I wanted a new start. And cutting off all the hair was the perfect way of starting."

"You look beautiful." He hugged her.

"Do I really?" She touched her hair, still unsure of her decision to cut it all off.

"Absolutely. How are you feeling this evening?" Her father asked with concern.

"It's the best day I've hard in weeks. Thanks." He hugged her.

"Don't mess up my makeup."

"You and your mother..."

"Her and her mother what?" Jordan said as she came to the top of the stairs. She was flawless. Her hair was swept up. Makeup was top notch. Her burned orange, strapless gown was fitted at the bust and flowed down into a floor length princess gown. She had a split in the right place to show off her beautiful leg with pure perfection as she glided to the bottom of the stairs."

"Wow, Jordan, you look..."

"...perfect, flawless, without a doubt the most beautiful woman you've ever laid eyes on." She finished his sentence.

"All that and more." He kissed her on her cheek as not the muss up her makeup. "So, you're finally ready?"

"Perfection does take time, even for Jordan Campbell-Dean."

"Well, Miss perfection, let's get going, you don't want to be late to your event." Zechariahs said to his favorite two women. As he opened the door Sascha was standing on the porch in front of them. "Sascha, what are you doing here?"

She had been crying. She was upset and could barely compose herself. She hugged Zechariahs, a source of strength she knew was there.

Jordan came to the other side of her husband and took in the scene before her.

"What's going on Sascha?" Jordan tried to feign sympathy for a woman who she had known had been screwing her husband for nearly thirty years.

"It's Alex. He hasn't been home in almost two days and he doesn't answer his phone."

"What does that have to do with us?" Jordan snapped back.

"Jordan!" Zechariahs tried to calm his wife. "What happened?"

"I don't know. I'm scared Mr. Dean. He never leaves without checking in. Can you please help me?"

"We're on our way to my ball. We can't do anything for you." Jordan was not pleased by this intrusion.

"It's okay. Jordan, you and Paige go on ahead. I will meet you there. I will contact Cole for her and then we can go on with the night. Okay?"

"I'm not too happy about this!" Jordan made her point known.

"I know, but I promise I won't be late." He kissed her for assurance.

"Yeah, mom, he won't be late. Let's go." Paige didn't know what was going on, but he wanted it to be quailed before the whole night would be ruined. "We'll see you there." He guided her mom away from the door and the two of them headed to the limo parked outside the door. Jordan was looking back taking in the two of them as they hugged.

They entered the limo and drove off. Zechariahs still held her in his arms. "When was the last time you heard from him?" He asked her.

"Two nights ago. He was going to a meeting. I'm scared Mr. Dean. I'm scared." She held onto him tighter.

CHAPTER 93

Kameron sat in front of the vanity applying the last of her makeup. She was on hour two of getting ready. She knew she had to be the pentacle of perfection at **the** event of the Atlanta social scene. Her dress fit like a glove, and though she was four months pregnant, there was no sign of the baby. Her weekly doctor's appointment yielded good news as her doctor told her that she was progressing along without any problems in her pregnancy. She looked beautiful, but felt at ease with her secret pregnancy, but felt horribly as she knew her body was changing and couldn't do anything about it.

She looked at the clock on the vanity and realized that it was nearing seven-thirty, and Malek hadn't arrived home—this wasn't like him, she thought. Though she wasn't worried about Malek, she was more worried that his mother's venom would spew if the two were late. She would ultimately be blamed for their tardiness and Kameron wanted no parts in that. Now that her father was dead, she knew she would have to play the game in order to keep her lifestyle, because her future was definitely uncertain at the moment.

Malek walked in and stopped in the door way. She saw him in her reflection as she applied the last bit of mascara. "You're late! I don't want to hear your mother's mouth! Hurry and get dressed!"

"Thornheheart is your father!"

"Excuse me?"

"Senator Thorneheart Kincade is your father."

"What are you talking about? Get dressed, Malek." She tried to be nonchalant about the accusation.

"He's the one who has been stealing money from my company. He's set up this dummy corporation to smuggle *JEM*, that drug, and you are his daughter that was helping him."

"Do you know how that sounds Malek?" Kameron was scared. Her life as she knew it was crumbling around her. Malek was ravenous. His anger seethed through his teeth and he was gnashing at her.

"You bitch! It wasn't enough that you were fucking that ex-con Rory, you are aiding in taking down my father's company by associating him with these drugs!"

"Rory, that con who killed your brother?"

"I found out everything. I've been investigating you for weeks. Try and deny it. I have pictures, paperwork, and anything else to implicate you in this whole thing. Tell me you didn't know about the Russian actress your father hired. Tell me you didn't know about the money! Tell me you didn't know about it all!!! I have this envelope full to prove otherwise." He threw the folder with everything he needed to convict Kameron at her. It landed on the vanity. All was strewn before her. Her lies, deception, and scheming was now in black and white. She couldn't say anything. Her mouth dropped. He grabbed the back of her neck, and pulled himself closer to her ear.

"Malek you're hurting me!" She said with a whimper trying to get him to release her.

"You evil, vile bitch, why would you do this?" He wanted to know, give her some sort of out. Would she be forthcoming with her motives?

"What choice did I have?" Her tears were flowing. "You had my life in your hand with that stupid contract! I had to do something. When my father came to me with the idea, it sounded perfect and I wanted to pay you back. It just got out of hand. I didn't know about the drugs. I swear. It just happened."

"My family's name could have been ruined by this! And for what your father's revenge and petty jealousies?"

"Your father did him dirty!"

"My father won those contracts fair and square. He's the American dream. Your father didn't like it, so he plotted and schemed to take him and his family down. And he goes so far as to do this!" Malek's grip on her neck was tighter.

"Malek, I'm sorry! Let me go!!! Please!"

"No court in their right mind would convict me if I murder you, you merciless bitch!!! Give me one good reason why I shouldn't kill you."

"I'm pregnant." She grabbed the ultrasound that was in her opened purse." He let her go instantly.

"You're lying."

"Look at the date Malek." He did as he was instructed.

"That's today's date." She was telling the truth. He continued, "Is it mine?"

"Look at the due date. I'm four months pregnant. That's to the day that we fucked and we discovered Kevin's death." She stood up. She was showing off her flawless figure in her tight Versace. He looked her up and down trying to find the baby, a tangible sign that she was carrying his child. "I won't start showing until month five." She knew what he was doing.

Malek was noticeably taken aback. His anger gave way to joy. Tears began to well. "What does this mean?"

"We're going to be parents. So what about what you know?" Kameron was beginning the biggest plea bargain of her life.

"You want me to sweep this under the rug and pretend it never happened?" Malek was conflicted. He had always wanted a child, and wasn't sure if was ever going to get it. And now he was going to be a father. On the other hand, his family business and name was tarnished by her actions and he couldn't easily let that slide. She had committed a crime and she had to pay for it. But it was he that put her in this position to begin with. If he hadn't made her sign the contract, she wouldn't have gone to these lengths.

"I'm in debt to you for the rest of my life, Malek. I will be the mother this child needs. I will be your wife and lover you want and desire. I won't ever leave you. Do we have a deal?" Tears were flowing.

"You better do that thing I like." He said with a smirk.

"Not every night." She knew he was leaning towards her deal.

"Okay. We have a deal. We have to keep up appearances. We will be married soon. I want my child to have a name." Malek was implicit in his desire.

"This is my new life." She said with a slight grimace.

"Mr. and Mrs. Malek Dean."

"Is that what our Christmas cards will say?"

"Yep and our stationary and robes." He laughed. The tension was broken. "Let's get dressed before my mother gets angry."

"That's the last thing I need." She sat down to touch up her makeup and her hair that was messed up during the altercation. She felt horribly as she got ready to put on her smile and make everything seem okay. She had a made a deal with the devil, and he had got the upper hand. She knew what she had to do for her life to be what she so desired. The sacrifice would not only be for her future, but her child's as well.

CHAPTER 94

"Yes, 1433 Seaborne Ave. Okay. Just call me when you're here."
Jordan had arranged a car for Mya, and she was calling to confirm when it
would arrive and the driver was late. She carefully took a load off and sat
at the counter top as not to disturb the sleeping baby, or her gown she
barely fit into. She wanted to back out, but she knew that Jordan would
have a coronary, seeing as though she had arranged for her gown to be
custom made to fit her figure. So, she happily complied with the custom
made gown, town car, and night mingling with the Atlanta social scene.
After all Kevin was dead, but she was still a Dean, as was implied by the
child she carried.

Upon sitting, she noticed the stack of mail that she hadn't gone
through all week. Usually she took it with her to the office, but between
the meeting with Alex, Dontavious, and meeting with various other people
about Kevin's murder, her mail remained unopened and on the countertop.

She began to flip through the stack, and discovered bills, coupons,
catalogues and other various mail items that she was used to, until she
came upon a manila envelope. It had no return address and the opening
was sealed with clear box tape. The stamp from the post office said
Dekalb County, but her house was in the same county, so she didn't think
twice. She opened the envelope and discovered a stack of handwritten
letters. She was confused, as she began to read it.

Unknown to her, the front door crept open. Cole snuck in. He silenced his phone which had begun to ring. It was Dontavious, by the caller i.d. He put it in his pocket and slowly made his way to the kitchen, where he knew the letters would be. He had been in this house so many Friday nights for dinner with the three of them. The only woman who he could ever be open about his sexuality with was Mya. And when the three of them were together for those dinners, nothing really mattered in the world. But he was there on a job. He had gone to Rory's place and got rid of the letters, and Emory, of course, told Cole he had gotten rid of his. So, the only person still left was Mya. He hoped that he could get to the letters before Mya had read them, but as he peered in on her at the counter, she was in the midst of reading them.

Mya read to the end of the letter. Rory had finally revealed Kevin's real killer. And it was to her surprise his friend, partner and confident, Cole. Rory had laid out the whole plot in this letter Mya was no longer ignorant of the situation. She picked up her cell phone and dialed Dontavious' number. It went straight to voice mail. "Call me back. I received some letters from Rory. I know who killed my husband. It was Cole..."

She was knocked unconscious by a chloroform laced rag that Cole held over her face. The cell phone hit the ground, but didn't end the call. What was said next was caught by Dontavious' voice mail.

Cole held the unconscious Mya with one arm as he dialed Emory's phone. "Yeah, I got her. She had read the letters. I'll take her to the warehouse, not a problem. We'll deal with her and Alex later after the ball." He hung up the phone and took her out the back door, as not to alarm the neighborhood, even though it was now dark outside.

Mya's phone was on the floor. The phone called ended.

CHAPTER 95

Dontavious tried once more to call Cole, but still no answer. He was already dressed and waiting for him at the condo. It was getting closer to eight and Brianna had been expected him an hour before. But with the last minute work for his father and other things, he had decided to wait for Cole and the two would go together.

He looked at himself in the mirror and found that he look quite nice. He hadn't dressed in a tux in a while, and he felt good about himself. At that moment his cell phone alerted him that he had voice mails. There were two. He put the phone to his ear and heard the first one: "Hey, babe, it's Cole. Got caught up with some work. I'll just meet you at the ball. Sorry sweetie. Love you. Bye." Dontavous felt silly as he had been trying to reach Cole all this time, and he had actually left a voice mail on his phone. He smiled. He knew he had found a great man. And he felt secure in his relationship, something he hadn't felt in weeks since the night Cole came home smelling of cologne from someone else.

The next voicemail started and to his surprise it was Mya. Mya revealed all to him, and sinking feeling came to the pit of his stomach. Not only did she reveal that it was Cole who killed his brother. But on the end of the voicemail, he heard a scuffle and the voice of his lover on the end revealing that he had taken Mya to a warehouse. What warehouse he thought. Mya and her baby were in danger. He had to help them, but didn't know how quite to do that. Everything he thought he knew was done.

He thought for a moment as to how to go about finding her. His first instincts were to call Cole, but with the information he knew, he thought about the one person who he felt could help him with this issue. He dialed a number he thought he would never call again. He frantically spoke once the person opened the phone, "I need your help now!"

CHAPTER 96

By nine p.m. the ball was in full swing as the elite of Atlanta's social, political and entertainment circles intermingled at Jordan's famous Harvest Ball benefiting Alzheimer's research. People draped every inch of the huge Fern Bank Museum. Chatter about this year's incidents, ups and downs of the Deans, littered the air, but all that was trumped by the presence of Jordan. And as all good Southern people, they hid their animosities, and gossip with smiles and a cleaver compliment to the hostess who was making her rounds. Everyone exclaimed how much they loved the ball and how impressed they were by this year's venue and theme.

"Jordan, great job once again." Emory stated as he approached with his young wife on his arm.

"Thank you so much Mr. Mayor." Jordan snidely replied.

"I detected some sarcasm."

"As you should. You won't have that post for very much longer my darling."

"The voters will determine that my darling." His phone rang. He looked down at the i.d. and saw that it was Cole. "Well, my job is never done. Have a great and successful evening." Emory glided off with the new wife and casually made an exit.

Liam, the curator of the museum, approached the two of them: "How did everything turn out Mrs. Dean?"

"Everything is remarkable, Liam. Thank you. Every article you will read tomorrow will have nothing but praise for you and your staff." He was delighted.

"Thank you Mrs. Dean. Well enjoy your evening." He left.

"We've done a great job Mrs. Dean." Brianna exclaimed. "Where could my date be? He's usually on time. He is ex military, right?"

"Yes. The famous Dean Ball and not a Dean in sight." Jordan was angry. Her perfect night was being ruined by the absence of her family. She was trying to keep tabs on her daughter, who she was making sure was coping in her first big social even since the incident, and was trying to balance the flow of food and drinks to the crowd. On top of that concern, she knew her husband was still with the woman he had been sleeping with for years, helping her cope with the disappearance of her son. And her two sons, neither one were in sight. Dontavious was usually so punctual, but was no where to be found. And Malek, she feared, had been caught up in some mess created by the Kameron, a woman who she detested and hoped would move on with her life, leaving her son behind. So, all these thoughts, compounded by her insatiable need to keep a smile on her face to prevent the world from knowing what was going on, held her hostage at her own event.

"Mom we're so sorry to be so late." Malek said giving his mother a slight hug and kiss.

"Malek, you know how much I detest tardiness. Was it this neophytes' fault?"

"No, it wasn't Kameron's fault. I got caught up with some work things." Malek tried his best to explain.

"And how are you doing Mrs. Dean?" Kameron chimed in, letting her know that she was present.

"Well. And you Kiki?"

"It's Kameron, and I'm doing well. My, don't you look beautiful." Kameron barely squeezed out without being nauseous.

"Thanks darling. Couture does have its benefits."

"That it does. Malek arranged to have this made for me. Doesn't it look great?" Kameron twisted the knife.

"You do clean up well. But at the end of the day it's just a dress and makeup." She had a slight smile.

"Well mom, Kameron will be on our way. We have to mingle. I've spotted a couple of investors." Malek said trying to quail the situation.

"Darling, may I have a moment with Kameron." Jordan said very politely.

Malek knew this wasn't a good idea. "Mom, I don't think this is the right moment..."

"No, I'll be oaky. I'll join you soon." Kameron said assuring him that she could handle herself. Malek was not too keen on the idea, but did as she had asked and left her side.

"Mrs. Dean, I'll be back with you shortly. I'm going to call your son." Brianna said as she took her leave.

"Kameron I'm going to make this very clear to you. I don't like you!

"I wouldn't have guessed." Kameron quipped.

"I know about your contract with my son. The one he made to keep you in his bed and at my company?" Jordan spat it out very frank.

"We all meet each other in different ways. Some have E-Harmony, others dating services, but I had a contract. I'm not ashamed."

"What amount of money would you need or want to get you the hell out of our lives!" Jordan answered. She was serious.

"Jordan I love your son." She lied. "I'm not going to leave him. You're stuck with me...well at least for the next eighteen years." Kameron clued her in on her new secret.

"You're not saying what I think you're saying." Jordan hoped and prayed this day would never come.

"Congratulations. You're going to be a grandmother once again." Kameron said with smile. "Have a great rest of the evening, **mom**." She smiled, "Oh, and I'll send a cordial of Hennessy over in a bit. Still like it neat?" She chuckled a bit as she walked off to be by Malek's side. She hated that she was tethered to Malek for the rest of her life, but she loved the fact that she was setting up a war with many battles with the matriarch of the Dean family. This would be battle that she would fight for years to come.

Jordan hated this night even more. Her family was no where near, but all was calmed within her, as to her surprise, Paige took to the stage and started to sing. Her melodious voice filled her heart with pride and joy. Her daughter was beginning to start her life over again and this night would be her first step.

CHAPTER 97

Mya was tied to her chair. When she finally awoke from her induced sleep, she wasn't sure of her location, and was quite groggy when she did finally open her eyes. She was in a dank warehouse, surrounded by crates. She began to panic. She was made aware of her tied hands when she tried to move with little success. "Help, someone help!" She screamed the best she could.

"It's no use. No one can hear us." Alex said to her. He was weak. He was tied up next to her and the two of them were prisoners not of their doing.

"Alex, what are you doing here?" She was relieved that she wasn't the only one there.

"I was knocked out and brought here two days ago. Do you know how you got here?"

She tried to remember, as it all came to her. "I was at my countertop reading mail, and the next thing I know I'm here." Mya was confused and scared. Her poking around for Kevin's killer had gotten her run off the road earlier, and now it had lead her to her new prison, so she feared. "I know everything Alex."

"What do you know?" Alex inquired.

"Cole killed my husband. Emory and Thorneheart are involved in this somehow. I don't know how, but they are."

"I confronted Emory about it. He admitted it all. It was all for that drug *JEM*."

"Kevin got close to the truth didn't he Alex?"

"Yes. That's why they had him killed."

Tears began to flow. "He was only trying to protect this city." It all boiled down to one simple fact for Mya. Her husband could finally rest in peace. The truth was finally out. But no one would ever know if either one of them didn't escape their prison.

"And it was all for money. I hate to admit it."

"I'm scared Alex. What do you think they'll do to us?"

"Get rid of us. Why wouldn't they?" He admitted a truth he didn't want to face.

Dontavious and Percy sat outside the warehouse on Peachtree Street in the still darkness. Percy had led him here and let him know that this was indeed where Emory had helped bring Alex to a couple of nights before. "Are you sure this is it?"

"Yes, we brought him here." Percy answered him.

"Why didn't you tell me this the night that you were spilling your guts?" Dontavious demanded.

"I didn't see the relevance. And I didn't put two and two together until tonight when you called." Percy explained.

"Here." He handed him a glock that he took from Cole's condo.

"What is this for?" Percy demanded.

"You might need to defend yourself. I'm not leaving without Mya and Alex alive.

"Can't we call the cops?"

"The mayor and the cops are in this up to their eyeballs. They aren't helping." Dontavious concluded.

"I don't know..." Percy stated.

"You still have a good shot?" Dontavious inquired.

"Still the best marksman in the group." Percy replied.

The two entered the warehouse in a conspicuous door Percy had entered with the unconscious Alex. They were into the belly of the warehouse and the smell of drugs was strong. They glided on the side of the walls as they navigate by way of moonlight.

"You're awake Mya." Cole said entering the area in which they were located. "How do you like our hub for JEM? Isn't it great?" He said with a smirk.

"Cole, how could you? Kevin did everything for you. He was like a brother to you."

"He was fucking with my money, hon. Nothing personal. I did love him like a brother, you're right."

"You have a sick sense of what family is Cole." Alex spat out.

"And Mr. Gallardo, you now have company. Aren't you happy?"

"You are a sad excuse for your badge."

"Your city pays me shit. I had to do what I had to do." Cole said to Alex.

"So, what are you going to do with us? We know your secrets. We know everything." Mya stated ostentatiously.

"Just waiting on word from Emory." Cole said. He went to the crate and opened one to inspect the new arrivals. He picked up a bag of pink powder, *JEM*, pure and hadn't been cut and readied for distribution. "Isn't it beautiful? This stuff will hit the market and make us billions. People need something to distract them from this horrible economy and life in general."

"You're killing millions, Cole." Alex tried explaining.

"Darwin said he best, 'only the strong survive.' Or was it a Motown song? I tend to forget." Cole stated trying to be funny.

"It looks like they've doubled our order. This is wonderful." Emory stated as he entered the clandestine room.

"Yes. I think this will go just as fast." Cole retorted.

"I see you got the widow of Kevin." Emory finally laid eyes on her.

"I went to get the letters before she could read them, and she was there, already indulging her curiosity." Cole explained.

"Did you get rid of the letters?" Emory asked as a second thought.

"Of course. Once we get rid of these two, everything will be set.

"Justice will prevail Emory. All things done in the dark will come to light. Trust me!" Alex mustered up.

"Karma, zin bull crap, whatever you associate that with, it's not anything I have to worry about Alexander."

"Emory, you were working with my husband to take down the drugs in this city."

"Yep, and as soon as he got too close to the truth, then I had to get rid of him." Emory stated with no compassion. "And now his wife and child will be joining him shortly."

"How do you plan on doing this? You can't hide bodies forever!" Alex stated.

"You'd be surprise." Cole stated with a smirk. He had killed ten people that were involved and knew about this situation, and up and until this moment, no one knew how and when they had taken place.

Emory walked over to the crate and looked at his new supply. He was happy about it. "Cole, this shit will be shipped out tomorrow morning. Make sure the contact is taken care of. Also try to make their murders as painless as possible. We try not to be that heartless. I have to get back to the ball so that I can have an alibi. Speed it up as well buddy, your boyfriend can't suspect anything. This plan is almost fully executed."

"Will do Emory." Cole stated as he pulled his gun from its holster. Emory made his way out of the room, and there was a loud boom that echoed throughout the room. Cole turned around and was thrown by the sound, so much so he took cover. "What the hell was that?" He made his way toward the direction of the sound with gun in hand. To his surprise when he exited the room, he saw Emory dead on ground, blood oozing from his abdomen. When he looked up he saw Dontavious and Percy holding guns on him, one of his personal guns from his collection was the first one he recognized.

"Dontavious..." Cole was surprised and shocked. He was backed up in the room he had just exited.

"I heard everything." Dontavious was near tears.

"We can talk about this. Work something out." Cole was pleading, even though he had gun on the two of them.

"We can't work shit out Cole. You killed my brother and you were responsible for all of this! You're sick!!!"

"Babe, I was doing all the rest for US!"

"You didn't even know me when you killed Kevin. Stop the lies! Just let Mya and Alex go, now!"

"I can't do that. Emory..."

"Emory is dead. Any more excuses." Dontavious was pissed. His anger was searing.

"Babe, we can work this out! I love you." Cole said in a last ditch effort to save his ass.

"You have never loved me. You were paid by Thorneheart and Emory to be with me. I know that for a fact. You all used my insecurities to bring me in on your awful plan to destroy my family." He was crying.

"Please, Dontavious, this isn't you. You can't kill me." Dontavious was noticeably affected by this confrontation that he was shaking, so much so that his hands with the gun in it were shaking as well. Cole saw this as a weakness and thought this was the perfect moment to strike. Cole cocked his gun back and mad motions to shoot Dontavious. Percy saw the reaction and counteracted blasting Cole to the ground. "I'm shot. I give up." Cole said as he lay on the ground, without his gun and helpless.

"Did you give my brother the satisfaction?" A single gun shot to Cole's head killed him. Mya yelped. He untied Mya and Percy untied Alex. Mya hugged Dontavious. "Are you okay?"

"I am now." Mya said with relief.

"How did you know where we were Dontavious?" Alex asked.

"Percy told me. He helped me figure this whole thing out.

"So, this is the famous private I've been hearing about?" Mya stated.

"Yes, one in the same." Percy stated.

"Oh, I think we have a problem Dontavious." Mya said.

"What's wrong?" Dontavious inquired.

"My water just broke." Mya held her abdomen. She started labor. The four of them exited the warehouse with their wounds and memories.

Police and others swarmed the warehouse within an hour. Kilos of the drug were confiscated and truth of what had been going on was revealed. Percy was held as a hero, and Dontavious and Mya were praised for their commitment to finding the truth about what had happened to Kevin.

Sascha was happy to have her son back home without a scratch. And Jordan was happy to have her husband back home after he helped her.

Mya gave birth to a son Kevin Zechariahs Dean, Jr. He was a beautiful boy. He weigh almost eight pounds, even though he had come early, he was in perfect health. He was a perfect mixture of his mom and dad, but favored Kevin more-so. Mya was happy to hold this little person who would be with her for the rest of her life. She was no longer alone in the world. Dontavious, who would become Kev J.'s godfather, was by his sister-in-law's bedside. He vowed that he would never let anything happen to him, not as long as he lived. Something good did come out of this whole tragedy of Kevin's death, but Mya had wished that Kevin was there with her to share this particular event.

As Alex entered with flowers and a rattle for the littlest Dean, the family had come full circle. He was once again in the fold.

The letters that Rory sent to his chosen few were not completely destroyed. Alex had a copy and so did Emory. When news of what the letters contained hit the media, it all but solidified Zechariahs' position as mayor. Everyone wanted to believe in change and they felt that Zechariahs could provide it.

EPILOGUE

Life for the Deans was back to normal by February when Malek's son was born. Sebastian Malek Dean was born on an unseasonably warm day at Crawford Long Hospital. He was loud from the get go, and mother and father bonded over this little bundle of joy that would inevitable join them for the rest of their lives. Malek promised to give his son everything he could ever want and assured him that he would also protect and love him always.

The welcome home party was held at the Mt. Paron Road Dean Mansion, and everyone in Atlanta's top echelon of society was there welcoming the Dean's newest arrival. This was a perfect beginning to a life that Kameron could have only dreamed of for her child. Even though she was in a loveless relationship, she knew that her son would have everything he could ever want and more. And that fact made her happy and peaceful in her current situation.

Kev-J. and Sebastian would be the only grandchildren Jordan would ever have and she tried her best not to discriminate between the two. She found it quite hard seeing as though she couldn't bare the presence of Sebastian's mother Kameron. Their intense battles through Sebastian's child hood would be legend as Jordan came to grips with Kameron's intrusion into her family.

The Deans are the American dream. It didn't come without its struggles. Though money and power reigns supreme, this family isn't without its ups and downs. This cover family tries its best to hide its dirty little secrets, shortcomings and lies, but unsuccessfully they have all been revealed. But as Zechariahs said in his toast that day at the Welcoming party for Sebastian.: "Long live the Deans, the family, the name, the Dynasty."

THE END